*By the same author:*

**UNDER THE DAM**
*and other stories*

**THE SHIELING**
*and other stories*

**TEA AT THE MIDLAND**
*and other stories*

**IN ANOTHER COUNTRY:**
*Selected Stories*

*All available from Comma.*

First published in Great Britain in 2015 by Comma Press.
www.commapress.co.uk

A CIP catalogue record of this book is available from the British Library.

ISBN   1905583745
ISBN-13   978 1905583744

Supported by
**ARTS COUNCIL
ENGLAND**

The publisher gratefully acknowledges assistance from Arts Council England.

Set in Bembo 11/13 by David Eckersall
Printed and bound in England by Berforts Information Press Ltd.

# THE LIFE-WRITER

David Constantine

# About the Author

**David Constantine** (born 1944 in Salford) was for thirty years a university teacher of German language and literature. He has published several volumes of poetry, most recently *Elder* (2014). He is a translator of Hölderlin, Brecht, Goethe, Kleist, Michaux and Jaccottet. In 2003 his translation of Hans Magnus Enzensberger's *Lighter than Air* (Bloodaxe) won the Popescu European Poetry Translation Prize. His translation of Goethe's *Faust, Part I* was published by Penguin in 2005; *Part II* in 2009. He is also the author of one previous novel, *Davies* (Bloodaxe, 1985) and the biography *Fields of Fire: A Life of Sir William Hamilton* (Weidenfeld). His four short story collections are *Back at the Spike* (Ryburn), *Under the Dam* (Comma), *The Shieling* (Comma), and *Tea at the Midland* (Comma). This latter collection won the 2013 Frank O'Connor International Short Story Award, and its title story won the 2010 BBC National Short Story Award. *In Another Country: Selected Stories* was published by Comma in 2015. David lives in Oxford where, until 2012, he edited *Modern Poetry in Translation* with his wife Helen.

# 1

THEN ERIC SAID, I don't want to be like that colleague of yours, Dennis What's-his-name, I don't want to be like him, clinging on, nothing else in his head every minute of every day, nothing only clinging on. I don't call that living when all you think about is staying alive. He halted, they looked at one another, and the man Eric did not want to be like appeared in the cold gap in their conversation, the man whose only thought was not to die, who had no other interest, no other conversation, nobody else's doings, hopes, fears, interested him in the least, nothing in the world outside himself, no past, present or future, nothing, all he thought about and spoke about was how not to die. He trawled the web for cures and the last he hit upon was carrot juice. He carried a large bottle of it in his briefcase and took a glass on the hour every hour in whatever company and wherever he happened to be. Nothing else, no other food or drink. Just in time, he said, I've found the one thing that will work. To his wife, family, friends, colleagues, strangers he became a living horror, his black eyes, black as anthracite, burning brilliantly in his sunken face. And that was what he was remembered for: his final year when he thought and spoke of nothing but staying alive, the potion supposed to cure him dyed him through and through, and his frightened eyes shone blackly from the holes in his yellow head. No, said Katrin, I don't want you to be like poor Dennis, of course I don't. But you can't just give up. I haven't, Eric answered. And I promise you

I won't. But it was as though some current or the tide had felt for him, found him, and was beginning to exert an attraction no amount of love would be able to withstand. He would turn, sink, and be taken away from her, far far away, quite beyond her reach. The onset of that remoteness showed in his face sometimes like the vagueness in the face of a pregnant woman, the look of belonging elsewhere, a look Katrin could not bear. He took her hand across the breakfast table. I can't complain, he said, I've had a good life, only two years short of my three score years and ten, that's not young, think of the people at school and university with me, dead already several of them, ten, twenty, forty years ago, let alone the poets, painters and musicians you write about, so many of them dying so very young. I can't complain.

It was early January, the low sun entering lit up their kitchen in a strange orange light. The strangeness horrified her, all their familiar things, his mother's dresser and the blue china on its shelves, his cookery books, his saxophone leaning in the corner by the music stand, she wanted them to stay exactly as they were, familiar and ordinary, let the room be always as it was, day after day, without effulgence and transfiguration, no lurid sunlight entering with the lie that sorrow is beautiful and fit to live in. Katrin stood up and began to clear the table. Eric watched her. Since the diagnosis, her face had altered, it had set hard into the struggle. I will age her, he thought bitterly, I will close up the years between us. She had taken the breakfast things to the sink and stood there turned away from him, looking out into the small garden at the birds she fed. They would die when they were due to die but in the meantime, in a wintry sun, they flitted, settled, flitted, each after its fashion, in their various lovely colourings, restless, quick, all hungry. There was grey in her short black hair. Sadness lay on her neck and shoulders, visibly heavy. He went and stood by her, embracing her. He kissed her neck. Will you work at home today? he asked. I shall go out and do my shopping. I thought we'd have a cassoulet. And I've found some very nice wine. You'd like that wouldn't you? She nodded. Yes, I'll stay home. Yes, I'd like your cassoulet and your wine.

But first he would go out into the rather dark conservatory along the north side of the house, and at the far end of it, in his smoke-hole, he would read the paper, do the crossword and smoke a cigarette. At the start of their marriage she had hoped this banishment when he wished to smoke would cure him of it. Instead, he grew to love the place and the routine. He sat there among her plants, did the crossword quickly, sat there contentedly reading, smoking, thinking. And she had thought he might give up the habit, to please her! She hated the smell of it on his clothes, on his breath, in his hair, his beard, his flesh. But he shrugged and smiled, those were the facts, nothing could be done about them, he mused affectionately over her and over himself, they were as they were, what more was there to say? His cancer was not a smoker's after all, so why stop smoking now? He liked the habit, it made a large part of his contentment among her plants and seeds, the half hour after breakfast, he enjoyed it, and Katrin would surely not begrudge him that uncomplicated pleasure.

Katrin left the dishes – Eric would do them when he came in from his shopping – and climbed two flights of stairs to her study in what must once have been the maid's room, under the eaves. She had no desire to work. If she turned the computer on at all it would be to dispatch the most necessary emails as quickly as possible and to study online a high-protein, low-carbohydrate diet a colleague had recommended as efficacious when all else failed. I *can* complain, she thought. If I were your age it might be bearable. You have had forty-five years of your life, your life with others, that I haven't had. All very well for you to say you can't complain. What about me when you leave me here, aging alone and we were never young together? But that was a thought which, even as it formed, more or less consciously she pushed to the back of her mind. Let it lodge there, if it must. Later, during passages of grief in which love and its sorrow took the form of self-recrimination, she accused herself of harbouring that thought as one might a grievance, for some future occasion, to be brought up and deployed in an argument against the person you could not live your life without. Such a sad and cruel argument. For by then he was not there to answer back.

Promising Katrin that he would not give up, Eric was honour-bound to co-operate in her efforts to extend his life. He agreed to her getting a second opinion, and commiserated with her when it matched the first. Further along the way, very sick from the chemo, he let her radically change his diet. He had no appetite by then and lost nothing by compliance. He saw she would grieve worse if, afterwards, she could not be assured that together they had tried everything. For that was the heart of the matter: that they should stand together against the thing which would separate them. He complied, for her sake more than for his own he let her have her way – which she suspected, at times knew certainly. It felt like betrayal, like standing shoulder to shoulder in a matter of life and death with a person you cannot trust. She told him so, she cried out in anguish, Oh you don't want to live! You have given up. You want to leave me. Then he took her hands, sat her down by him, and did his level best to explain himself. Do you think I love my life less than Dennis What's-his-name loved his? How can you say that I want to leave you? I love my life and you are the best part of it. Then why won't you fight? she answered. I do fight, he said, and I will. But only for me, she said, you're only fighting because I ask you to, not wholeheartedly, you don't have faith. Then he confessed that the diagnosis, the moment it came, seemed to him correct and final. I saw a dead-straight railway line, he said, like the one I used to cycle to as a boy, the west-coast line that passes under the East Lancs Road, we stood on the bridge and watched the express come at us, nearer and nearer, till it vanished us in the tremendous noise and the steam. Like that, the armoured head of an express locomotive, coming down a dead-straight track, very fast, but in slow-motion. I saw my sickness as an unalterable and ineluctable fact, coming at me in slow-motion, very fast. And I remembered an old teaching: the fact is fixed, but my attitude towards it is mine to fashion as I please. So I decided I would live by that teaching, to the last. And to be honest, I have surprised myself. First, that I ever remembered the teaching – I suppose it surfaced in answer to my case – and then that I have tried to live by it. So that's what you meant by not giving up? she said. Yes, he answered. The fact: in how I view it I have a sort of freedom. All on your own, she said. All on your own in your head. You have left me already. You have left me all on my own. No, no, he answered. But it wearied him, he closed his eyes, the space behind them filled with hopeless sorrow. Katrin went to her room and wept in rage and shame.

Wordlessly, they came to an understanding. He would fight in her sense, which meant he would align himself loyally with her in trying to stay alive. She, for her part, would leave him free in his philosophy, in his idea of a sort of freedom against the inevitable. She knew he complied out of love for her, not in faith. He knew she hated his acknowledgement of the inevitable and that she thought his freedom in the spirit amounted to nothing much. In her view, he'd have done better to pit the energies of his mind wholly against the very idea of death. He could be her comrade in the struggle to save his life; but in his struggle for a freedom of mind against the unchangeable fact he was on his own, she could not join him, he did not even want her there, she could be of no use to him. But her adamant denial made him uneasy. As the weeks passed and the fact bulked ever larger, ever more solid and unquestionable, he feared they would part in disarray, at odds, leaving things unsaid and undone that would trouble and perhaps torment her afterwards. So he pleaded with her, We must make some preparations, I can't leave you ill-prepared or you will suffer worse than need be. She saw his agitation and out of pity agreed to discuss whatever he liked. She saw the mortal illness staring out of his eyes at her and the cold certainty of his death reached like a lover's hand towards her breast. Still she fought back. She said to herself that she would do all he asked *as though* it were certain he must die; and reserve to herself, in her innermost heart, the right of denial, the right to continue fighting to make him live.

Eric told Katrin very simply some things she knew already, things they had agreed without fuss or pathos at a time when death had no shape or presence in their lives: that he wanted to be cremated, that the funeral should be simple and secular, that he wanted his friends, even the oldest, to be there if they could. Some music: jazz, a blues, Schubert. A brief address, if she wished it. And a poem of her choosing. Then about the money, which he had always attended to more than she had: where everything was, what her situation would be. She would get his full pension for a year, after that it would halve. But there was also a life insurance policy, she would have to write to them. Also their savings. All the documents would be on his desk. And she must stop the payments to Edna. That obligation ended with his life. She nodded, none of it mattered. And he asked her for two promises: that she would keep up relations with their common friends, and that she would carry on with her work, she must not waste her talents. She promised, but remotely. And to finish, he said – and this was very important to him – he wanted nothing left between them that still needed to be mended or forgiven. Was there any such thing? He begged her to let him make amends while there was still time or to forgive him if it was beyond repair. She shook her head, blankly. You forgive me? he asked. Of course I do, she answered. But truly there is nothing to make good or to forgive. She could think of nothing, her mind was blank. It grieved her to turn her thoughts to faults and blame. So it was in a tone of remote and formal response that she asked him had she herself any amends to make. None, he answered. And he forgave her for any wrong she had ever done him? He nodded and smiled. But to her it was all shadows, it had no sense, she was doing what he bade her do, as well as she could, but the only real thing was how thin his face had become, how thin and white his beard, and his death stared out so hard at her from his widening eyes that her will to oppose it suffered a shock. I'm glad about all that, he said, patting the back of her hand. Thank you. And relief, almost peace, came over his features. He closed his eyes, he slept, she went away to prepare his evening meal.

As Eric got weaker, time seemed to slow, almost to halt. Perhaps more than ever before, he and Katrin became capable of present life. The hospital delivered a bed, which she made up for him downstairs in the front room, so that he could rest there during the day. Both knew and neither said that it would become his only and his final room; but in the meantime, for an interlude, there was no sense of such a future in it. The light came in plentifully through the big windows, everything was clear and just as it should be, their books and music, flowers, pictures, the furnishings they had chosen together. They would sit side by side listening to music – blues, jazz, a choir, a string quartet – neither saying a word. All was familiar, and infinitely new. They had space and time to listen with due attention. There had been abrupt accelerations in his illness, and phases of crisis, haste, anxiety, fret and exertions and demands beyond their strength; so now their peace and quiet in the downstairs room were a great kindness. The year bore very slowly into spring, but for some hours of every day the dying man and his wife felt cradled, exempted, their life allowed a pause and an abeyance. They were not *waiting*; at least, it did not feel like that; they were *attending*, and not upon an approaching and imminent thing but on where and who they were and what they were doing in the present tense.

They read aloud to one another, in turn, she took the book from him when she felt his voice tiring, she continued in her voice while he closed his eyes, recovered his strength and attended to the reading, to the lives of fellow human beings in poetry and fiction. They sat very close, and each in turn, in a low and familiar voice, converted the signs on the page into living sense.

For more than a year, on Thursday afternoons, Eric had read Proust to a man called Anton with motor neurone disease, the son of a Russian émigré and once an outstanding surgeon. He prepared the week's pages meticulously; tried every difficult sentence aloud; walked a mile across town and read out Proust in French to a man encased in a respirator, tubes feeding him, tubes emptying him, who signalled the life of his mind with an eyelid and whose adamant wish, should the machinery fail, was to be resuscitated. Even after his diagnosis, Eric continued these readings. He saw no reason not to. He still did the daily crossword, smoked a few cigarettes, shopped astutely for the evening meal, spent much of the afternoon preparing it, practised his saxophone, kept up his Russian, read a poem or two – why should he not continue with Anton a little way further into *À l'ombre des jeunes filles en fleurs*? So he read Thursday by Thursday, hour by hour, and walked home across the town, until the illness took him up into its appointments and its sessions and leached his strength and constricted his being in the world. Greatly weakened then, more and more confined to the one room downstairs, his reading aloud to Katrin and his being read to by her became a wondrous extension, countering his own reduction, it lifted him up and out again across frontiers of space and time into the lives of others leased into further life by the imagination.

At first, out of a sort of tact, Eric and Katrin read things they could finish at a sitting or perhaps over a day or two – a single poem or a few by the same poet, a complete short story. But then one morning without comment he reached for *Silas Marner*, easefully they settled down to it, entered it again with all the time in the world, dwelled in it, handing the book at leisurely intervals to and fro. There was no hurry. It was deeply familiar and deeply strange, their living having shifted into a space of greater attentiveness, the book gave ever more of itself, it met them differently, with new pathos, longing, satisfactions, shocks of enlivening pleasure. They were newly moved by it, moved on, further, strangely, in their thinking and feeling. They read books they had read before, even twice or three times before, books they had shared for years. Eric had always extended the borders of his reading. He was open to suggestions, he read reviews, ordered from catalogues, in three or four languages he had always been on the look-out for new things he would enjoy. Now that was over, and with Katrin he turned to what was to hand, there close on the shelves – which did not feel in the least like a diminution of curiosity, but more like a quickening and an expansion. No sentence, no paragraph can be read quite the same way twice. A sequence of poems, a chapter, a whole story, a novel, all open and go on opening infinitely. So there was no perversity or defiance in beginning a work of poetry or fiction they would not finish. They felt it to be a living and moving thing, alive in all its parts in every fibre, it was not made to be exhausted, it was made to delight and outlive them. So they had reached Book IX of *The Prelude*, 'Residence in France', when their reading had to stop.

Their lives simplified. He was dying, she nursed him. Now and then his brother, his son or a friend phoned, for news; one day Daniel visited and stayed for the afternoon; and every day she had half an hour out of doors, to shop or just to walk, and a neighbour came in, to watch. Katrin slept on the sofa and woke every three hours to give Eric the morphine that eased his pain and let him sleep. It was a phase of life, an ordeal, she measured out her strength for it, knowing it would end, not wanting it to end. She read to him, but now he could not attend so well. When she paused, she saw that his eyes were on her, on the fact of her reading quietly to him, he had attended less to the words, more to the fact of her, of her caring for him, of the two of them close together in their marriage. He took her hand, asked her again to promise him that she would look after herself, resume her life, continue her work, see people, keep up with their friends, make new friends, she had many years of life ahead of her. But all this she felt to be a cruel distraction: why must he divert her thinking from now, from being with him, from easing his pain, her strength was all measured out for that and when that ended, so she felt, she would have no strength and need none. He was mortally sick, but mortal sickness was better than death, he breathed, he conversed with her, he made his love for her palpable with his hand and with his eyes and he knew – it showed – her love for him, they were there together in the downstairs room in their own home, he was sick, he would die, but not yet, not for a while yet, and meanwhile it was now and time, in pity, had slowed almost to pausing and every minute of his still being alive and their still being together counted, mattered, it was added to the sum. So she shook her head when he pleaded with her for assurances about her afterwards – stood up, cleared away a glass and a cup and saucer, refreshed the flowers, put on the music he would like.

It was early February, cold nights and the moon becoming full, becoming large and brilliant, a flat white pockmarked face of cold, a hard disc beaming at the earth, at the house, at the walls and doors and windows, reflecting the coldness of outer space, passing it on and magnifying and focussing it on homes whose warmth, if let, will always, and very quickly, leave. Katrin drew the curtains tight, but they were not thick enough to keep out the sense of the moon's acute white brilliance. And the light shone through the windows of the front door, lay on the wooden floor in the hall, showed as a thin blade, like a visible draught, at the threshold of the sick-room. It made her nervous, and Eric could not get warm. She fetched him another blanket, kept the heating on.

Katrin rose at three, to give Eric his morphine, and found him awake, alert. I was waiting for you, he said. She gave him the capsule. I didn't mean because of the pain, he said. I'm doing well tonight. I've been remembering something. I wanted to tell it you. Help me sit up. I want to tell it you properly. She helped him, arranged a cover round his thin shoulders, sat by the bed and took his hand. His face was a wonder and a horror to her: so gaunt, his wisp of beard, his stained and carious teeth, but through all that, chiefly out of the deep black eyes but also from the lips, came something like joy, hilarity, a sort of anarchic and youthful glee. Listen to this, he said, gripping hard at her hand, his voice low and wondering, marvelling, as though he could scarcely give credence to the story he would tell her.

There were four of us, he said: Smithy, Vince, Daniel and me, the first two are dead and I soon will be, so that leaves Daniel, ask him if you like, he'll tell you how he sees it. We were done with school, as good as, we'd all got places for October, and somebody had the idea, Why don't we meet up in France, end of August, when we've earned a bit of money, why not? We went to the Central Library and looked at a Blue Guide, for the South, and pretty well at random decided on Vizille. Who's ever heard of Vizille? Nobody. But the Guide said the town had a rue Elsa Triolet, so we agreed: three days running, 10 in the morning, 6 in the evening, whoever gets there first, sit in a café on the rue Elsa Triolet for an hour, morning and evening, three days running, and watch out for the rest of us, all coming our different ways and aiming at the 29th, 30th, 31st August, 1962. I went back to Kelloggs in Trafford Park, on nights, £7, 2 shillings an hour, double time Sundays, triple on the Bank Holiday, I was on a conveyor belt, last position, where the packets come through filled and my job was putting in the plastic spacemen, a free offer, collect the whole set, paint them yourself, little grey naked plastic spacemen, hundreds and hundreds of them every night. I earned the money for France. And now this, listen. His face was hectic, as if through the crust of the years, through age and sickness and the cast of death, with a brutal strength delight was breaking out. I got the 66 bus into town, he said, and walked up Market Street to London Road Station, as we still called it then, not Piccadilly, London Road, because that's what it was, the road below the station, and where people turned left up the slope to the trains, there at that junction stood a signpost pointing along the road that went on its way, and the signpost said: London 186 miles. And night after night in Kelloggs, dropping spacemen into cornflakes, I'd had that signpost in my inner vision, as the place to start from, for Vizille in the south of France. It's the old A6 from Carlisle over Shap Fell, through Preston and the heart of Manchester and out into the Peak District, Buxton, Matlock, joins the A1 at Luton… I stood there for a minute, at the signpost, touching it, and then off I went down the London Road in my hiking boots and a rucksack on my back, nothing much in it, Rimbaud, a notebook, washbag, sleeping bag… And before I'd gone two hundred yards, at a traffic lights there was a lorry waiting and the driver's mate looked down and said, How far you going, son? London, I said. Hop up behind, he said. We'll take you as far as Chapel. I can see him now, he had a fag in his mouth and white dust on his hair, his eyebrows and his overalls. And the tailboard where I sat, leaning against the cab, all there was dusty too, all the gear, the ropes, the straps, the tarpaulins, all white dusty, they were delivering in Manchester from a yard near the quarries in Chapel-en-le-Frith. Eric's voice cracked, his features jolted. Hush, said Katrin, soothing his hand as though he were her sick and feverish child. Later, she said, have a sleep first, tell me the rest later. No, no, he said, now, it has to be now. I sat amid the dusty tackle leaning back against the cab and watched the London Road spooling out from between my feet. Was ever anybody happier than that? Oh in no time we were out through Stockport and through Hazel Grove and Disley and into the gritstone and then the limestone land! It was only mid-morning when they set me down in Chapel. I had egg and bacon and a mug of tea and, when I felt like it, I was in no hurry, I found my road again, walked a little while, stopped, turned, and put up my thumb for another truck. Think of me then, Katrin, never forget me then, that lad gaily assuming the land and its roads and traffic would never be anything but kind to him, he raises his thumb and a truck stops, after that it's a vicar in a Morris Minor, an elderly couple in a camper van, a fisherman riding a motorbike and sidecar, How far you going, son? It's a few miles at a time, through the Dales, the limestone so white under the sun it hurt your eyes, the watercourses deep dark green and secret, little by little down the London Road that never thought further ahead than, it might be, Matlock, pottering along, till suddenly, a vivid red, it's a BRS all the way to the depot in Brent Cross, hour after hour, the driver a big man, I remember his big hands on the wheel, the blond hairs on them, his blond moustache, his puffy face turning my way as he talked and talked, about the war, how the war had done for him, how his mate from school died shot through the eye right next to him, his grief, his terrible rage, how he'd killed a German when he needn't have, just to be even for his mate from school, a big blondy man who was on his knees already and his hands lifted up for mercy, and he bayoneted him, a fine big blondy bloke with pale blue eyes, when he shouldn't have, for revenge, and saw his face still and always would, his face and his uplifted hands, asking for mercy. Katrin stood up. That's enough now. She walked to the curtains, parted them a little, the moon glared at her full, there was nothing between her and the flat white pitiless face of the moon that passes on the heat and light of the sun to earth's small habitations in a cold illumination humans cannot bear. She shut the moon out, turned, Eric was beckoning her, his hand like a claw, she leaned over him, Hush now, she said, sleep first, let's both of us sleep, tell me the rest later. How I set off walking through London, Eric whispered, how somewhere along the way – it was nearly dark by then – a postman halted in his van, asked me where I was making for, Dover, I said, Jump in, he said, and he took me out to an eating place on the A20, I couldn't say where, a big place, all lit up, and the traffic hurrying past, ask in the carpark, he said, there's always people making for the ports from here, good luck to you, son, good night. Katrin laid her fingers on his lips. He gripped her hand, hard, kissed it, There's more, he said, so much more, I've hardly begun, I'm not on the ferry yet, ask Daniel, so good it all was, so good.

# 2

DURING THE FUNERAL, and after it when the mourners came back to her house, Katrin continued in the almost rapturous state she had been lifted into by the last hours of Eric's life. It was over, accomplished, her strength had sufficed. And now meticulously she would attend in every detail to every thing that needed to be done. She allowed advice, but followed it her way; help, but she directed it. She accepted condolences, and herself extended them to whoever had been saddened by Eric's death. She was courteous, gracious; almost constantly she smiled, her eyes shone with the beauty and solemnity of his death, its profound and unique importance. And she exulted: we were alone, I held his hand, I spoke to him last, he saw me last, I closed his eyes. Above all: my strength sufficed, I saw it through. She was sovereign over the afterwards. It should be just as he wanted it, all just right: the three pieces of music, the poem she would read, Daniel would speak for five minutes. When in the brief gap between the previous committal and Eric's not enough orders of service were laid out, Katrin was coldly angry. Her arrangements faltered. It took a couple of minutes to make good the error. Then things proceeded, she smiled at the clerk, forgiving him. And throughout, smiling, attending to the details, she was remote, she was enclosed alone in the fact of his death, and there she rejoiced, she had sole cure of him, she had gone to the very brink with him, seen him over, she alone, no one else.

As the mourners assembled, they were all, without exception, strange to her. Scrupulously she had invited all of his oldest friends she knew to be still alive; several came and most she had never met before. But the strangeness lay also over people she knew well. In Eric's son, Thomas, a stout man of forty-five with a very round and childish face, she could see no family likeness whatsoever; and in Eric's brother, Michael, so much likeness it was repellent. Close neighbours and the few friends and colleagues of her own, she felt she had known them once and now she, or they, had slipped, so that they faced one another oddly. In part, of course, it was the black everybody wore. In that costume they had a role, they were figures in a ceremony, each stood for grief on an occasion of mourning. So in that sense, being for a while figurative, all were themselves estranged out of their normal lives, and dressing in the mirror they had known it and had felt solemnified. Also, although they were assembled for a common purpose, around a death, and all connected to that centre, a coffin, an absence, many were strangers to one another, never having met before or so long ago, half a century ago in some cases, the names they were offered and remembered didn't fit the present faces and appearances, they were ill at ease as the dead man himself would have been after so long a gap, nothing much in common in the interim, the threads from school and university long since severed, near-impossible to take up again, and hardly worth it.

Katrin passed among them like a good hostess, smiling, embracing, saying a few words, offering food and drink. All interested her because all in varying degrees had been touched by Eric's life. She attended particularly to those who had known him as a boy or a young man, before she was born, long long before she had met and fallen in love with him. She was drawn to them, but how odd they were, how remote, mostly heavy and bald, in suits they never wore except at funerals, gauche, drinking quickly, a bit loud and hearty in their desire to belong, for a couple of hours, to the thing all there had in common. Any wives with them drifted loose, out to the margins of the occasion. Katrin smiled and went to and fro, and sensed that her cold exaltation passed like a draught through the company. She was concentrating, she had a purpose, she marvelled with pride and satisfaction at her composure.

Katrin stood in the bay window with Daniel, looking out. Behind them the mourners made a hubbub that did not concern her. None of it was intelligible, the words had all gone under in a generalised social noise. Her back felt safe. Daniel said, Did you invite Edna? Katrin's consciousness tore a little. She glimpsed a further afterwards in which it would be necessary to ask Daniel many things. A shudder went through her, which he perceived. Forgive me, he said. No, no, she said. I did write to her when he died, I did invite her, she never answered. And I asked Thomas to tell her she would be welcome but, as you see, she isn't here. Daniel nodded. She is very embittered, he said. Then both stared out in silence at the cold sunny street where the housefronts, the cramped front gardens, the tightly parked cars, were all in place as though nothing had happened. Katrin held a bottle of wine in each hand. She bethought herself of her role, she was returning into it, when a small elderly woman wearing a duffle coat, a black cloche hat, red stockings, and carrying a yellow rucksack, appeared, as it seemed, from nowhere and halted, looking lost, at Katrin's gate. Ah, said Daniel. The woman smiled at them, made a questioning sort of gesture with her black-gloved hands, and stepped briskly up the path. Daniel raised his eyebrows, shrugged, took the bottles. Katrin went and opened the door. Oh, Madame Swinton, said the new arrival, je suis désolée, oh, excusez-moi, madame, je suis Monique. And she continued in rapid French – which Katrin could not quite keep up with – to explain that she had got off at the wrong railway station, was quite lost, by the time she reached the crematorium everything to do with Eric was over, all his party had gone, somebody else's service was in progress, she had come on as quickly as she could, to meet Katrin and to see Daniel again after many years, and how sorry she was, she had dreamed vividly of Eric the very night he died – and she stood there on the doorstep, appealing to Katrin and beginning helplessly to weep. Again there was a tearing in Katrin's consciousness, again a frisson of pure terror. She foresaw, she felt already, how in the near next phase of the afterwards she would be assailed. But for now, still exalted, seeing the older woman's grief, she took it into her own, into the centre of the whole occasion, herself, his widow. Monique stood on the threshold, childish, a waif and stray. Katrin brought her in, embraced her, helped her off with the rucksack and duffle coat, noted the short black dress she wore, as for a party, and how poignantly it sorted with her face that was like a mime's saying more than it can bear. Her small hat had gone askew. Then in a rush Monique pulled off her gloves, flung them down, with stained and quick little fingers undid the rucksack and dug out a package, which she handed to Katrin. Je vous ai apporté ça, madame. Un petit souvenir des années soixante. The wrapping was a couple of pages of *Libération*, the thing itself was a fired black bowl decorated inside with a single red rose and outside with a sparse motif of small clusters of cherries. Ça vous plaît? Katrin nodded. She held the bowl on her palms. This too, since it was beautiful, she could take into her high solemnity. Again, saying nothing and with a look of the greatest seriousness, she nodded.

Daniel appeared. Ah, he said, seeing the bowl. Monique turned her smudged face his way. Tu t'en souviens? For answer he kissed her wet cheeks. Katrin smiled now on both of them. She saw how they *belonged*. Merci, Monique, she said. Soyez la bienvenue dans cette maison. Then she left them together, bearing away the bowl as though for a ritual, but fearfully, feeling the world lurch and her steps to be very unsure. She went into the middle room and laid it down among the last books Eric had ordered and that had arrived after his death. There she stood for a moment, conjuring up the resolve to go back into the big front room, into its noise and utter strangeness, in among all the people in their suits of woe, their faces lifting towards her, all well-meaning, full of friendly pity, and this swell of grief and friendship would bear her up again, their kindness would help her, she was apart but it would strengthen her, she would manage, she would get through to six o'clock, when all, every friend and relative, would leave as arranged, as promised, and she would be as she was, alone, entirely alone, to broach the long afterwards, the life without him.

Daniel and Monique were the last to leave. She took his arm. On the street, lamplit, they looked back once at Katrin standing in the bay window. She watched them out of sight, an elderly couple, the tall grey-haired man stooping, the small woman clutching at him, yellow rucksack, red stockings, respectful black, they had visited her out of Eric's youth. She drew the curtains.

Katrin began to clear the house of all that was left of the funeral party. She worked fast, concentrating. She hastened on what remained of her exaltation towards the completion, into his absence. She had to be alone for that and the house had to be spick and span, as though she must leave it presentable, not knowing when she would be able to attend to it again. She concentrated, her strength was limited, she mustn't waste any.

Two hours later the house was just as it should be, all the materials of hospitality were put away, the chairs were back where they belonged. That done, she climbed the stairs, step by step an ever more leaden effort. Pausing at the bedroom door, in the light from the landing she contemplated their bed. Some things, she ascertained, are unimaginable, however hard you try. She stepped in, closed the door, stood in darkness, felt forwards, and fully clothed curled herself up small on the counterpane, her face in her cold hands.

For a week she did nothing. Or whatever she did to stay alive and to persuade the neighbour, looking in, that she was managing, none of that survived the present in which it was done. Vaguely she remembered a faint amazement that anything could be so bad and yet not actually fatal. Life continued, it insisted, it bore you along through the motions of living. So a horror she had not known before entered her like a disease that you will never again be quite rid of, you are the host of it now, its abode, it will come and go as it chooses: the horror of knowing that life without the spirit is possible, you can live as a dead simulacrum.

After a week Katrin left the house for an hour. She walked by the river whose banks had been set in concrete, so that it would not flood. She no longer wished to sit still in a chair or lie curled on the bed. All her exaltated feeling, her sense of his death as a solemn and beautiful thing, her pride in having seen it through, all that was in tatters. Now she could not bear to be still, her thoughts tormented her too much. She decided harshly against herself. The end was a mess, she had made it worse not better for him with her denials and her measures. She should have helped him in the philosophy he had tried to follow, for in the event he could not manage it alone. Often she saw him quite at the mercy of dying, not master of it, not fashioning his own sense of it freely. She saw him wretched and in pain and nothing in his eyes but revulsion and fear. Death hauled him off and that was that. In her remembering, she had to go back some weeks to hear him say, I can't complain. And that philosophical voice hardly comforted her. Rather, in her state of restless self-torment, it called up the sad riposte, All very well for you! And she fell again into the bitter feeling that her loss was greater than his, harder to bear, impossible to make up, because in losing him she lost her strength and now she would never have compensation for the years of boyhood, youth and manhood he had lived without her, ignorant of her existence. She had seen him frayed and battered by suffering at the end; but very easily she could imagine him, once he was through, resuming his sense that life had treated him well and he couldn't complain. And she saw him, with that advantage, turning all his concern towards her: she must look after herself, make the most of her life, live gladly, as he had. And how should she do that without him?

This running colloquy with him distressed her more than it comforted her. Every other person lapsed, she was inhabited entirely by him. She felt that he had not passed away but had passed on, into her, and there he lived, in her, not jealously, not desiring to confine her further life, but wishing her well, urging her to live, to keep up with old friends, make new ones, get on with her work. And all that benevolent admonishing worked futilely on the fact that he, the admonisher, was necessary to her doing what he asked.

# 3

KATRIN – DR KATRIN Szuba – was a writer of brief lives, rather in the manner of Walton or Johnson but her subjects were insignificant figures of European Romanticism. At Kraków she had written a doctorate on Byron and the Polish Liberation Movement of the 1830s in which, as she readily admitted, she had said nothing new but which had so gratified her father, whose own career had been a failure, that, dying soon after the conferment of her degree, he had, to thank her, sidelined her brothers and bequeathed to her the library of nineteenth-century Polish, French, German and English primary and secondary literature which walled the landings and half the attic of the big house she must now live in alone. It was during her years of postgraduate study, scrupulously following up references in collected works and letters, that she had discovered her real interest: the lives of men and women who have the allure, the passion, the structures of imagination, the longings, the disappointments, the hectic ambition, the devotion, the folly, the grief of their great contemporaries, but not their talent. That difference – the gap – began to fascinate her. It troubled her, it moved her to pity. The gap: that which they do not have and cannot, however hard they try, whatever they sacrifice, make up. So Katrin began to assemble an anthology of these characters. At first she had to make clear to colleagues that she was not searching, as many academics were, for men and women who did indeed have talent but who by chance or – especially the women – because the social order disregarded them, had been overlooked. The people she was drawn to wished to be poets, painters, musicians, lived as though they were, perhaps even believed they were, but on the evidence of their work were not. What made them fit to be written about, in Katrin's view, was that they lived their lives without the thing they needed and could not acquire: the gift. Each lived a unique life, but at the heart of each was the common lack. Therein, for Katrin, lay their poignancy.

Katrin discussed her characters with Eric. He did not feel them to be so very poignant. In his view, they did what they wanted to do, they had a purpose, they lived it. And perhaps having talent or not having talent was a distinction that, *existentially*, did not matter much. Some without talent became famous in their day; they had the public corroboration many geniuses themselves never had. Quite likely, Eric said, they died believing they were what the public said they were. And what did they care, dead, when a later public thought differently? Still Katrin stuck to her project, there was something in it, for her at least, her instinct told her so. And she saw, and after his death developed the insight, that his refusal to think of her people as poignant, let alone tragic, in part reflected his own view of himself. He knew what he wasn't; and on the whole he knew and liked and approved of what he was. He had many gifts, which he relished and developed up to a certain point. They contented him, he felt no urgent need to go beyond. On the gifts and achievements of others he looked with benign admiration, envying no one. He was as he was, he enjoyed himself. A hedonist, Daniel had called him in his brief address, a rational and humane hedonist. He did not die feeling he had fallen short; he died contented with his life. The gap, the lack, the wanting to make up – that was all Katrin's.

Again and again as he lay dying, Eric had urged her to go on with her work. Such a good idea, he said. People will read you and take these lives of yours into their own. But she looked away, her mouth clenched tight in worry over him. It was quite possible that people would read her, as he said. She had a contract with a university press, they would bring her book out as soon as she pleased and at a reasonable price, in paperback. Like Eric, they seemed to think it would have readers. Of the lives she had in mind, a couple had appeared already, she had lectured on a couple more, and always the response had been encouraging. There would be nine in all. Indeed, that was the working title: *Nine Lives*, altogether propitious, as Eric said. But steadily, from the day of his diagnosis, her interest in them lessened. During this lessening there were points, like milestones, when she realised, with a spasm of horror, how far into disinterest she had come; and at the last, still some weeks before he died, it settled into her as a cold certainty that these other lives did not matter – perhaps they never had, or why now, under the duress of his dying, could she let them go so easily and with no regret? Why were they and her once so keen involvement in them of so little avail? Why were they not strong enough to help? Almost she felt herself to be dying with him as he died, to be narrowing, drifting to an end. No life interested her but his, his life was all she wanted to call her own.

Katrin sat at her desk. After a while, a vacancy, she switched on the computer. There were 237 unopened emails in her inbox. She switched the computer off. From that high room she had a view east over roof-tops to where they diminished and the town ended. More distantly, beyond the motorway, rose the high moors; and although they were never quite visible, not even when snow transfigured them, still the sky over there had a height, largeness and openness that seemed to want, in reciprocation, miles and miles of empty moorland far below.

Behind her the ceiling sloped down to a low wall in which was a door into the attic. Too uneasy to contemplate the eastern sky and in dread and panic at what the blank computer held, she turned on her chair and faced the attic door. She was in a state in which distress, anxiety, panic, rise and rise into something akin to paralysis but fraught with a desperate need, and inability, to move – panic in stasis, no act imaginable that might bring release; confinement in unease without opening or issue in any direction; unbearable, but implosion and annihilation the only conceivable way of ending it. Her breath came in quick sobs, her heart leaped and twisted like something hooked, her hands wrung at one another. Then in all that, like the ghost of herself quitting an uninhabitable body, she stood up, moved crouching under the ceiling, went on her knees at the door, pushed it open, felt for the light, and looked in. A greater height had been managed in there, up to the rafters, and her father's books were ranged as high as possible wherever that could be done. At the sight of them she retched. So why had the ghost of her, like a somnambule, knelt at the door, looking in?

On the floor in the far right-hand corner of the attic, pushed up against the books, lay Eric's brown wooden trunk with its broken brass clasp and one of its leather handles replaced with a double loop of rope, the trunk badged with the stickers of dispatch and delivery by British Rail and British Road Services half a century ago, and upon the trunk stood five or six full brown-paper carrier bags.

The trunk itself and the bags upon it were nothing new. They had gone into the attic like the dead father's books when she and Eric married and moved, on account of her new job, from Surrey. They were out of sight and from one year's end to the next they were out of mind. For Eric himself they were sided away, they belonged *back then*, in another country, they were done with and, like much else, only kept because on the whole he did keep things he saw no compelling reason to get rid of. They shocked Katrin now as much else did in the strange light cast over her familiar world by his illness and death.

Still in a state akin to sleepwalking, Katrin bent under the low lintel, stood up again in the roofspace and knelt before the trunk and the carrier bags. One by one she moved the bags to the floor. They were filled with letters. She lifted the lid of the trunk. On the lining, in neat block capitals, was written: ERIC SWINTON, 35 HEATON STREET, HIGHER BROUGHTON, SALFORD 3. And layered underneath were many bundles of letters and postcards, some still tightly bound with string, others released from elastic bands that had perished. Even this was nothing new. The letters were not something unknown in a strange location. They were documents of his life before he knew her, and the attic was where they were kept. It was no secret. Now and then consulting a book in her father's library, she had noted her husband's carrier bags and trunk, but only as a fact and one that troubled her far less than did the legacy of her father's books. Eric's past had always been open to her. When they first met, whatever she asked, he answered candidly, just as she did all the questions he put to her. So she knew about his first marriage, the divorce, his bringing up the child alone, his two or three romantic attachments along the way. And before that marriage, concerning his years at school and university, if she enquired, he told her what she wanted to know. So she knew about Monique, a little. Katrin could have outlined the man's life story up to the point at which she entered it herself and they continued it together. True, she always had to ask, he needed prompting – his unfinished narrative at death's door was unprecedented – but she never had the feeling he was guarding secrets. She asked, he answered. He never seemed reluctant or reticent. Rather, so she felt, all that past life was over for him, he didn't need it, he was content in the present, in the new place, with her.

No prohibition lay on the trunk and the carrier bags. He had never asked her not to read his letters. He might have destroyed them himself when he was well or she would have done it for him in his illness or now after his death, had he said that he wished it. No, he did not forbid her. But as she knelt there now before the open trunk, she could feel his concern, she could hear him saying, Don't bother with all that. Come away. But having lifted the lid, she knew with a quite peculiar shock, that however lovingly he urged her not to, she would disobey. The ghost of herself, leaving her body whose torment had become unbearable, had gone by instinct to the thing there all along and close at hand: the one thing her soul desired, which was to know him as he had been before she loved him, to fetch his early years into the years she must now live without him. Katrin had stopped trembling, her heart still raced but now with an excitement caused by the revelation of a purpose. She did not want to live a life without desire. And now, kneeling before the trunk and the bags full of letters, desire, for good or ill quickened in her.

# 4

THERE ARE THREE strata of letters in the trunk (and those in the carrier bags would perhaps make another two). They are bundles of years and of many different writers. Katrin takes out a letter from a bundle that has fallen open: 3 February 1976, posted in Woking, the Queen's head on a turquoise 6½p second-class stamp. In the same loose clutch there are another three with the Woking postmark. Katrin opens one, it is from Edna. She puts it back in the envelope quickly. She digs through to the lowest stratum, takes out a bundle still fastened tight with string, the letter uppermost is postmarked Garmisch 13 July 1962, two 20 pfennig stamps bearing the head of Bach. Katrin pulls the bow, the string undoes, the letters and cards relax, perhaps thirty of them, quickly Katrin checks their dates: earliest April 1962, latest that December, several from France. Katrin sits back on her heels, the letters loose between her hands in her lap. She stares up at the rafters. Then abruptly, leaving those letters on the floor, the lid of the trunk still open, the carrier bags in a cluster by the trunk, she goes back into her workroom, closing the attic door behind her and turning out the light.

Her body feels better, as though she has come back into it, found it habitable after all and will now be able to manage. She stands for perhaps five minutes at her desk, looking out over the computer east towards the enlargement of the sky over the invisible moors. Then she turns, takes a deep breath, and goes downstairs one floor into the room that had been

Eric's study. The room is as it was, a cheerful clutter, all his many interests, the many beginnings, the years and years. She will look neither right nor left but strides to his desk and sits there before a space which he cleared entirely for the documents having to do with her future finances. This is as she expected; but unexpected, and harder to bear, is an A4 sheet of his writing, in a hand that looks determined to be clear, to make the letters, the words and the figures large and clear. Katrin sees the effort, the hand's weakness, its struggle to be steady; and this is more than she can bear. She hurries from the room, stands on the landing, leans her face on her arms against the wall, and weeps. It is another lapsing, the virtue going out of her, the letting go of her hold on a life fit to live. But it passes, or she forces it to pass. She goes along the landing to the bathroom, swills her face, stares at the image of herself, dries her face, returns to the room and to his desk.

He has listed the sources of income he told her about at a time when she could not bring herself to attend. He has set out what it costs annually to run the house: gas, electricity, water, council tax, insurance, phone etc. And he writes: Stop the payments to Edna. And Thomas is doing well, he does not need any help from you. And, as you know, there is something for their children in my will. Even if you stopped working you would have enough to manage on. But I think you shouldn't stop working, I think it will help you if you carry on working and are with your colleagues. Your work matters, you will do more than I ever did, your book is a wonderful idea.

Katrin hurries downstairs and sorts quickly through the accumulated and unopened post for anything having to do with her finances. She finds a letter from Eric's pension fund, another from the life insurance company. They offer her their sincere condolences, they tell her what the payments to her will be, the insurance exceeds Eric's estimates. Katrin nods, she wants that basis settled. She phones the surgery, asks for an appointment as soon as possible, they have had a cancellation, can she be there by 12.30? She takes a shower, changes her clothes, dresses warmly for the cold outside, and by 12.45 Dr Gracie has agreed that she must have sick leave, three months, see how she gets on. Katrin goes home, phones the department, tells them she will not be back for three months, the doctor will write to the Registrar. Everyone wishes her well, they miss her, but she must get better, they understand how hard it is for her. Katrin thanks them all, sends everyone her love, puts the phone down. She is playing cautiously, she has given herself three months. But before that term is up, if her resolution holds, she will resign her post, postpone her book indefinitely, and concentrate on doing the one thing she desires to do.

Now there are 257 emails in her inbox. But she has a new attitude towards them. She deletes, unread, everything from the University, which is three quarters of the sum. Then those from her publisher, she opens them, glances at them, deletes them all, but writes one brief reply: she is grateful for their sympathy, she is unwell and cannot work, she will take up everything again just as soon as she is able to. That is another substantial clearance. The rest is junk – she annihilates it – or from friends, some hers, more Eric's, and dealing with these, especially the latter category, she becomes alert in a way that is novel, and troubling, to her and she pauses, wondering. It is the project! Knowing what she wants to do, she knows what will serve it. From now on everything and everybody will be more or less serviceable. What can't help, she will ignore or discard. This is novel to her. She looks at the names of the emailers. Some of them may be useful. So she takes care, she is beginning to muster her resources. In her life-writings before she has only dealt with the dead whom it is easier, with a quiet conscience, to sort in the light of the project. Now she will sort the living. So be it. What she desires to do is what she *has* to do. She is already learning the way of it.

Three o'clock, she has not eaten, she presses her left hand against a very slight pain under her ribs on the left side. No food appeals to her, but she goes down to the kitchen and prepares something in accordance with the diet she introduced for Eric and has kept to since.

# 5

Dear Daniel,

As I said, I've begun with 1962, and this is as far as I've got with a summary of that year. Please fill in or correct anything you can. I enclose photocopies of a card and a letter you wrote to Eric in April, at Easter, when you were in Paris. There are three or four references I don't understand and a couple of words I can't decipher. I've marked them and I'd be so very grateful if you could help me out. Then, even more important, here are also copies of four letters you wrote to Eric that summer. Do you still have his to go with them? At the funeral you said that, like him, you generally did keep things. What joy it would give me to match your letters up during that important summer! I didn't tell you at the funeral but I tell you now that the day after your visit, two days before he died, Eric suddenly began to speak about your rendezvous in France, in Vizille, all in a rush he began to speak about it, but he was too ill to finish, he only got as far as a place somewhere on the road to Dover where a postman had dropped him. Oh I can still see his face at the moment when he had to stop! So youthful again and excited. He said I should ask you to tell me the rest of the story, for surely he told you everything that happened to him on his way to meet you in Vizille at the end of August 1962. Forgive me, Daniel, I must ask you, you were his closest friend and if I can learn all there is to learn about that journey I feel I shall have an entry into the whole truth of him when he was a very young

33

man and the world opening up to him. You will do this for me, won't you, as his friend and now my friend too? I saw in his eyes that night and I heard in his voice how sorely he wanted me to know how much the story mattered. Perhaps he thought it would help me if I truly comprehended what it felt like for him then on the threshold of his happiest life. To me that threshold is as passionate and glamorous as anything in the lives of the poor failures I used to care so much about, those who yearned so much and felt it so keenly in the very sadness of always falling short. Help me wherever you can, Daniel, won't you? And don't worry about me. I am doing well since I began all this. People have remarked on it. A colleague met me in town, when I had taken some old photographs in to have them enlarged, and she said I looked much better and would surely be well enough to come back quite soon. But, Daniel, I am thinking I shan't go back. I think I will first postpone it till October, and hand in my resignation before then. Don't tell anybody yet. I have easily enough money to live on, Eric saw to that. But do you think he would be cross with me if I give up work? I hope he will understand that I have to do what I am doing now if I am to hold on to any life worth living. I am not trying to become happy. But I do want to stay alive in a way that will not disgrace his name. You understand, don't you?

    With love

    Katrin.

Almost daily Katrin goes into the attic, takes out a bundle of letters from the lowest stratum, undoes the fastening, checks the postmarks to get some idea of the span of time, then carries the bundle through into her workroom. There she puts on an old jacket Eric used to wear around the house, it smells of him still, his lighter and an empty packet of Gitanes are still in one of the pockets. Wearing Eric's jacket, Katrin works on his early life.

It is true, as she wrote to Daniel, that Katrin has begun at the year 1962; but in order to understand that year, which seems to her to be the entry into the truth of Eric's life, she is doing what she always has done in her biographies: she is composing a detailed chronology of the life before and after the crisis or sudden shift or accelerated transition which interests her particularly at that stage of her work. So in Eric's case, either side of the late summer of 1962, she is collecting all she can from the years between his birth in 1943 and his marriage to Edna in 1964. And in addition to that, again as she always has done for the lives of her long-dead subjects, she is writing small portraits of the people who mattered to the hero or heroine along the way: parents, perhaps one or two other close relations, a teacher, three or four particular friends at school and university, any chance and brief acquaintances who somehow lodged and worked on in the subject's further life. All the surfaces of her workroom and much of the floor now accommodate the materials that are the makings of this chronology and these very brief lives. Out of a wardrobe on Eric's side of their marriage bed she has hauled three shoeboxes of largely unsorted and undated photographs, and another five crammed full with things such as birth certificates – Eric's own and those of his parents and grandparents – medical cards, a few death certificates, school and university exam results, a YHA card stamped by half a dozen hostels in the Peak District, old passports with their corners clipped, awards, badges, colours, testimonials, pay chits, betting slips, his portrait done in pencil by Monique, a Post Office savings book, concert, theatre and rugby programmes, cuttings from newspapers in four or five languages, a dozen I-Spy books (1954-5, diligently filled in), scores of receipts, some notable wine-labels, a collection of cigarette packets (Woodbines, Capstan, Dunhill, Senior Service, Craven A…. in fives, tens, twenties), bus tickets, lists (Russian vocabulary, shopping, reading, Christmas cards, jazz musicians…), the itinerary of a cycling holiday in North

Wales, a piece of shrapnel, several Woolworth's notebooks (none written in more than a page or two), a dog licence, a summons for riding a bicycle without lights, a ration book, an Old Moore's Almanach for 1963, a British Legion poppy, a scrap of Arabic, a code, a spell, a curse, and much (so much!) besides. The obscure subjects of Katrin's book, her Nine Lives, never came to her trailing such abundant material proof and revelation of their existences; and she realises now, considering Eric, how much easier it is to get at the figurative sense of a person's life, the sense that really interests her, when the documentation is fragmentary and sparse. To see Eric clearly for what he truly was and is, she must concentrate, keep her eye on essentials, not allow her vision to be muddled by all that the trunk, the carrier bags, the shoeboxes and the living friends will contribute as she consults them. Which is why she is so glad of 1962, beyond any doubt the year in which a person, her subject, was obeying life's chief command: become the one you are!

Every bundle in the lower strata contains perhaps a year, at most two years, of letters; which are not ordered chronologically, nor are the different writers gathered up separately. There is one exception to this rule, shocking Katrin when she discovers it: thirty-three items, all fastened together and all from one person: Monique. Most are postmarked Paris, 1962-63, their stamps are usually pairs of 25 centimes, ghostly Marianne on a red lake background. The last run of them, fifteen, between June 1963 and April 1964, are unopened.

Katrin leaves these letters lying in the attic. She returns to the writing of a very brief life (no more than five hundred words) of Eric's French teacher in the sixth form, who, going far beyond the syllabus, introduced the small class to Beckett, Sartre, Camus and the poetry of Aragon. He interests Katrin. She sees that he matters. He is strikingly good-looking, like Marcello Mastroianni in *La Notte*. He had great hopes of Eric. He sent him a copy of *Les Yeux d'Elsa*, published in London in 1943 by Horizon-La France Libre, 'Pour t'encourager,' as he wrote by way of a dedication, Christmas 1961. But she has Monique at the back of her mind, almost as a presence looking over her shoulder, as she writes about this schoolmaster. She wants to make him real in her account, but he does not trouble her, he is entirely benign, and though still among the living (he wrote her a kind note when Eric died), he is remote, he will never visit. But Monique came to her house, stood on the doorstep and wept, gave her the black bowl decorated with a red rose and red cherries. Often since then Katrin has summoned up her smudged face, her motley clothing, her easy intimacy with Daniel; but now, after the discovery of her letters, fifteen of which Eric never opened, Monique enters the workroom unbidden, anxious to speak.

What does Katrin know about Monique at this stage of writing Eric's life? He told Katrin that he met her in Paris in September 1962; that he went back to Paris at Christmas, to see her again; that they met for the last time early in 1963. She was born in Nevers, in July 1944, went to school there, moved to Paris and lived in various places behind the Panthéon, as an artist and a potter. Katrin can remember Eric telling her these few facts. It was just before they decided to get married. She had the feeling then, and has it again now, that he wanted her to know something important about him, so that she would understand the man she would be living with. In the event, he told her very little; and reaching early 1963 and his last meeting with Monique, he halted abruptly, shrugged, and stared hard into Katrin's eyes. In truth, she had no very passionate desire to know his secrets. That time was past and elsewhere. She loved him, he assured her again and again that he loved her, really that was all she needed and desired. She kissed him, they resumed their walk, and that was that. She *noted* that he found it much easier to talk to her about Edna, about his marriage, his mistake, as he called it, and from time to time they did discuss her, letters came from her, there was the continuing business of his payments to her

– Katrin said he should stop them, he wouldn't – but none of this mattered deeply. She felt sure of him and neither his marriage nor his Paris romance ever grieved her. It is harder now, far harder, as day by day she pieces together the life she was not part of. He is not there to tell her then is then and now is now. The now is splitting open and into it seeps, trickles, pours the country he had wanted nothing more to do with, the country he called 'back then'.

# 6

DR GRACIE IS a woman of 52 in remission from breast cancer. She will see Katrin once a fortnight, oftener if Katrin would like. She says she must get out of the house at least once a day, walk, be among people. She advises her to discontinue the diet she began for Eric and to eat normally, try to relish things. Katrin mentions the pain under her ribs on the left side. Dr Gracie examines her, says again that she should eat properly, there may be some slight inflammation, if the pain doesn't go she will arrange for a scan.

Katrin wants to obey the doctor. She thinks of Eric's shopping, the expertise and the gusto of it, his leisurely preparation of the evening meal. He would come to the stairs, call up to her in her workroom under the eaves, she came down, everything was ready, all just right, the table correctly laid, a red candle burning. He appraised and savoured every mouthful, they ate slowly, they talked. Now there is nothing, there is worse than nothing, she must sit, eat, think in an absence as alive as the years of presence were.

She does go out, it is April. She takes a walk they often took together, downhill through the old part of town, to the river, along by the old moorings, yards and warehouses that have become venues for the arts, places to eat, galleries of the past, along by the hurrying water and back to the streets again, uphill home. An hour's tour. Or, to place herself truly in the midst of people, she walks through the covered market, stands still for five minutes at its centre. But this does her more harm than good. For in all the purposeful coming and going, in all the cheerful clamour, she knows herself for what she is or soon will be: a shade, an empty shape. Her insubstantiality frightens her. Perhaps fear is the last feeling you can call your own, as you vanish.

Now and then she bumps into someone she knows. She starts up in a lively fashion, talks brightly, gives the best possible account of herself, asks questions, attends. But she can feel the necessary energy leaving her even as she speaks and acts. And she believes this lapsing away is visible to her interlocutor. They know. Doubtless to one another they say, Katrin isn't doing very well.

At heart Katrin does not want to live. Only her work, her life-writing, enlivens her. She hurries home, puts on Eric's jacket, continues. She has a photograph of him on her desk, taken after the diagnosis but before the sickness claimed him for itself. It was their anniversary, he has a glass of champagne to hand, he looks her full in the face, smiling. He is enjoying the occasion. How carefully he considered what they would most like to eat and drink. How he savoured it all. Now Katrin feels she is not fit to be looked at by his image. She feels with ever greater certainty that he would not like her to be doing what she is doing. Has she kept her two promises: friends, her work? Scarcely. Friends phone *her*, they email, she answers as cheerfully as she can. And as to her work, she is working more hours a day than ever before, she has no other commitments, very few distractions. But surely he would be uneasy about the nature of her work. And yet she can't imagine him forbidding it or even begging her not to do it. He would speak his mind: that he fears she will harm herself. But then he would leave her be. He was never a tyrant. Live and let live, was his motto. And writing his life is the only way that she can live.

23 April 2012

Dear Daniel,

Thank you so much for your letter and your notes on my little chronology and your explanations of the mysteries in those letters. I should have thanked you sooner but I was a bit low for a few days. It is bound to be like that and I am better now. My writing about Eric is going well and I feel helped by it. So don't be worried. I'll email you a couple of passages then you will see for yourself that it is not sentimental or morbid. I try to treat him like one of my subjects. I hadn't realised you were on your own in Paris that Easter nor that you were the discoverer of the famous hotel. I wonder if it's still there. One day, all being well, I shall go on a research trip to the 5ème and 6ème: Perhaps I should stay in that hotel? I am overjoyed that you still have the letters he wrote to you and I agree it would be much nicer to see them − the real things − than the photocopies. So do let's meet. I could come to London. Dr Gracie says I need to make excursions, and to meet you again and to hold Eric's letters would surely be the sort of treat she has in mind. Meanwhile, for your attention when you have time, here are copies of a letter you wrote to him *poste restante* in Nevers, 3 September 1962, and also − what a relic! − a *telegram* you sent him 5 September, *poste restante* in Nemours, saying, as you see, YES GO TO MONIQUE. How lucky I am that you keep and remember things! I feel there is so much you could explain to me, if you would be so kind. Email me a date when we can meet.

With love

Katrin

PS I have found Monique's letters but I haven't read them yet. I must. To be honest, Daniel, I am fearful of them.

Katrin fetches up a card table from Eric's room, sets it against the wall in hers, puts his photograph and two bookends on it. That done, she goes into the loft for Monique's letters and ranges them one behind the other in line towards her from the wall. She flicks through, checking the postmarks. They are exactly in order. Every now and then comes a postcard, twice a telegram. Thirty-three pieces of evidence all told. She pushes them away and aligns them along the far edge of the table, between the bookends and up against the bare wall. Now she can begin.

The first envelope is addressed to Eric at 35 Heaton Street. Katrin takes out the letter: 7 rue Tournefort, Paris 5. le 25 septembre 1962. She begins to read: Eric, chéri, j'arrive pas à croire que tu ne sois plus là. Mon corps, le lit, tout l'appartement, nous n'y comprenons rien... But before she has read half the page she decides this way of going about it will not do. She fetches the A4 notebook – the third – in which she drafts her chronologies and portraits and makes comments day-by-day on the progress of her work. Next to it she sets the big Harraps from Eric's room. So far she has transcribed all the letters and cards directly on to the computer but now, with Monique, she will proceed differently. She will copy out each letter long-hand, in ink, on alternate lines of her notebook and on the empty lines between, in pencil, she will make a translation of the French.

Translation is a mixed business. As you bring a foreign writer across you mix her language with your own. All translation is, more or less thoroughly, an appropriation. Your language, into which you bring the foreign, is your own tongue, your speech, your voice, your accent, your tone, the expression of your characteristic demeanour in the world. And Katrin, as she now transcribes Monique into her own hand and then, in her own hand, translates her, will thus doubly appropriate the foreigner from across the Channel half a century ago. In her own hand she will put Monique into English, the language that has almost evicted her native Polish. At the same time, the translator is not proof against the writer. How should she be? To translate you have to be open. Opening enables you to partake of your foreigner; or makes you unable to resist. Opening, you may slip towards becoming the one you are translating. Perhaps Katrin even wishes it. So in this ceaseless to and fro – a kind of fighting, a loving quarrel – Katrin transcribes and translates the letters Monique wrote to Eric fifty years ago. Her French improves rapidly – her passive understanding, at least, of the already written sentences. She knows she would still have trouble holding a conversation or composing letters of her own in French. But by evening, after the first three letters, Katrin understands Monique pretty well.

Daniel emails and suggests they meet soon. He can answer all her questions and tell her much besides. And he asks should he not spare her the travelling? He would enjoy a trip west, if he caught the first off-peak train he could be with her soon after twelve. Will she let him take her out to lunch? That could be the excursion the doctor ordered. And they will have their conversation and he will hand over Eric's letters. Katrin is touched by his kindness, she replies at once: yes, he must come to her if he would like that, but she will give him lunch at home, just as Eric would, and of course he must stay the night if he possibly can, they will talk at leisure, there is so much to say. Back in a trice comes his brief reply: Wonderful, and many thanks, I'll do just that, I look forward to it.

Katrin crosses to her table against the wall, to work. And seeing the letters, the notebook, the dictionary, and turning then to take in the contents of the shoeboxes and the opened bundles from the loft, all the documentation now covering every surface and half the floor, she feels in a rush of sadness and fear that neither soon nor ever again will she have a dear friend home to give him lunch and supper and a bed for the night. It is finished already, that sort of thing, before it began. Nobody must see this room and her in it in Eric's jacket in the midst of her life-writing. Is it shame? Is it a fierce *pudeur*? Whatever it is, it amounts to a prohibition of all ordinary friendliness and sociability. She wants nobody home but her subject's ghost, not till the work is done and everything returned to secrecy in the attic and the cupboard by their marriage bed. And when will that be? Years, perhaps never.

She checks the train times, she emails Daniel: would he mind after all if she did the travelling? She feels she needs to. There's a train gets in at 12.23. Will he meet her? Does he know a quiet place nearby? He answers at once: of course, just as she prefers, he will be there.

Katrin contemplates the hundreds of items from the shoeboxes which, for an overview and to make significant juxtapositions, she has laid out on the floor. With the photographs she has not been able to do much more than sort the black and white from the colour. Shall she take a few dozen along for Daniel to ponder? And the cast-list of *Fin de partie*, entrance-tickets (*tarif réduit* or *gratuit*) to the Louvre and the Musée Rodin, a cinema-ticket (Cluny-Palace), a theatre-ticket (Comédie Française, in the gods), a copy of *Libération*, 18 October 1961, a stray page of Rimbaud's *Une Saison en enfer*, a bare postcard of Rodin's 'Fugit amor', the front of a cigarette packet (Gitanes) with what look like train-times scrawled (not in Eric's hand) on the back? All these ephemera, hoarded for half a century, not ephemeral in fact, they have lasted, but they matter only to her now, the widow, who needs help if she is ever to give them their due in the life she is writing.

In the quiet coach Katrin reads through her transcriptions and translations of the first tranche of Monique's letters and cards, 25 September – 1 December 1962. She is by no means sure she will show these to Daniel. She has brought the two telegrams with her – 3 November, 2 December – and these she will show him and ask him about because they seem to be important for the story, the plot, of Eric's life at that point. For five minutes she stares out of the window, ignorant of where she is, and not caring. But she sees that the banks are flowery and the trees are in leaf and blossoming. Sorrow circumscribes her all the time and everywhere, she wraps herself in whatever protection she can fabricate, but it is a poor habitation, it lets in the sorrow, slowly or in a rush, slowly or with sudden violence she suffocates, sorrow being an atmosphere inimical to life.

Katrin shudders – and switches on her laptop. Everything of Eric's life already composed is in the colossal memory of this small machine. No other document houses in there. Like the A4 notebooks, this slim travelling companion was bought for her one purpose. With three clicks she summons up the makings of his life: the advancing chronology, half a dozen portraits, a list (almost a bibliography) of the chief materials she is using, two or three substantial passages of the life itself, all from childhood, with some family history preceding them, easiest to write, so that is where she began. And questions – for herself, for Daniel, for anybody he might suggest if he cannot answer. It is all correctly done; and as she reads a page or two of the continuous prose, she takes a writerly pleasure in its clarity, its matter-of-fact tone. She loves the English language, always has, and over the years and when it became the language of her love and marriage, she has loved it more and more. Eric commended her grasp and deployment of it. Still, it is not her mother tongue, which, writing about him, she is glad of, it is his language, not properly hers, and in it, getting better and better, she approaches him. And as is often the case when a speaker and writer becomes adept and expressive in a foreign tongue, Katrin feels herself liberated and allowed to say things, and to say them in ways, which her mother tongue would baulk at or forbid. She knows that soon she will have to attempt a writing for which clear matter-of-factness will not suffice, she will have to say wholeheartedly what love is like, what love and the concomitant grief are like, what it feels like, loving and grieving and not wanting to live and yet hoping, somewhere deep down or far at the back of the mind, that it may still become possible to want to live.

At Reading, looking away from the screen and out at the life outside, Katrin has an apprehension of violent chaos. The platforms are being rebuilt, there is too little room for the press of people in an anxious hurry for their trains. She sees a woman with a baby violently jostled, her face shocked by it. Katrin's courage begins to disintegrate. Why did she think she would be able to cope with London? She packs up her things, sits tight, closes her eyes, striving to hold together an identity. Half an hour later she is delivered into Paddington among thousands who, to her, seem to know who they are, and why, and where they will go next. Daniel is waiting at the barrier. She sees in his face how she appears to him, and she bows her head in shame.

Then it is better, he is courteous, carries her bag, she takes his arm. He stoops, walks slowly, perhaps just for her, he seems to be reflecting on the fact of the two of them proceeding through the crowd together, and in a shy way, like a boy, he is attentive, he glances again and again at her, to see how she is managing. Katrin's faith revives. He is Eric's oldest friend, of course all will be well, or at least bearable, on his arm passing through this multitude of strangers. From nowhere the word 'covenant' comes into her mind. There is a covenant between them, between the three of them.

They arrive at an Italian restaurant in Praed Street. I think we'll be all right here, he says. I'm almost a regular. It's early, we should be all right. But at the door Katrin halts. It is a cheerful place, there are photographs and paintings of Verona on the walls, the rose-marble amphitheatre, Juliet's balcony, the Alps stepping closer in a wintry sunlight. There's a table free, they could sit face to face and talk. But she can't do it. Forgive me, Daniel, she says. You should have come to me after all. But I was ashamed. And now here also I am ashamed. Forgive me. I can't do it. There are so many things now that I cannot do. No matter, he answers, he takes her arm, turns back to the street with her, a taxi halts for him, she closes her eyes, he is Eric's friend, they are bound by the covenant, he will look after her. Ten minutes later they are in a tranquil square. I often come here, he says, especially at this time of year. See how leafy it is, and listen how quiet. Sit here now, I'll be back very soon. Flits away, aging ghost of a boy of eighteen, reappears. A picnic, he says, with a plastic beaker of wine. I quite often do this. And it is nice to have company.

Katrin sips at her wine. Eat as well, Daniel says. You must eat. She obeys, a little at least. Being told what to do is a gentle thing. She eats a few mouthfuls, and for an interlude the pasta, the sips of wine, feel like kindness itself, a bodily kindness. He watches her, and nods. Then quickly and with relish he eats too, drinks half a beaker at a gulp, wipes his mouth and says: Eric was working at Kelloggs, nights, he cycled in for 10 and back home at 6. He earned good money. I was in a place near Garmisch, I was a courier, I only got my keep and a few tips. But we were high up, in the clear sharp air, I took parties out most days though I'd never been higher than Snowdon before that. Near the end, when I was wondering how to get to Vizille, a woman gave me a bicycle. It had been her son's and he had died in a climbing accident, she said. So I cycled to Vizille, I took my time, I didn't arrive at the meeting place till the morning of the third day. There were half a dozen cafés on the street in question but I only remember one, the Café Elsa, it had a red awning, under which sat Eric, reading. I watched him for some minutes across the street. He was entirely absorbed. A few people, a few cars, now and then a bus, passed beween us, but there he sat, again and still, when the view cleared. The thought of our two journeys, the very thought of our arriving in that almost arbitrary place *by design*, moved me greatly, and still does. It seemed you might decide on a thing, conceive and formulate a desire, and then set off and accomplish it. How I loved him! And often since then I've been moved by that moment, but from a different perspective, so that I see both of us, Eric at his table, already an *habitué*, and myself just arrived out of the high mountains, and I love, admire and rejoice in both of us then and feel again, and am glad of, my friendly advantage over him, seeing him, contemplating him, for some minutes, before he raised his eyes from his book and saw me, the arrival, his friend.

Eat a little more, Daniel says. Sip a little more wine. And I'll tell you more. There is more and more to tell. What was he reading? Katrin asks. *L'Homme révolté*, says Daniel. He had been given it the first morning by a man – a sort of itinerant scholar, he said – who as soon as he finished a book looked out for someone to hand it on to. We sat there for a couple of hours, first with a coffee then with a carafe of wine and the cheapest sandwich. After that we found a way into the big park and lay around all afternoon by the lake. Did he tell you about his journey? Katrin asks. Not till that night. At 6 we went back to the Café Elsa, in case the others turned up. I was hoping they wouldn't, and when nobody did and we were making our way out to where he had left his things, he told me that when he got to Vizille, and began to wait, he realised I was the only arrival he was hoping for.

He had found a hill about a mile outside the town, to the east. I hid my bike in a ruin close to the road and we climbed up to his camp with a bottle of wine, a bit more bread and cheese and some apricots. And that was when he told you? Katrin asks. Yes, when we were lying side by side under the stars. When I think of those stars now I feel them to be very close above us and somehow audible, like a distant rapids.

Katrin leans back, with the plastic bowl and the plastic beaker in her lap, and shuts her eyes. In its accent and in the rhythms characteristic of their local speech, Daniel's voice is close, and feels to be getting closer, to Eric's. She gives herself up to wholly listening. He told me all this in a wondering tone, says Daniel, as though it were the fabulous account of someone else's adventures. At that place on the A20, where the postman had dropped him, he did not have to wait long.

He hung around in the carpark and when a likely couple came out, a man and wife about as old as his own mother and father, he accosted them politely and asked would they take him towards Dover, if they were going that way. They were and they would. The husband was an off-duty policeman. During the war everybody hitched, he said. So why not now? As long as you're careful, said his wife. She chatted about their son and daughter. They'll have it better than we did, her husband said. No more wars and a decent education. Coming to Dover, he drove to the port, though it was out of his way. The cars were in line for the next sailing. Just walk along and ask, said the policeman. All you want is your passage across. On the other side they put you out and you do as you like. That's what our Jack and his girlfriend do. Works every time, he says.

So Eric did as Jack and his girlfriend had always done: he walked down the line of cars and vans, looking. Pretty soon he saw a Hillman Minx with space on the back seat and when he paused, the driver wound the window down and nodded. Just to the port, Eric said. The driver nodded again; reached behind and opened the door. His wife turned in her seat and smiled. The line moved off. At the barrier, the driver presented the three passports. On board, Eric felt embarrassed. Why should they want his company for the crossing? But they took him with them to the cafeteria and the driver, unspeaking, brought tea and pastries for them all. The wife smiled. You making for Paris? she asked. Yes, said Eric. We're going to Dunkirk – well, somewhere near Dunkirk, she said. The husband nodded. Eric in a rush, into their silence, said that really he was passing through Paris and heading on down to a place the other side of Grenoble that nobody had ever heard of, to meet one or two or maybe even three school friends. Then he told the man and wife the whole plan and how after working for ten weeks in Kelloggs he had set off down the London Road out of Manchester, and how lucky he had been and what kindness he had met with from strangers. After that, he asked would they excuse him, he wanted to go out on deck and would come back and find them later. He stood on the deck in the dark and watched the lights of Dover fade and the lights of Calais brighten. There was a wind, he said, and the sea made a mighty rushing noise, parting white around the prow and trailing white astern into the black. When he returned to the cafeteria he found the woman alone. She told him not to mind her husband's silence. He had been at Dunkirk in 1940, and very suddenly, and to her great surprise, he had wanted to go back there, or to the place near the Belgian border where the retreat had got stuck in a terrible traffic jam and his best friend, not twenty, had been killed when the German planes came over. He had wanted to, but now he wasn't sure, and perhaps they wouldn't go there after all. He's quite chatty normally, she added.

Daniel stands up and walks to and fro in front of Katrin. To and fro, to and fro. Then he sits down again, offers her more wine, she shakes her head, he pours himself half a beaker and drinks it off fast. And rather absently and without conviction he begs her at least to eat another mouthful. These bits of lives, he says. Fifty years later I can still recall faces, phrases, tones of voice, of people I encountered travelling. People reveal themselves. You meet, they show you something – perhaps a good deal – of who they are. Then you go your separate ways, you will never see them again, but bits of their lives will lodge in you for ever. That Dunkirk soldier and his wife, Eric met them, I didn't, but when he told me about them under the stars on that hill outside Vizille and when I tell you about them now, how living they are to me, though very likely dead, and perhaps in you also they will continue living.

Once they were through Passports and outside the gates, the husband and wife shook hands with Eric and wished him a safe journey. You'll want the Boulogne road, the husband said – that way, along the shore. I'd get my head down somewhere soon, if I were you, and make an early start in the morning.

It was already past midnight. Eric set off towards Boulogne. There was very little traffic. He could hear the sea close on his right hand. He walked for perhaps an hour under the moon and stars, not anxious at all, so he told me. But when he left the road he found that he had come within sight of a cluster of lights and that the beach was not open, as he had assumed it would be, but was enclosed by a broken wire fence within which were buildings, perhaps warehouses or hangars. Too tired to retrace his steps to the open dunes, he crawled through the wire netting and in at the smashed door of the first shed. It was a vile place, he told me, smelling damply of ruin. But he felt his way into a corner, unrolled his bag and lay down on the concrete floor, his head on the rucksack. He thought he must have slept at once, perhaps even for three or four hours. A faint lightening had entered through holes in the roof so that he saw signs of another's passage or lodging – an old mattress, bottles, tins, a few rags, a tattered bag – along the far wall. The place disgusted and thrilled him in equal measure. He had an idea of himself as a vagrant who lay down in foul places, commended his soul to the guardian angels, and slept. And when he woke, Eric says, he lay there for a while amid the dereliction, taking it all in. He saw rats, he heard the snuffling of some larger creature at the broken door. Not until the light outside was definitely sunlight and the first cars were passing, did he pull on his boots and creep from the shed, and through the fence, to the road. The first driver he hitched picked him up. He was in Boulogne as the cafés opened. He washed himself, he ordered coffee and bread and sat at a table in the window, watching.

Katrin opens her eyes. I think I'll get the early train, she says. Can we walk back to Paddington? How long would it take? Half an hour, says Daniel. He packs up the picnic, insists she takes what she hasn't eaten, for the journey. They leave the garden. Last week, he says, when I knew we'd be meeting,

I looked at the map to see if I could work out where Eric slept that night. I'm sure it was very near Sangatte – where the tunnel comes up now, where the big camp was. That's an odd thought, isn't it?

At the barrier, saying good-bye, Katrin says, You'll tell me the rest another day, won't you? Daniel nods. Then she asks: That telegram – YES GO TO MONIQUE – does that mean you arranged it? Yes, says Daniel. I met her at Easter. I thought Eric would be glad of a place to stay. And her letters, Katrin says, I've put them in order, I've begun to transcribe them. The last fifteen are unopened. Eric never read them. Ah, says Daniel. – Does that surprise you? – Yes and no. – Do you think I should open them and read them? – Daniel shrugs. Katrin, he says, one way or another you have to get through this business. And I don't even know what would help and what wouldn't help. Katrin nods. Neither do I, she says. But you will tell me the rest of his journey, won't you, and how he got back to Paris and found Monique? Yes, I will, says Daniel. As a matter of fact, he cycled back. I gave him the bike the woman in Garmisch had given me. I wanted to be in the mountains again. He gave me his rucksack. We said good-bye at the Café Elsa, he pedalled off out of town towards Grenoble.

# 7

DR GRACIE'S SURGERY is spacious and light. She has a couple of landscapes on the walls – lake water reflecting light, sky behind hills through which a path is climbing – and also a painting by Gwen John of a girl reading. On her desk, in a clear space on the left, she has photographs of her husband and their two children. She wears a soft blue dress and a coral necklace. Her hair has recovered but is greyer than it was. Her glasses give her the appearance of a studious schoolgirl. Behind her there is a garden, an apple tree in flower. And the scents of the garden, a breath of warmth, and birdsong enter the surgery through the slightly opened window.

There has been a silence, the timbre of which, for both women, is thoughtful. Then Dr Gracie says, Tell me what you fear most, Katrin. Say your worst fears. Katrin answers at once. The first is that I have got Eric's cancer. The second is that my life was nothing till I met Eric and has become nothing again now he is dead. She halts. Then she adds, And that really even when he was alive and I loved him and he loved me, even all that life amounted to less, much less, than the life he'd had already before we met. Dr Gracie nods. The cancer is very unlikely, she says. But I'll get you a scan as soon as possible, which won't be all *that* soon, things being the way they are, but soon enough, and in the meantime you must try not to worry. I'm not really worried, Katrin says. Perhaps I was wrong to call it one of my two worst fears. The second fear is much the worse. It is so bad sometimes the first doesn't count at all. Part of me wants to have his cancer. Yes, says Dr Gracie, I was afraid you were thinking like that. Why do you feel you are less than his life before? I've been reading his letters, says Katrin, mostly those written to him fifty years ago. He didn't say I shouldn't. He didn't tell me to burn them without reading them. And I've been talking to his best friend, who knew him back then, and everything he says makes me feel that my second fear, the worse one, is reasonable. – And you can't stop enquiring into Eric's past? – No. Not now. – Not even if it's harming you? – No, I can't stop now. And I don't know that it is harming me. I only feel alive when I'm finding out more about Eric.

Dr Gracie never hurries you. Time slows and even pauses in her room. She allows silences during which it is birdsong you hear, not the ticking of a clock. Katrin stands up. I'll go now I've told you the worst, she says. Dr Gracie nods. People find different ways of getting through, she says. Maybe deep down your life knows what it wants. Maybe, says Katrin. Maybe it wants to die. Dr Gracie shakes her head. I don't think so. And even if it did we could help it change its mind.

Katrin puts on Eric's jacket and sits down at her table facing the wall. It is two days since she saw Dr Gracie and two weeks since she saw Daniel and in that time she has not had the courage to continue transcribing and translating Monique's letters. Instead, she has done easier things, still troubling (everything is), but do-able in a mechanical sort of way. Whatever she can date among the photographs and the contents of the shoeboxes she has begun sorting into folders year by year. So, for example, into 1952 goes a train-ticket to Morecombe, an envelope bearing a two-penny stamp of George VI and the imprint GOD SAVE THE QUEEN, and a black and white photo of Eric and his brother Michael walking with the scholars. Such early miscellanea are touching enough, and collecting them into strata and juxtapositions is a satisfying task. But even in this, the accumulating richness begins to abash her. Her own childhood feels needy in comparison. Year by year, as Eric's life enlarges, hers diminishes. And yet in a sense he was nothing out of the ordinary. His family had their griefs and their troubles, and even as they made their way, did well for themselves and their two sons, they were of the times, the times were bearing them along, the ethos encouraged them, they had possibilities which they worked for and seized. Perhaps that is what Katrin is overfaced by now: that in another country, a quarter of a century before she was born, the times were moving, opening, lifting the citizens up after war, loss, much hardship. Perhaps it is only that: the opportunities, and that in all the struggle there was hopefulness, a belief. She comes later, grows up into the disappointment, and there she must bide, without a comrade to encourage her. She has the strange and unhappy feeling that on 24 August 1962, setting off for France, he went far ahead of her and she would never catch up.

As a preparation for her return to Monique's letters, or still prevaricating, Katrin composes another small section of chronology:

1962
Easter (15–23 April): Daniel in Paris, he stays in the Hôtel Malebranche, meets Monique, stays with her.
1 June–21 August, Eric working nights at Kelloggs in Trafford Park (and occasionally – when he has to – still attending school)
24 August, Eric leaves Manchester
28 August, arrives in Vizille
31 August, Daniel arrives
2 September, Eric leaves for Paris, Daniel for the Alps
Eric's route (partly Daniel's supposition, from what Eric told him): Eybens, Grenoble, Saint-Égrève, Voreppe, Voiron,

Morestel, Bourg-en-Bresse, Mâcon, Charolles, Digoin, Decize, Nevers, La Charité-sur-Loire, Sancerre, Briare (west bank of the Loire, all D-roads), Montargis, Souppes-sur-Loing, Nemours, Fontainebleau, Melun, Évry, Vitry-sur-Seine

8 September, he arrives at Monique's, 7 rue Tournefort

25 September, he takes the boat train to London

26 September, back in Salford

4 October, Oxford

October-December, letters, cards and two telegrams fom Monique

End of Michaelmas term: Eric takes the boat train to Paris

Katrin opens a letter postmarked Paris 24 November 1962. Between the folded sheets of thin blue paper is a photograph of a young woman slipping her blouse off down her bare arms behind her back. The image is reproduced, from a different angle, in a large square mirror standing on a wooden settle and resting against the wall on her right. Her head is lifted and she gazes unsmiling and with something like disdain at the photographer and indeed at whoever views her undressing in the photograph. On the back, in Monique's hand, are the words 'Tu m'aimes?' Katrin leans the photo against the letters aligned between the book-ends along the wall. She stares, taking it in. She says aloud, I have never looked like that. She lays the photograph face down on the table, closes her eyes and conjures up Monique, her yellow rucksack, red stockings, black cloche hat, as she stood on the doorstep after the funeral saying she had dreamed of Eric and beginning to weep. The face of an old woman, crumpling and smirching like a child's.

Katrin goes down the two flights of stairs, into her kitchen, and takes up the bowl, Monique's funeral gift, from off the shelf among the crockery Eric inherited from his mother. The doorbell rings. Katrin starts like a thief in her own kitchen, holding the bowl. It is late afternoon. She feels the intrusion to be monstrous, wholly wrong, coming from an elsewhere before she had become what she is now. She shakes her head, not in refusal but in bafflement at this astonishing importunity. It rings again, piercingly loud and shrill. But she stands with the bowl in her hands, averting every atom of herself. She stands until she feels sure that whoever rang has gone away. Then she hurries back upstairs and sets the bowl on the card table with the photograph of Eric at their anniversary.

But the doorbell has frightened her. Suddenly she fears that *she will not be allowed* to finish her writing of Eric's life. Something will intervene: her health will fail, her friends, her brothers or the authorities will remove her from her workplace. She will never carry it through, she will never recover.

To counter this panic she takes Monique's photograph and kneels on the carpet with it among the scores of black and white photographs to which she has not yet been able to ascribe a definite date. She sorts through rapidly with her fingertips and has soon assembled Monique in five more images. Back at her table, she lays them all out like a hand of cards, and behind them, against the letters, she stands the girl undressing. She contemplates them, glancing often at the photograph of Eric taken six months before he died. She steeps herself in that montage of images. Soon she can work. She reads the letter of 24 November and transcribes it into her notebook. Then the next, 3 December. She understands both very well. How he must have suffered. Then really to take it home into herself, slowly and carefully on the lines left vacant between the lines of French, Katrin translates Monique's letters into Eric's mother tongue.

Paris 24 November 1962

Eric, my darling, I miss you. Do you miss me? If you do, it is not enough or you would not be able to bear it in the strange place you are in now but would appear suddenly in my room in the middle of the night and surprise me with happiness as I did you when all this began. You tell me how you spend your days but it doesn't make any sense to me, life is short and doing without what you enjoy seems very stupid to me. But perhaps you enjoy being told what to think by old men who were never young or so long ago they can't remember what it felt like? I am not sure whether Daniel is still my friend or not because I have told him several times to tell you to come and see me but if he has he has not done it well enough. So far as I know, you are still where you were and must be content there, I suppose. Thank you for your letters. Your French is pretty good. I expect you are getting better and better marks for your proses and translations so at least I am good for that. I don't think my English will ever improve. As everybody knows, you have to go and live among the speakers, and I don't want to do that, and wouldn't, not even for you. It is freezing cold here and I've no money left for coal and wood. I sleep in my clothes with every blanket and coat on the top. One good thing about you is how warm your body is. Really, it is your duty to appear *bodily* in my bedroom and not just as a spirit when I try to get warm by conjuring you up. Oh what a swine you are! I expect you have servants bringing you grog and hot waterbottles every night. I am not working much at present. My hands are too cold and besides I can't afford the clay and the colours. Anne gave me a pair of gloves, the kind that leave your fingers bare, and wearing them I can at least draw and paint a bit. I have done some nice things – an old woman going through the bins along our street, some winter jasmine, Anne in her warm red coat sitting at my window – which I will show you if I ever see you again. They make fun of me here. They say I am moping for my English boy. They say I am *unfree*. Well, they can say what they like. Supposing I do love you as you swear you love me: it is possible to love and still be free. In fact, love should set you free. I went to the Luxembourg yesterday morning. There was a fog and the people were moving down the avenues and the paths like spectres. All the sounds were muffled. Where the sun should have been there was only a faint lightness which sometimes intensified and the sun became visible, but only as a silver disc, like a small full moon, and soon vanished again. But there was enough light for the big trees to appear in their drapes of hoar frost, grey silver and dripping. I met Jean-Luc, he was trying to photograph these phenomena. Paris is the most beautiful place in the world and where I live is the most beautiful part of Paris. You could make a living here by teaching fat businessmen English and I wouldn't be so cold at nights. Think about it, English boy. Monique

Paris 3 December 1962

Poor darling Eric, I was only teasing you, of course your studies are important – perhaps you will be very rich one day – and I'm sure your professors teach you to think for yourselves. Yes, I will come and visit you in your funny college, I promise, but not just now because I haven't any money. Also I want you to come back to Paris first. This is where we fell in love and seeing you again will be easier for me here and perhaps for both of us because you love this *quartier* nearly as much as I do so you will almost be coming home when you come back here but Oxford sounds very strange and foreign to me and I think I should find it hard to be at ease with you there. But we shall see. I have done some designs for pots, mostly cherries and roses, red on black, lovely shapes, and when I can get back to the wheel and a kiln, I'll do some proper work and then I shall feel better. The cold is getting worse here, as it is with you also, I think, so I spend a lot of time in our café, they don't seem to mind us sitting around for nothing. Well, it's not quite for nothing: I gave Maurice a vase I made in the summer, he has put it in a place of honour behind the bar, I should think it will be worth a fortune one day. You remember Yves? He has packed up and gone south and not just for the winter but for good, he says. People come and go, and at present, so it seems, mostly they go. I walked for hours yesterday, I went to the places I love best and that we went to together when you arrived in my life and I wanted you to love them too. Remember? The length of the Luxembourg to the Odéon, that café, Pont des Arts, Les Halles, all the long way to Père Lachaise, the Mur des Fédérés and Clement's tomb, there were more red roses on the hard earth. Remember my shoe fell apart and you tied it up with string? Coming back it was getting dark, I collected a few wintry things at the Marché aux Fleurs, they were clearing away, the river is full and moves very fast, what a quick death you'd have if you ever felt like dying. I was so tired when I got back, I fell asleep on the bed and woke up very cold. I didn't tell anybody where I was going and when I went to the café – quite late, to warm up – I told them lies when they asked me where I had been. You didn't say anything about my photograph. Perhaps you don't like it?

Write soon.

Monique

Your other letter has just come. You mustn't ask me questions like that. You don't own me. What if he does pay me? I need the money.

Katrin ranges those two letters on the left, continuing the series she has already transcribed and translated. She sits back, staring at the wall. It is time she went downstairs and made herself an evening meal. The thought dispirits her. She has no appetite, the effort will be great for no enjoyment. Yet she knows she must eat. Appetite and enjoyment are a bonus. You do not have to enjoy doing what you must do if you wish to live. All that matters is: you do it. She agrees with that precept. But reaches for the next letter from Monique, 4 December 1962. Opening it, she finds that it is not a letter at all. There is nothing in the envelope except a postcard of Bonnard's *La*

*Sieste.* On the back of it Monique has scrawled, Ça te gêne s'il me baise après? Or – there seems to be an emendation half way: Ça te gêne qu'il me baise après? So either (as Katrin translates it in her head): Does it bother you if he fucks me afterwards? Or: Does it bother you that he fucks me afterwards?

Downstairs in the kitchen Katrin turns on the radio. A junior minister is saying that he can see no reason whatsoever why the state should fund the humanities. She opens the fridge. There is some soup left, from two days ago, and some cheese that might still be all right. Warming the soup, she turns off the radio. They never had a television, but a daily paper was delivered, Eric read it thoroughly, did the crossword, she read it after him. And the radio, yes, they listened to the news and often to programmes having to do with important matters, past and present, at home and abroad. And they discussed things. Katrin puts the soup, the cheese and the end of a loaf on the bare table. All ceremony has deserted her house. In silence, eating without pleasure, she allows herself to be possessed again by thoughts of Eric and Monique in the bitter cold winter of 1962-63. His jealousy deepens her bereavement. She feels that he suffers and she can do nothing about it. But she suffers too: she was never Monique. The want never can be made up. Suddenly the house is unbearable, it is too big, it has too many rooms, every one of those rooms is empty. The sadness wells up in her. Really, it is too much to ask that she wish to live. Sadness and panic, only those, for evermore. All day has been sunny, she has seen it through the window, the spring swelling into summer, and now at dusk she feels, again, what she has missed, what she has not been part of but it passed her by, outside the window pane. All day, indoors, she has fed herself on an absent life, on love in the form of grief, and there is no nourishment in that. She is learning that you cannot live on sorrow.

Turning on a lamp in the front room, Katrin goes out for an hour – down to the river, along it, uphill home. Letting herself in again, she feels that day by day she will become less able to face these homecomings. The house abhors a vacuum, it fills up with absence, the air is thick with the fact of absence. She stands in the dark hall, backing the front door to, facing the stairs and wondering how anyone so possessed by grief should climb night after night to her marriage bed.

In the front room the phone rings. Katrin sits on the sofa, where the bed was in which Eric died. The phone rings and rings. Then it stops. She sits. Perhaps she will turn to stone like a woman in the myths. It begins ringing again. Because the noise is unbearable, she lifts the receiver. Ah, says Daniel. You're there after all. I was going to tell you the rest of the story. But very likely I'm too late. I expect you were already on your way to bed. He has been drinking, she can hear it. No, no, she says, how kind of you, do talk to me. Suddenly she knows that he is lonely, there is fear and sadness around him, he is afraid of the long night and has phoned because he wants some company. And it is as though something opens in her that had been tight shut, a lost faculty. His polite voice continues: she is tired, shall he not rather phone her tomorrow, when would be a good time? She wonders at his voice, and at her quickened sense of the undertone of it, his loneliness. Then in haste, as though she might lose a chance that will not come again, she interrupts him, No, no, Daniel, you must tell me, but wait one moment, wait there, I'll be back... And hurries up to the bedroom, seizes the duvet, drags it downstairs, wraps herself in it on the sofa. Now, she says, now tell me. Oh but first, Daniel, just one thing: Monique, she sent him a photograph, she tormented him, why did she do that? Ah yes, says Daniel, the photographs: Jean-Luc, he was good, he would have been very good indeed, you know. I've got a dozen more of her somewhere, done by him. I don't suppose you'll want to see them. But I've got them somewhere safe, if you ever do. They are very beautiful. He killed himself in 1964. Nothing to do with Monique. There is a silence, like the slow silent collapse of the grounds for further talk. Quick, Daniel, says Katrin, tell me the rest of Eric's journey. Tell it me, I won't ask any more questions, but I'll be listening, not sleeping.

So Daniel begins, in a low rapid voice, the phone seems to recover the accent he had as a boy, the tone, rhythms, local timbre of his voice back then, which was Eric's too, or near it, near it and yet different, alive in Daniel but as though for an interlude the dead man were given his voice again and were telling her the story himself, as though he had arrived at the meeting place, full of the journey, brimful of his adventures, and spoke in a hurry so that she should be the first to know and the passion of it would be hers to share with him. Yes, says Daniel, sitting in the window of that café in Boulogne, watching the waking street, you can imagine how pleased he was with himself. He had come through a night in a place where dossers lodged with their cans and bottles among rats, and there he sat now, free as a bird, with bread and coffee and the money to pay for it. He said good-bye to the *patron*, who wished him *bonne route*, he felt bowled along by the good wishes of the whole wide world, and coming to the Paris road and seeing the hitch-hikers strung out along it, in ones or pairs every thirty yards or so, he made no pause at all but strode on, greeting everybody courteously as he passed, quickly, as though he would do the 150 miles on foot if he had to, but his intention, of course, was to get clear of the competition, to walk on until he was singular, an old trick, and it worked. A mile or so after the turn-off to Le Touquet, marching fast and alone down the N1, he hooked a 2CV, whose driver, a widower in his late fifties, was bound for his monthly assignation with a widow in Belleville but this time, unbeknownst to her, to ask her to marry him, hence the large bouquet of red roses on the back seat. He dropped Eric at the Porte de Clignancourt, there treating him to a glass of wine and a sandwich and telling him more about his years as a prisoner-of-war in Silesia and the death of his first wife, Berthe, of tuberculosis, in 1946. Things will be better for your generation, he said. At least, I hope they will. And then, says Daniel, this hopeful widower uttered a sentence which must have impressed Eric forcefully because he repeated it to me, that first night outside Vizille, in French: Si le fascisme revient, ce n'est pas la peine d'avoir des enfants ou de planter des arbres.

It was early afternoon, says Daniel, a Saturday, a fine day. Studying the métro map and his road map of France, Eric decided he would take the 4 as far as St Michel, surface there, and make his way towards the N6 down the Seine. He was in no hurry. He strolled, observing people and things. The life of the great barges, family life on the water, the gear, the dogs, a sleeping cat, the fishing rods, the geraniums, the ready bicycles, everything delighted him. He waved like a child to all and sundry and felt blessed among mortals when anyone waved back. Moment by moment, not in fits and starts but steadily, the world and his apprehension of it were opening up. From nowhere the word *éclosion* came to him. Whether he walked or stood, sat down on the embankment and read, lay flat with his hat over his face and dozed, he felt the softly insistent pulse of his life in the world opening – felt it, he could almost hear it, in the air or in his breathing of the air, a pulsing. The noises of the water – waves, engines, klaxons, gulls – and of the cars and vans, the trains, buses, the surfacing high-riding métro, these and much more were the distinguishable individual tones and accents of the city's life, and they were all borne up in a vast calyx of being whose pulse and heartbeat he felt to be his own.

Are you still there? Daniel asks. Yes, yes, Katrin answers, reaching out from within the duvet and switching off the lamp. She had drifted into a rapt enjoyment of the tone, rather than the text, of Daniel's speech. It is like that sometimes when you ask a person the way. He answers, he launches himself into directions, explanations, commentary, advice and beginnings again, his eyes never leave your face, all he wants is that you should be helped and directed by him towards where you want to be, and soon, he is so compelling, you cease attending to the information and are taken up instead into his kindness, into gratitude that he deploys his local knowledge so generously, you love the look on his face, his gestures, his earnestness, his giving himself up wholly to the fulfilling of your request, so that in the end, nodding, smiling, at a loss how to thank him, you leave him pleased, both of you pleased, and though you know at once that as to your route you are none the wiser, still the encounter has enriched you, it has a virtue quite other than that of precise instructions, which of course you still need and must ask someone else for and make yourself listen to with the other sort of attention.

Daniel continues, I suppose he crossed the river at the Pont de Tolbiac, but after that, though I have tried, I really can't follow him with any certainty. The roads have changed beyond all recognition, the old ones vastly enlarged or supplemented or replaced by the autoroutes. Modern maps are quite useless. But perhaps it doesn't matter. The important thing is this: somewhere – let us say Charenton – he bought a bottle of wine, some bread and salami, a couple of oranges, and asked the way to the old N6. By now it was five or six o'clock, he had left it late to begin getting clear of Paris, and what I love about this passage is his *insouciance*. He progressed very slowly, in short local lifts, people going out for the evening took him along for a while. Thinking about it these last few days, I've come to the view that he advanced not much further than Montgeron. It would be dark by then. When he described his journey to me under the stars outside Vizille he was himself unsure where he had spent the night. He told me that he felt suddenly dog-tired, he left the main road and made his way west half a mile or so, beyond the streets and the houses, into a rough park, he thought, or perhaps a wasteland, and there he drank some wine, ate one of his oranges, and lay down. The sky was clear, a long goods train passed close by, he could hear traffic faintly on the N6 and he had a sense that there might be water not far off. It felt, he said, like a between place, a remainder. Then he closed his eyes, says Daniel, and slept at once. Are you still there, Katrin? She is drifting on the borders, wavering between the states, warm, helpless, and it is the helplessness that most appeals to her. She will float away, listening like a child to stories. Already far off, still she picks up the anxiety in Daniel's considerate voice: he wants her there, awake, he wants her, two hundred miles away, listening while he tells her about his dead friend whose journey fifty years ago has become a wonder to him. Yes, she says, I'm still here. Do tell me the rest, Daniel. She means it, she does want him to talk, and she wants to listen, but in this drifting, dissolving fashion, warm, snug in a duvet, helpless, listening to a voice which is close in her ear and as remote as the dead are to the living, the beloved dead, so close, so present still, but very distant, gone impossibly far away, that is how she listens now, and helplessly, like something adrift on the turning tide, the shore may be close but it has no attractive force, the tide will turn and decide, all the drift will be away from the land. Still she says, Yes, I'm listening. He woke in a mist, Daniel says, drenched, in a total and silent stillness of white mist, shivering, but as though it did not matter whether he were cold or warm, all he knew for certain – and with a passionate delight – was that he lay on the ground in a whiteness, alive, wide-awake, having shifted during a passage of sleep into an elsewhere, a new way of being, so strange, says Daniel, I can hear the strangeness of it still, I can still hear his voice, not the particular words – though he did his best, we knew they were not adequate – but the tone and accent of them, so thoroughly steeped in strangeness. Then he heard the water, its utterance through the cries of birds – some curt, like barking, some elongated in a musical gargling, and shrieks, howls, a choking, screeches, an imbecilic chattering, and one that sounded like several tongues being scrambled through ventriloquy. So that, he thought, is what water sounds like when the daylight wakens it. He lay drenched and shivering on the earth and listened, taking it in, and I took it in from him, for ever. No point in getting up yet. He lay there. It was light. He would wait for the sun. Vaguely and partially some trees were visible. And next, first alarming him then gladdening him, came bipeds, his own species, but older, upright, purposeful, they strode out of the mist along the path by which he lay. Bonjour, they said, one after another, Bonjour, Bonjour, Bonjour, singly, at intervals, all so purposeful, humping their gear, the great hampers, the many rods and nets, they were booted, caped, hatted, the mist shone grey and silver on their moustaches, Bonjour, Bonjour, and lying there not a yard clear of their path, looking up, to each in turn Eric said Bonjour. Then they had passed, one after the other they came out of nothing and went into nothing, out of nowhere into nowhere, passing by Eric in his brief length of space and time, and each and every one of them, briefly materializing, courteously wished him good-day. They had all tramped through, a dozen, two dozen, three dozen, and around the water, each to his place, they were settling amidst their equipment, for the daylight hours of their Sunday, unspeaking, concentrating, staring at a float, each solitary among his own kind, kith and kin with the birds who cried and shrieked and sang and hunted ferociously in weed, water and mud, for the wherewithal to stay alive another day. Eric lay, no warmer, waiting for the sun. First signallers of it were the larks, he heard them far above him, invisible, in the light, he lay in his seam of cold fog and high above him the larks were singing already, they were already in sunlight under the blue of heaven, small creatures packed to bursting with the power of song, they rose, held steady, sank, rose up again, carolling. He lay there listening, certain that long before the cold and damp did him any harm, he would share the daylight with the larks, the Sunday, the day for worshipping the earth and the life of the earth under the empty and rejoicing sky. The mist passed over into the state of clarity, and Eric took cognizance of the left-over land he was lying on. He reached out for the second of his oranges and lay a while longer in the warm sun, his damp bag steaming.

Katrin wakes in the dark and does not know where she is. Bit by bit a world reconstitutes itself: sofa, duvet, a voice, the phone. But then the mind, instead of anchoring her where she was when she fell asleep, suddenly cannot hold off the inrush of a feeling of loss. And it is not her grief, her constant state, but more like the feeling you may carry with you out of the night's last dream – a dream whose plot, figures and images have dissolved but the feelings they bodied forth have come through. It is sheer loss, heartbreaking loss, in which there lives a cruel suggestion of forfeiture. The loss was her doing, she let something go, by inattention she forfeited it. Still only the feeling, there is no cause or object that she can recall.

Then comes an image, still not a reason or explanation, but a concrete thing in which the loss is made visible. She sees a pair of hands, cupped together, tilting down towards her. And there precisely, in those offering hands, lives the moment of loss, the sorrow of forfeiture.

Katrin reaches out and switches on the lamp. It is three o'clock. The phone has fallen to the floor. What was the last thing she heard Daniel say? That Eric woke in a mist, shivering; fishermen came by very close and all of them said Bonjour; then there were larks, the mist disappeared, he lay in the sun eating an orange and getting warm. How much longer after that did Daniel continue speaking to nobody?

Something in the course of the night has strengthened Katrin. She has slept on the sofa which stands where the hospital bed stood in which Eric died. But it is not that, not that she has come through an ordeal. She has no sense of an achievement by force of the will. It is the story. All she did was listen to a familiar voice continuing a story. It lives in her now, she can dwell in it whenever she pleases. Even the thought that she left Daniel speaking to nobody does not grieve her unbearably. There is a covenant between them, she will confess, apologise, he will forgive her and gladly make up to her whatever she has lost. Things can be remedied. She switches off the lamp and goes back to sleep till there is daylight outside, a car passes, a neighbour calls good-bye to her daughter leaving for work.

Katrin busies herself. She sets a place for breakfast, eats and drinks with some patience. And she thinks of the hands that, cupped together, surely contained something and offered it and nobody was there, nobody's palms, nobody's lap, opened to receive the precious and offered gift. This is a dream grief, so shiningly concrete she feels she may track it down and assuage it. She goes out at once, shops for lunch and supper, and then on impulse, pleased with herself, goes into a café and sits there quietly for twenty minutes, watching the street and not anxious that she might be seen.

Back home, it is late morning, she puts on Eric's jacket and prepares her desk to continue transcribing and translating Monique's letters. Then she goes downstairs and phones Daniel.

Katrin, he says, what a nice surprise! But are you all right? Is something the matter? Daniel, she answers, I have to ask your forgiveness. I fell asleep last night. I am afraid you carried on telling me the story and nobody was listening because I had fallen asleep. There is a silence, which to Katrin seems long and is painful. Daniel, she says, are you still there? Did you hear what I said? Will you forgive me? I woke up again at three in the morning, terribly sad, in a feeling that I had lost something. And of course it was the rest of the story I had lost, by falling asleep. What do you remember last? he asks. He does not sound aggrieved. His tone, Katrin senses, is that of a man abruptly obliged to realise that he was even more lonely than he had supposed. Not foolish, not betrayed into making himself ridiculous – talking to nobody in the middle of the night about the journey fifty years ago of his friend who has died – no, not ridiculous, but it is as though a shaft has opened up in him, a well-shaft, and he peers down and sees no end or measure of his loneliness. Katrin, he says, I never noticed, even at the very end, do you know I am not sure I addressed you even then, I can't even be sure that when I finished the story I asked were you still there or wished you good night. I was talking to myself, I was carried away on it, for nobody but myself. Daniel, says Katrin, that is not true. The last thing I heard was the larks in the sky above the mist and the last feeling I had was of warming – of Eric in the sun, warming. Another silence. Then his voice is quite different. Ah yes, he says, the larks. And before that, Bonjour! And now it is midday and sunny here. So you missed the lady of a certain age, driving a Peugeot 203, who, somewhere south of Auxerre, offered him afternoon tea and a bed for the night, which he politely declined. And the van-driver, leaving Avallon, who reached him a wad of pornographic photographs out of the glove compartment and asked was he interested in art. And the OAS man in a Chrysler who screeched to a halt near Chalons-sur-Saône, flung open the door, hurried him in, and warned him that if they came to a roadblock he must lie on the floor, for they would not stop and very likely the police would open fire. Yes, I missed those things, says Katrin sadly. No matter, says Daniel. They are three among many. Perhaps I should write them down. Perhaps I should write you the whole journey, from Heaton Street to the Café Elsa, and send it to you, for your records. It is midday, sunny in London, sunny two hundred miles west, and again, as in the night, hearing Daniel's voice, something shifts in Katrin, opens. She is a biographer, she has written brief lives of obscure poets, musicians and artists long since dead. And now, for her own salvation as it seems, she is engaged in writing her husband's early life. She has a great deal of material, almost ravenously she is collecting and collating more and more. But when Daniel offers to write the journey down, give her a script in a letter, or in an email that she might print, it comes to her as an important revelation that in this at least, in the journey, she does not want more documentation, she wants the voice of a friend – Eric's friend, her friend – telling her the story that she will attend to passionately after her own fashion and for her own good which she will find her way to the best she can, with many detours and wrong turnings. No, she says, please don't write it down, Daniel. There are many things still that I shall want you to write down for me – dates, facts, bits and pieces of chronology – but the rest of the story of the journey that I missed, or heard in my sleep perhaps, tell it me again, will you, when you have the courage to, please do. Another silence. She can hear him breathing. Listen now then, I'll tell you the ending, we can fill in the rest some other time, but the ending you need now, and when I woke this morning, I thought of more of it, I discovered more in it, so listen now.

Katrin sits on the sofa as she had done, listening, in the night, but now it is day, the room itself is sunny, cars pass occasionally or people on foot, and faintly she can hear the strange cries of children in the playground of the primary school two streets away. Leaving the N6, says Daniel, Eric had been taken some distance down the N85 and dropped at a cross-roads just south of Éclose, where his truck-driver turned off left to deliver feed at a farm near Saint-Didier-de-Bizonnes. About midday, 28 August 1962, an unpromising place, not much traffic. Eric sat on a kilometer stone, reading, his bag on the ground between his legs. It was hot, the road came out of, and soon vanished into, a haze. Eric sat (from his point of view) midway along a stretch of visibility. Whenever the chance of a lift came into view he stood up and raised his thumb. But the few vehicles were travelling fast, doubtless the drivers noticed him but barrelling along down a dead straight road they were disinclined to halt. Eric wondered about walking back to Éclose, or on the three or four miles to Champier; but he was in no hurry, he liked being where he was, sitting in the heat on a kilometer stone, reading. After a while he did not even stand up when a car, a van or a truck came out of the haze and approached at speed on a surface that wobbled like mercury. He sat, raised his thumb, resumed his reading. I should say he very much liked the idea of himself that day by the roadside reading, waiting without impatience, Daniel says.

Strange, Daniel's voice over the phone in daylight. It goes back down the years and in the accent of *then* retrieves the journey into the room here and now. Katrin keeps her eyes wide-open, she is aware of the life out of doors, and of the daylight from outside pouring in. But at the same time she is rapt by that story in that voice into a condition akin to darkness, sleep and dreaming. It is as though she has a cloud around her, invisible, transparent, allowing in the daylight world, and yet wrapping her around in a state which is inviolably other. She is wholly there, in the story, at that crossroads on the heat-hazed road, she is present where for her very life she has to be. And all that is required of her is that she listen.

When Eric looked up, says Daniel, it was the straight N85 he scanned, where it emerged out of the haze in a silver rippling. He paid no attention at all to the local and unnumbered road behind his back. But it was from there that his lift arrived, slowed at the junction, signalling right, and halted. The driver leaned across, opened the door, and said: Grenoble? And that was it, the last helper along the way. He was a man in his late sixties, white-haired, softly dressed in faded blues, driving to visit an elderly relative on the east side of Grenoble. He was courtesy itself. My name is Claude Bresson, he said, shaking hands. All his bearing, without affectation, was gracious. He encouraged Eric to talk, asked where he had come from, what his hopes for the future were. He drove slowly, there were thoughtful pauses in the conversation, then he nodded and asked another question. He complimented Eric on his French which, lift by lift, had indeed improved. His own language was formal, he made sentences as though he were writing them down, and all with the accent and modulations of his local habitation in the deep country he had emerged from along a road known locally as 'la rue de la vie dessus', the hamlet of Brieux, where his family had lived for generations, where he still lived with his wife and her father in the house he had gone to the first war from, and come back to, by great good fortune.

Before they had gone many miles down the *route nationale* Bresson asked Eric was he in a great hurry to reach Grenoble. I should like to show you something, he said, a particular place. It wouldn't take long. It would be half an hour at the very most out of our way. Eric answered that he was in no hurry at all, he should be glad to see the place. So they turned off east at the next crossroads, through fields of maize and one or two small vineyards, to a circle of woodland, curiously distinct, a domain apart. Here the road, little more than a track by now, ran alongside a wall, whole lengths of which had tumbled. Bresson halted at a ruined lodge, a pair of rusted open gates, a drive curving in under the trees. We can walk now, he said. I used to come here when I was a boy, with my friend. This is the farthest our mothers allowed us to cycle. It was already ruinous and abandoned then. I call by once or twice a year, to see how it looks and to mark the differences. And after you and I had talked for a little while, I thought I should like to show it to you, so that you will perhaps remember it. The drive led to what had once been a lawn and a formal garden. Eric mentioned the basin of a vanished fountain, some toppled and broken statuary (he remembered a head of Pan, the hands and pipes lying several yards away), and everywhere the elms, ash, sycamores had invaded and were thriving. Of the house itself, three walls still stood, but as though they wouldn't for much longer. Jackdaws lifted out of the empty and roofless space and hung in the air above it with much noise. It's a little worse every time, said Bresson. Or better, if you prefer a wilderness. But I wanted to show you the lake. They left the drive and by a path that was smothered in dead leaves, skirting the garden and the house, they reached an oval of black water, the lake. It has shrunk, you see, Bresson said. Back then it seemed immense to us. We fished from the landing stage over there. An enormous pike was said to inhabit the waters, far longer than the span of our arms and with teeth and jaws that would rip your hand off. To one another we boasted that we would land him one fine day – and had nightmares that we might. So fishing was a mixed experience. And visit by visit, borrowing tools from home and telling nobody, we built ourselves a raft out of timbers in the boathouse and poled across to that far side where there's a sluice to lower the waters, if need be. Such an adventure it all was. But the lake has shrunk since then. Every year the trees advance into the mud. The place was utterly still, Eric said. I suppose nobody but Bresson ever went there. Forgetting me, contemplating the water, after a while he shrugged and said we should be on our way.

Then, in the car, continuing slowly towards Grenoble, Bresson spoke at greater length about Fabrice, the friend he had cycled to the ruined *manoir* with – how the older he got, ever more vividly more and more details of their friendship came back to him. So much between them *went without saying*; in many ways different, they matched, they were consonant, each knowing the other as well or better than he knew himself. And then the war: same enthusiasm, same regiment, same company, same platoon. And he lost him on the Somme, in an attack on the ruins of a village called Guillemont, lost him horribly, helpless to save or comfort him, and like many other details from so long ago Fabrice's agony came back to him, lying awake at nights, the screams and delirium of it, his slowly dying through all of a day and the following long night, alone and beyond anybody's reach. Then, Daniel says, he asked Eric's pardon for burdening him with such things and said he sincerely hoped that all the new generation would be spared them.

They drove into Grenoble about four. Conducting him to what he called his usual café, on a terrace overlooking the Isère, Bresson asked Eric what he would like to eat or drink. The words he used, says Daniel, lodged in Eric's memory ever after, for their courtesy: Qu'est-ce que je vous offre? he asked.

The rest, says Daniel, was unimaginable. The relative Bresson visited, an aunt in her nineties, lived alone on the east side of the town, in the village of Échirolles. Arriving there, Eric said he had a mind to walk the five or six miles to Vizille. He was in no hurry. Bresson said that would be a very good idea. There's a track and then a footpath, he said. You pass a lake, a castle, and, best of all, a view will open up that you will never forget. Eric thanked him, opened the car door, reached behind for his rucksack and made to get out. One last thing, said Bresson – un petit souvenir. I want to be remembered kindly by someone as old as I was when I went away from home into the first of the wars. He took a small cloth bag from the glove compartment. Hold out your hands, he said. Make a cup of them. And into that warm and containing space, out of the crimson pouch, in a glistening slither, he tipped a dozen, two dozen, three dozen small thin silver coins. Treasure, he said, from back then. Eric stared. As I said, says Daniel, it was unimaginable. After a while Bresson held out the open pouch. Best pour them back in, he said. Eric made a chute of his hands and the coins like a shoal of flashing fish slid with a tinkling out of sight. Bresson drew the pouch shut and handed it back to him. For safekeeping, he said.

Eric walked the last miles like a dreamer. He found the way without difficulty as though he had known it in a previous life, its character and particular beauties came back to him. The lake lay open under the blue sky, around its shores very quietly rippling. And at Haute Jarrie, coming to the ruined castle, he had Vizille below him, and beyond, risen up white and lit almost horizontally by the declining sun, stood the Alps. He sat there for half an hour, the coins in their crimson pouch in his hands. Then went down, crossed the main road, and pretty soon found the hill he would camp on for the next four nights.

Are you still there, Katrin? Daniel asks. He startles her out of a state of listening which is as unlike the everyday waking state as is sleep itself – a sort of trance, but keenly attentive, lucidly observant. Yes, yes, she says, this time I have heard every word. The hands, the gift. What in the night and on waking she felt she had lost or forfeited, it is given her now in broad daylight. That was the evening of the 28th, Daniel says. I didn't get there till the morning of the 31st. So for three nights Eric lay on his own under the stars, and thought of his journey lift by lift, stage by stage, through all its variations of tempo, mood and pitch, to the climax: the slide of silver coins into his hands, and the white Alps that had stepped up close in the evening sun. And when I arrived, that night under the headlong spate of the Milky Way, in a rush like that of the stars themselves, he told me it all, and to finish, like a conjuror, his *pièce de résistance*, he sat up, produced the pouch and tipped its silver into my cupped hands, so that I should have the feel of it, he said, the cold slither and heaping, and never forget it, the gift from back then, on a hilltop under the stars.

# 8

THERE ARE FORTUNATE people who, looking back, recall a childhood in which the sun was always shining. First holidays especially, by the sea or among the hills, return like paradise in a lasting sunlight. Rather in that way, Katrin will remember her visits to Dr Gracie. Surely now and then it must have rained; of course, the window was not always open; some days scent and birdsong must have been absent. But when Katrin, looking back, recalls Dr Gracie's room, the heart of the memory will always be light, spaciousness, stillness, patience, in a lasting early summer.

How's the pain? Dr Gracie asks. Much the same, Katrin answers, pressing her hand up under the ribs on her left side. But I have a date for the scan. – Which I'm sure will set your mind at rest, says Dr Gracie. And straight after it, says Katrin, I shall have a few days in the Peak District, with Eric's brother and his wife. They live at Ashford-in-the-Water. I've never been there before. You'll like it, says Dr Gracie. I used to go near there as a child, to a place above Cressbrook Dale. I've been thinking lately I'd like to go back with my own children. Perhaps we shall. Perhaps you will make me organise it, by your example.

On an uplift of confidence Katrin tells Dr Gracie about the night when she realised that Daniel needed to talk to her just as much as she needed to listen to him. Also, she says, I sat in a café on my own for twenty minutes and did not panic. Very good, says Dr Gracie. But don't be discouraged when things become worse again. Really, it's best not to think of it in terms of progress along a line – and certainly not along a straight line. In fact, sequence, progress, degrees, anything linear, and, above all, anything *serial*, these are not helpful concepts for the mending of your life. I mean, you don't want to discard Eric, do you? You don't want to think of him as a burden and an impediment you must get rid of and move away from, to live. You love him and he loved you. It is grief devouring you, not love. You have to convert grief back into what it was: an abiding love. You don't want to throw it off and leave it lying by the wayside. Altogether, the wayside is an unhelpful image. This is not Pilgrim's Progress. You are not making for the Celestial City.

After one of the silences to which that room is so hospitable, Dr Gracie says, And here's something else, connected with the unhelpfulness of thinking linearly: Being ill and being well are not opposite, or even distinct, states. In varying degrees they partake of one another. So you are not setting off from the state of illness on the road to the state of being well. You will always be ill and well, in a continuously shifting mixture. All we want – and it is a big thing to want and to attain – is that illness doesn't become or continue to be so strong that it thwarts you, reduces you, and spoils your life. Everyone lives in that struggle whether they know it or not. And it is better to know it, because then you will be watchful, you will always be on the look-out for what will help your life and be wary of what will harm or hinder it.

Dr Gracie has spoken more than she usually does, and more insistently. She leans forward, engaging Katrin's gaze. You do understand me, don't you? You want a life of your own in which grief becomes love again and works for the good of your life. You will always be haunted – why should you not be? – sorrow will always shadow you and some days and nights it will come in very close again. But don't let it stay close for long. Sleeping and waking with sorrow will leach away your strength. You don't want that, and nor would Eric want to watch you trying to live like that.

She looks tired suddenly. Katrin thanks her, says good-bye. The sun streams in, the blackbird sings from the apple tree whose blossom is drifting clear of the shapes of fruit.

Katrin puts on Eric's jacket and sits down at the little table facing the wall. Her scan is tomorrow. The following day she will travel via Manchester and Buxton to spend a few days with Michael and Sheila in Ashford. But now, having assembled all the materials, she will force herself to do something difficult: write an account of Eric's arrival in Paris and the first period of his love for Monique. She has copies of letters written by Eric and by Monique to Daniel; letters to Eric from Monique and from his father; and notes on her conversations with Daniel and on Eric's own occasional remarks to her concerning that time. She lays out also a few contemporary photographs of Eric and Daniel, in one of which, taken by a stranger, they are sitting together in the Café Elsa, each raising a glass of wine as though to life itself. And against the row of Monique's letters along the wall (all opened now, all read) still stands, as it has for some weeks, the photograph of her undressing in Jean-Luc's studio. It belongs later, of course, in late December; but Katrin wants her there in that pose as the very sign of the romance that, in Katrin's account, Eric is now entering. She writes:

Eric arrived in Nevers late on 5 September 1962 and early the following morning collected a letter from his father and one from Daniel at the main post office. There were other routes to Paris, needless to say; but, according to Daniel, he wished to pass through Nevers because he was haunted by the voice of Emmanuelle Riva in *Hiroshima mon amour*. He had many of her lines by heart. This, for example, 'Avant d'être à Paris, j'étais à Nevers'; or this, 'C'est à Nevers que j'ai été le plus jeune de toute ma vie.' She played a young woman of Nevers who, during the Occupation, fell in love with a German soldier and had her head shaved for it when the town was liberated and her lover killed.

Eric re-entered Paris at Vitry-sur-Seine and rode in along the left bank. Time passes differently when you travel, and the ten days since he was last by the river, admiring the barges, saluting their families, felt like months. Or (perhaps another way of saying the same thing), he felt that the shift and opening in his life could not be measured by any sequence of ten days. Daniel had told Eric very little about Monique. But he was glad of the arrangement, it would save him looking for a hotel. He thought he would stay a couple of nights and then head off towards Calais and home. It was an anxious and complaining letter from his father in Nevers: why had he not written more often, when would he be home, surely he must get himself ready for university? (Katrin makes a note that all the letters Eric had from his father then and for the next couple of years were of that kind. She resolves to question Michael on the subject.)

Eric left the river at St. Michel and cycled up the boulevard, looking odd but no odder than many others, as far as the rue Soufflot. After that, uphill, he made his way on foot, pushing the laden bike. (Katrin spreads out her map of Paris, follows with a forefinger: Soufflot, Panthéon, Clotilde, Estrapade…) At the junction with the rue Tournefort, Eric bought two oranges and a bottle of red wine. Reaching no. 7, he leaned his bike against the wall, took his shopping out of the pannier, stepped back, and looked up. The building was high and rickety, with many flowering balconies, washing lines, iron balustrades, open windows, aerials, and above all that: blue sky, criss-crossed by screeching swifts. Monique's bell was the highest of a dozen or more. The bottle in his right hand, extending a finger, Eric rang, and waited. No answer, he rang again. Still no answer.

Katrin halts. Her courage lapses. She can't write even a small passage of pain. She stares at the photograph of Monique undressing and the worst of it this time is the girl's almost disdainful self-possessedness. In Katrin's broken-off account Eric stands on the pavement with a bottle of wine in one hand and two oranges held against his heart by the other. He has stepped back a couple of paces and is looking up to the top floor, the blue sky and the swifts. Quickly Katrin writes, And all the while she was watching him, she stood at the window of the café opposite among her friends and they watched him waiting for an answer on the pavement. Katrin puts down her pen, flicks rapidly through Monique's letters ranged in order along the wall, and takes out and opens the first of those fifteen that Eric never read, never even opened. She finds the passage and translates it thus: Eric, my lost love, it is a small thing perhaps but among the many bad things I did sometimes I think the worst is that I let you stand waiting on the pavement looking up while Jean-Luc, Yves, Alice and the others stood around making fun of me and perhaps also of you. And now you won't write and forgive me this first thing, let alone all the others, and it will make no difference if I tell you that when at last you turned and saw us all standing in the window in our café I loved you there and then, you were so foreign and childish with your gifts of wine and oranges and your funny bike, and so beautiful your body was, so skinny and hard, and your face and arms and legs sunburned after that long journey from under the Alps. And your expression when you saw us and knew we had been watching you, your look of being at a disadvantage, foolish, at our mercy, at *my* mercy, you poor boy that I was cruel to from the beginning, it breaks my heart now when I see you smiling in puzzlement at us behind the glass in our own café, and raising the wine and the oranges as though to propitiate us all, there at the outset.

Katrin sorts through her documents, leafs back through her notebooks, and writes, See also Eric's letter to Daniel, posted in Calais 25/9: When I slept out last night I kept seeing her as I saw her first when I turned and she was there in the window of the Café Amyot with all the others and now that I've got this far away from her I feel her the way sometimes when you sleep out your back feels cold and however you turn you can't make it feel warm. – And this, Monique to Daniel, 26/9: In case you think it was so quick because I felt guilty for looking at him behind his back, it wasn't. It was so quick because I loved him at once, as soon as he turned round, and then I did what love told me to do.

Katrin goes downstairs and into the garden. She sits at the small round iron table where sometimes, not often, it is rather a sunless place, she sat with Eric for coffee or tea. She sits for five minutes. She feels as you do when you know that soon you will have to be sick but you have a deep childhood horror of being sick and you put it off as long as possible, hoping the need will magically vanish, but of course it won't, very soon, as an adult, you will have to hurry to the place where it is proper for you to be sick. Meanwhile you sit, hoping against hope that it will go away, and the horror of it builds up in you as though it were the stuff in the stomach itself. Katrin feels like that. After five minutes combating it, she hurries back upstairs to her table facing the wall and writes:

The letters, some conversations, plus how I imagine it: He wheeled his bike in under the stairs. She took his bit of shopping, he carried his panniers, up five floors to the very top. Inside, he went straight to the open window and looked out. Before him the roof-top life extended, acres of it, higgledy-piggledy, slates and panes and aerials and chimney stacks, all angles, all manner of shapes, materials and surfaces, all their colouring, every nuance of every texture visible. He viewed the city's canopy and heard, out of the canyons of the streets, its muted tumult. She came and stood by him. She wore a short sleeveless brown dress, almost a shift. Ça te plaît? C'est beau, hein? Her bare arm touched his.

The kitchen was in a back corner of the room with the view, behind it ran a dark corridor, bathroom and toilet on one side, very cramped, and on the other her bedroom though which you had to pass to reach the place, not much more than a long broom-cupboard, where, she told him, he could lay out his sleeping bag on a camp bed. She worked in the front room, in the best light, and the clutter of working lay on every surface and all over the floor. The walls and the slopes of the ceiling were papered almost completely with paintings, sketches, designs and photographs. Can I stay a couple of nights? he asked. Stay as long as you like, she answered. I have to work but you won't mind that. And if you've got any money it would help, but don't worry if you haven't.

He went down to the street again, for some bread. It was early evening. The abundance of life made him giddy. Loud, bright and joyous, it crowded in on him, it overwrought his senses, so that he walked quickly to the breadshop and quickly back again, as though for shelter. She had cleared the only table of her work in progress and set it for two. Again he stood at the window, entranced. She brought a salad to the table then halved and slid an omelette on to his plate and hers. He poured the wine into two small glasses that had once held mustard. Everything was simple. She asked after Daniel – He gave me his bike, he said, and I gave him my rucksack. He wanted to go back into the mountains. – All on his own, she said, not as a question, rather as the statement of an unsurprising fact. But when they turned to one another, asking and answering, with no caution or forethought, only to learn, each to the other was extraordinarily surprising. It was like discovering a new appetite and becoming hungry to feed it. Listening and speaking were an equal pleasure. Her face was shapely, its features very definite. He watched her mouth, he watched it making the sounds and rhythms of her language. And for the first time in his life, as his sight and hearing attended to the vigour, quickness, allure, ever-changing expressiveness of this foreign speech, he felt also the deep otherness of a woman's sex, as though it were being shown to him, not as mystery, not to perplex or seduce him, but just as fact, as an astonishing fact, around which now all the tide of his life since leaving home precipitated. With her lips, teeth and tongue, with her eyes and with her restless hands she made her difference manifest, young woman to young man, so that he should acknowledge it and encompass it the best he could within his excited understanding. He drank quickly from the small glass, as though wine were something you could slake an increasing thirst with. Then suddenly – he had peeled and opened one of the oranges and set it on her plate with all its segments parting – tiredness rose up in him, he couldn't speak, he watched her further opening the fruit and slowly inserting it, piece by piece, into her smiling mouth. In a foolish amazement – which her eyes were laughing at – he watched her small sharp teeth bite into the crescent purses and release the juice. I'll have to go to bed, he muttered. I set off very early this morning. His mouth could scarcely form the foreign words. He stood over her. Bonne nuit, she said, offering up her hand that was like a child's, small and grubby, such a wonder to him he turned it this way and that and with naive solemnity kissed its bitten nails.

Katrin pauses. It is piercingly clear and present to her. Of course, she gets stuck for words, she can't write it into the sharp focus in which with the mind's eye and the heart she sees and feels it. But it is there in her, keen and bright as shards of crystal, and at the least wavering or dimming of the images all she has to do is glance at the photograph of the girl back then undressing, and immediately that evening and night, his threshold and entry, they hold and sharpen. Katrin knows that she is annihilating herself. She is conjuring up a past in whose light her own life withers. The better she does it, the worse for her.

Katrin closes her eyes and says aloud, He leaves her finishing the orange he peeled and opened up for her. He stumbles down the dark corridor to the bathroom. Everything is unfamiliar, he is *dépaysé* more than in any night under the stars or in barns, thickets or even his first accommodation, the sordid shed outside Calais on the Boulogne road. He finds his bed, strips naked, sheathes himself in the warm bag, and has just time to marvel at half a moon visible through the skylight a quarter of a million miles away, then sleep takes him. The next thing he knows he has woken and sees her standing over him. She is wearing a man's collarless shirt with the cuffs rolled up and the buttons undone to below her breasts. He contemplates her. She crosses her arms down and in one swift movement lifts the shirt up over her head and off. In what small light comes from the sky and through the glass oblong in the slanted roof he contemplates her nakedness, a faint whiteness, the black hair. Then she leans, feels for the zip of his sleeping bag and draws it slowly down the length of his left side. Viens, she says. And walks away from him and back to her own warm bed.

Katrin stands at the window and looks out beyond the town and beyond the motorway to where the sky and the moors below it make one vast domain of spaciousness and emptiness. She thinks her spirit would not survive five minutes in such a zone. Even in the contemplation of it she feels her person to be very slight, nothing really tethers her, she is without any effective connection, she would drift away, she weighs so little. And foreseeing such a vanishing she says aloud, And I will not have mattered. – How terrifying it would be to realise even for a second that every adherence, all relations, have disappeared, even for a split second to become conscious of there being no further possibility of belonging, no object of desire, and, without object or direction, the desire itself panicking and soon ceasing. Perhaps that consciousness would kill you at once, perhaps your spirit would flutter less than a butterfly in the killing jar, the atmosphere of no belonging, no connection, no adherence being to humans instantly lethal. How terrifying, and also, that emptiness, how attractive: to cease out there, be extinguished, be done with all the struggling, all the effort every day, every hour of every day, all the struggle to adhere to the world and to some few of its myriad people and places, all the exertions and the continual failings, to be done with all that, be rid of it, blanked out, unconscious in the infinite unconscious emptiness, how very attractive.

Katrin resumes her place at the cluttered table facing the wall and scribbles: Some details. She keeps her condoms in a small black-lacquered box on the bedside table on her side – the left side – of the bed. The lid of the box is decorated with the wide-open flowering of a single red poppy. When the time comes (which is not soon, first she wants to delight in him, to have him adore and please her for a good long time) she lifts the lid of the box, takes out the sachet and he watches her practised fingers tear it open. Afterwards she fetches the second orange from the living room. He watches her leaving and returning. He is not ignorant, but her self-confident lithe beauty unimaginably surpasses all the bits of knowledge he has so far assembled. She sits up in bed peeling the orange. It's yours really, she says. But we'll share it. She opens it, she halves it, their mixing fingers smell of it and sex. After that they sleep for a while. He wakes when she leaves the bed again. He listens, he hears her peeing, the word 'effrontery' comes to mind. He dozes, dreaming fast. Nothing is stranger than the rushes, gaps, lengthy elongations and total halts in the passage of time he has lived through in not much more than half the life of a moon since leaving home. She comes back, naked still, with coffee. This morning I've made it, she says. Tomorrow you do. Henceforth you make the coffee and wake me up with it. You will stay for ever. Oh how good it will be!

# 9

AT MACCLESFIELD THE ticket-inspector asks Katrin does she realise she needn't go into Manchester, she could get off at Stockport and catch the Buxton train there, earlier, on its way out. Save you an hour or so, he says. He is an elderly man with a pronounced northern accent. She is touched by his concern. Altogether, small kindnesses from strangers have affected her greatly on this longest journey since Eric's death. Thank you, she says. That is very kind of you. But I need an hour in Manchester. I have to check something. The inspector nods, pauses. She feels it would interest him to know what this something is, she feels impelled to tell him, there in the crowded carriage, speak it all aloud. These movements into the confidence of people she does not know! Of course, they spring from her solitude and its undertow of loneliness. The moment passes, the inspector goes on his way. Just as well, she thinks. But she adds his kindly interest to her fund of faith – faith in others, that they are trustworthy; and in herself, that she trusts or will learn to trust. She feels certain that her journey north will help.

An hour is more than enough. Katrin trundles her small case down the slope from Manchester Piccadilly, formerly Manchester London Road, and at the bottom, turning left, very soon ascertains that there is no signpost pointing to London, 186 miles away, any more. But she stands where perhaps it stood, where Eric began. Opposite, the buildings are glass and concrete, all new. She wants old brickwork, from back then. She walks along a hundred yards or so; halts at Store Street, a vast brick tunnel under the slope she has just descended. How many hundreds of thousands of single fitting pieces? Across the road there's Munroe's, there's the fire station. The mix is geological, breccia from the nineteenth century lodging in the modern. Perhaps here, at this junction, the truck was halted and the driver's mate leaned out and said to him, the boy in walking boots with a rucksack on his back, How far you going, son? The traffic is dense, the din and stink of it are hellish. But Katrin is in a place of her own making, intensely solitary, craving the ghost of the man she married, in a youthful appearance, as she never saw him, except as an image that floated into fixity, black and white, on the waters of a dark-room half a century ago. And how vivid and present he is to her! There on the kerb of the road whose ancient *raison d'être* has been obliterated, how definitely she can print the boy to whom this road was the clue into the places where his life would open!

Katrin goes for her train. The city is vast, the ways out of it branch finely and at every junction and intersection they falter, clog and choke. But from the ends of the platforms of its chief railway station, looking east, nowadays you can see the moors, extending north and south at a level indented height under the open sky. With the Pennine villages and townships the city annexed some of the moorland too; and in black canals, small unclean streams, flags, cobbles, dressed and blackened gritstone, still owns up to it. Very soon if you leave by train the city seems to loosen, particular roads and their directions clarify. With a map on the table in front of her, Katrin begins to grasp how Eric made his way. Again and again the rails approach, run alongside and cross the road he took. Through the slackening conurbation, in the opening country, the road recovers its identity, again it becomes a singular and important thing that joins one named place to another: Hazel Grove, Disley, New Mills, Whaley Bridge, Chapel-en-le-Frith, Dove Holes...

Katrin is met at Buxton by Eric's younger brother, Michael. As at the funeral, the family likeness shocks and rather repels her. But she knows he promised Eric he would keep an eye on her, just as she herself promised to stay in touch with his family and the friends he shared with her. So Eric is the presiding spirit here in Ashford-in-the-water, which generates goodwill.

Michael and his wife Sheila have just retired. She was head teacher of a primary school in Matlock, he was a senior probation officer in Derby. They will never lose interest in their work, he says, but now they will devote more time to the house and garden, the children and grandchildren, and to their own passions: Sheila's for choral singing, Michael's for geology. Their house, once a mine-owner's and before him an independent scholar's, stands on a terraced two acres a little outside and above Ashford, wonderfully light, airy, and with a steep garden that gives access through a small iron gate into the high fields themselves and so to the old workings, the spoilheaps, swallow-holes, caves and deep watery dales that will occupy Michael for however long he lives.

Sheila shows Katrin to her room. They stand at the window looking south over Ashford, the Wye, the A6, and beyond over high fields and densely wooded clefts. To Katrin, Sheila seems brisk and self-possessed. She has always had to keep a sharp eye on things – very often on several things at once – and in her working life among children she has grown adept at discerning human needs. Katrin feels herself being assessed, for hers. Michael will have told Sheila that she, Katrin, is struggling. Sheila will be kind. The connection between the two women is the husband and brother-in-law, Eric. Grief and kindness. Only that, only Eric. Katrin says, This is a beautiful house and you are very kind to me. Then, abruptly, That's the road, you know. That's the road he hitched down at the end of August in 1962. He had a lift from Manchester to Chapel-en-le-Frith in a quarry truck. I think he rode through Ashford with a vicar in a Morris Minor, but

I can't be absolutely certain. Thank you for this lovely room with a view of the A6. Sheila answers that, especially now, in summer, the road has become far too busy for their liking. That's one thing she won't miss in retirement: driving with Michael to the station in Matlock every working day. They have even thought of moving somewhere quieter. But the house has been their home for forty years, they bought it ruinous and have made it what it is now. The children and grandchildren love it, nowhere else would she find such hearths, big windows, high ceilings, such a garden, and Michael would be lost without the quarries and the mines. No, they have lived happily here, they shan't ever move. Katrin recognises, in herself and in Sheila, entirely different lives. When Eric was alive she might have set them more equally, or at least more comparably, side by side. Now her own abundance is all in the past, and much of it, she must concede, even in that past is not quite her own. Well, it can't be helped. This house is hospitable, the man and woman of the house will be kind to her.

They eat early because Sheila has a choir-practice in Bakewell. She is very sorry, she can't really miss it, she can't let the others down. And perhaps in any case Katrin and Michael would like some time to themselves, to talk? Katrin reassures her; and realises, with a start almost of shame, that in all her dealings with Daniel – meeting him in London, speaking to him on the phone, writing him letters and emails – she has conducted herself as though he, like her, has no life that does not touch on Eric's. He must have, of course; but never once has she asked after it and never has he intruded it into her obsessive preoccupation with his dead friend, her husband. But in Sheila's life Eric is accidental and peripheral. How strange that is: Sheila has a different centre, the circle of her life intersects only very thinly with that of Katrin's. And when, after siding the table and washing up and setting everything in the kitchen ship-shape and ready for breakfast, Michael sits down in his study with her among his books and fossils and minerals and asks her straight how she is managing three months on, Katrin feels the same: our centres are very different, our circles do intersect but not, after all, very fully. He is Eric's brother, three years younger, they lived sixty-five years on the same planet and yet, she thinks, he and I, in the matter of Eric, having Eric in common, do not after all have very much common ground. How can that be?

That evening Katrin feels unsteadied in her writing of Eric's life. If he were a subject she had chanced upon in her reading and had found compelling and had begun to write about him, such a jolt along the way might have been expected, she might even have welcomed it, she would have shifted her perspective and hoped by that adjustment to be getting a little closer to the truth. But Eric is not such a subject and Michael is not just another surviving witness whose testimony she might weigh and strive to assimilate into the evidence gathered from elsewhere so far. She sees at once when they sit down together in the room in which he is most at home, most content, most his own man, that Michael is grieving too but with a grief very unlike and perhaps even irreconcilable with hers. That is what unsteadies her. Indeed, she will leave their hospitable house feeling she has been put in question.

Hearing the car, Michael says, That's Sheila back. He stands up, hesitates and, awkwardly apologetic, goes out to meet her. Katrin sits. How long has he been listening for his wife's homecoming? Never mind, she says to herself, and lapses into her own thoughts. She sits; and when Michael and Sheila come into the study she starts like somebody suddenly woken and not knowing where she is. The singing has exalted Sheila, the radiance of it lingers on her face. Michael stands to one side, looking at her. This transfiguration is familiar but on every occasion it touches him, so that he stands shyly aside, marvelling at it in her. Katrin contemplates the appearance of it in both of them. They belong, their look is the sign of it. Michael has quitted the topic of his brother and now stands next to his wife who in a voice in which there is still an after-tone of singing says she will make a bit of supper since tea was so early because of her choir-practice.

The kitchen receives the light of the long summer evening. Sheila attends to Katrin, the unhappy guest; asks candidly how she is coping and begs her to say if they can do anything to help. Katrin feels her to be kind and resourceful in equal measure; but also that she, Katrin, can't – as Sheila means it – be helped. Soon Katrin pleads tiredness, she has had a long journey. She sees that they think her overwhelmed by sorrow. She *is* tired, she *is* sorrowful but more than that, as she embraces Michael and Sheila, thanking them sincerely, it is the need to steady her own understanding (against Michael's) that impels her to her room.

Katrin moves a small pine table to the window, opens her notebook, takes up her pen, and looks down over the village and the river to the quietening road. After a while, collecting herself, she writes:

Michael says he has no interest in Eric's journey to France. He knows very little about it, he says, and doesn't want to know any more. But he does know that it ended in Monique and about her he has no good feelings whatsoever. Indeed, he and Sheila were very shocked when she turned up in Eric's house after the funeral (I did not notice they were shocked) and the only mercy was that she missed the funeral itself. A good job Edna didn't come, he said. A meeting of the two of them in that house would have been very unpleasant. (The two of them and me, in the house Eric and I bought and lived in together?) When he admitted that he'd never had much time for Daniel either, I began to see that his real grief over Eric is mixed up with all manner of bad feelings that have their origins back then. He said, I lost him when he went to France – which sounded like one of those verdicts you arrive at about a life and stick to ever after because it makes some sort of sense if you don't look at it too closely. I imagine he has uttered it to Sheila more than once and that it will have become her statement on the subject too. When I mentioned the letters Eric had from his father – how anxious and complaining they were – he shrugged and looked at me as much as to say, Well there you are then. So Eric was a worry to his father, and also to his mother, of course, though she did not complain. And pretty soon he was a grave disappointment to both of them. And I – said Michael – being still at home, still going to school, had all that to put up with and Dad especially turned it on me and said he'd be damned if he'd let *me* act like that after all they'd done for the pair of us. And even when Eric finished with Monique it was no comfort to them. He told them nothing and anyway next minute it was Edna and getting married and leaving university a failure after all that work.

Dusk. The less and less traffic signals itself and feels its way with lights. Katrin watches the cars, a bus, a couple of trucks disappearing south. She writes:

There was an edge of bitterness in his voice. His story is almost (not quite) that he had to live respectably, set up a decent house and home, stay close to his roots, because his big brother, the family's first hope, didn't. But I should say it is his grief, the mixed feelings of his grief, dragging him back into hard experiences which were perhaps – for all I know – like a first bereavement, when Eric left him. But this house is so beautiful, and when Sheila came in from singing, how he looked at her, that is not the look of a man in a life he was *forced* to live. It is the grief working strangely, as strangely as it works in me, differently, because in our suffering we are all different, all singular and alone. He says Eric never had a home his mother and father and grandmother could visit and be comfortable in, so they came to him, in country they knew from childhood, the domain of healthful outings when they were children and the city was very dirty. And from his tone of voice you'd almost think he resented it, that they came to him, to his house and home, because Eric never had a place they felt easy in. Why, if it was so, does he not pity Eric? Why is he not simply glad and proud of his happy home? Perhaps he does, perhaps he is. Only for now the grief works in an ugly way in him.

I tell him I knew the parents and grandmother only in photographs, mostly black and white, and in the few stories Eric would tell me from time to time and especially in the last weeks of his life. His mother was still alive when I fell in love with him, he went north now and then to visit her and I begged him to bring her to us in our house, but she wouldn't come or he never did beg her for me. I tell him I lost my own family when I came to England, abroad, and that I feel I was no great loss to them nor were they to me. I tell him I loved Eric and only Eric truly, there was no before and it seems there will be no after. I tell him I am poor and that he and Sheila are rich beyond compare and that to me Eric was abundant life itself. He shrugs, he does not really want to know. He mistrusts me in what I am up to now, dislikes the very idea of it, rooting around *back then*, in the times he says he hates. He shrugs, but he glances at me curiously, as though there might just be something in me, in *it*, if he had the will to care. But his brother is dead, beyond reconciliation, he goes back even earlier than I do for the images of happiness, to his years as kid brother of the boy he idolised. And I say, You look back not just to happiness but to the bond of it, you and him, whereas I had no share in him then, I was not there, I was not even born, all that happiness is before my time. To which he replies, and it shakes me how emphatic his judgement is, Katrin, don't tell me you think his years back then were better than the years he lived with you. The stuff in France and at Oxford, don't fall for that nonsense. Then Sheila came home, he stood up to welcome her and I watched him staring at her face that shone with the after-light of singing.

At breakfast there is an alliance – tactful, compassionate, but still an alliance – of Michael and Sheila towards Katrin. How should there not be? They are husband and wife. Lying in bed, he will have recounted his conversation with Katrin, they will have discussed it and decided how best to manage the following day. 'How to play it' – that is the expression which occurs to Katrin over breakfast when Sheila, doing most of the talking, Michael listening and watching, asks Katrin would she like a trip to Matlock or Buxton, Michael has some work to do, shall the two of them go off and have lunch somewhere? Katrin admires her greatly and does not at all mind being ordered into place for the day. That is how they have decided to play it, she says to herself. Katrin, unsteady in her own way of being in the world, admires assurance, purpose, style, in other women and happily puts herself in Sheila's charge. She has slept badly, with pell-mell rushes of dreams, much babbling in broken Polish and German and interludes of open-eyed waking during which she lay in the dark of the strange house quite at the mercy of her sorrow and dread.

They settle on Buxton, via Tideswell, but change their minds only a couple of miles up the road when Sheila mentions that the dale on their left is Cressbrook. Such a lovely name, says Katrin. Such a lovely, lovely name. And suddenly, and as it were from nowhere, sorrow wells up in her and there, strapped in her seat and driving slowly along behind a tractor and trailer, she begins to shudder, she bows her face into her hands and tears force through her fingers as though she, one grieving woman, were the outlet into daylight of all the vast depth of that country's underground rivers and lakes of loss. At the junction, in the carpark of the Three Stags' Heads, Sheila halts, releases their belts and takes Katrin into her arms, holds and soothes her as nobody has since Eric was fit and well.

I think we'll have a cup of coffee here, Sheila says. And then why don't we walk a little way down the dale? Your shoes look strong enough and it won't be muddy. And after that, if you feel like it, we can drive into Tideswell, which is a very pretty place, and have lunch there.

Katrin wonders at the sudden violence of her sadness. It was the name, she says – just that. You see, my doctor used to come to Cressbrook as a child. And now she's in remission from breast cancer. And when I told her I would be staying with you in Ashford she remembered Cressbrook and said she'd like to see the place again with her own children who are grown-up, of course, and have already left home but would surely come away for a family holiday, if she asked them. She's a wonderful doctor. She gives you all the time in the world. I didn't tell you I went for a scan the day before yesterday. I've had a pain under my ribs on the left side, just as Eric did, so she fixed me up with a scan to set my mind at rest. She says she's positive there's nothing wrong. So that must be what made me cry like that.

They walk perhaps a mile down Cressbrook Dale. In summer that first stretch is dry and you must descend to where the trees begin before you will find the beginnings of the water. That is perhaps the greatest beauty of the limestone country: ubiquitous evidence of the work of water, and the self of it, the very body and soul of it, only becoming apparent now and then, according to weather, season, grace and favour of the terrain. The dampening underfoot, the quickening pleasure in the nostrils (almost on the tongue), of the mud, cress, meadowsweet, mint and leafiness – so much, so many shades, tones, textures and characters of so much, in a mild light and birdsong starting with the trees. Standing together by a small clear pool, watching the start and pulse of it up through the pebbles, Sheila says to Katrin, Just now, what you were saying about Edna, it's true nobody has a good word for her, but I must say that on the few occasions we ever met – at the wedding and now and then after Thomas was born – I had some sympathy for her. She didn't have an easy time, as I'm sure you know. Thomas told me at the funeral he was losing patience with her. He's near to telling her she won't be welcome in his house. She's her own worst enemy, he said. It was kind of you to invite her, but he was very relieved when she didn't turn up. And Monique there as well, says Katrin. Yes, Monique, says Sheila, the two of them in the house together, that might have been difficult. Not forgetting me, says Katrin. Of course not, says Sheila. The three of you. Though often lately, Katrin continues, it has seemed to me that I wasn't there at all, somebody stood in for me or I dreamed it, the whole day, until everyone left and then I became real again and it was unbearable. You were astonishing, Sheila says. Everyone said you bore up wonderfully well. And since then, Katrin continues, staring into the clear pool, seeing and not seeing its small insistent replenishing out of the ground, since that early evening when you all left I have been trying to put together a life in body and soul that would be bearable – just that: bearable – not very much to try for, you wouldn't think, but more than I have managed yet and more than looks likely in any near future. But you were saying – about Edna at the wedding – I looked out the photographs, of course, they were in shoeboxes with hundreds of others in the cupboard on Eric's side of our bed, I laid them out on the floor in my workroom, which you will never see, I will never let you or anyone else, not even Daniel, see the room in which I write my account of an important part of Eric's early life, and in those black and white photographs she is very beautiful, she has a *definite* face, like Monique's and like yours, when I see a face like that I think she knows who she is and what she wants and perhaps that makes at least some of the beauty of a young woman that she can look at you openly, she can bear being looked at, and I won't begrudge it her, on her wedding day, that she knows what she wants and believes herself fit to have it. Even perhaps that she believes she has got it. Sometimes when I look at the photos I think she looks almost triumphant. After all, she got him to marry her. But no one who knows the story before and after will hate her for that. I'm sorry, says Katrin, you were saying – forgive me, I talk too much. Tell me what you liked about Edna on her wedding day and on the few other occasions you and she ever met.

Let's start walking back, shall we? says Sheila, taking Katrin's arm and turning her away from their contemplation of the rising spring in the pool. Yes, let's, says Katrin. And you see how even in this beautiful place I am not really here and the only things I can concentrate on are not here at all but are elsewhere and fifty years ago.

I was only eighteen, Sheila says. Michael and I had only known each other a couple of weeks but he asked me to come to the wedding and meet his mother and father, so I did. His grandmother was there as well. I remember how uneasy they all were. Michael didn't know where to put himself. In the end he drifted to his family and scarcely spoke to Eric or Edna. As you know, the wedding was in church and she wore white. Daniel was best man and they didn't care for him either. I talked to him and, of course, to Eric, and after the reception, which didn't last long, I made sure I talked to Edna on her own for a few minutes. I felt sorry for her. She was only a year or so older than me. You're right, she did look beautiful but I wouldn't say she looked triumphant, not in the church, nor at the reception and not in any of the photographs I've seen. I'd say she looked determined, a bit defiant, she knew perfectly well what his family thought of her and him. I wished her luck. We'll be ok, she said. And that's my clearest memory of the occasion. She felt that by marrying Eric she had got the *makings* of happiness and she was determined they would go on and get the thing itself and prove his family wrong. Funny, I suppose her own side must have been there too but I have no memory of any of them, not even of her father who was in the RAF, I believe, and must have given her away. It was just her, Daniel and Eric versus the rest of the Swinton clan.

Katrin and Sheila stand aside to make way for a party climbing faster, a dozen or more, intent on the rim of the dale, they all in turn give a cheerful greeting which Katrin and Sheila answer with a nod and a smile. Perhaps one day I'll come here again, says Katrin, when I'm better. Meanwhile

Cressbrook will have to forgive me for not attending to it as I should have done. I don't know anything about the 'before' that you mentioned, Sheila continues, and not much about the 'after' either. Michael's family complained to me about Eric and Edna whenever we met and so did Michael when the bad mood took him. He didn't like visiting them and they never came here. When Eric came up to see his mother he stayed somewhere in Manchester and Michael met him there for an hour or so. And even after Edna left him, when you'd think he might be glad of us coming to help out a bit, he never invited us, we invited ourselves now and then, but I can't say we looked forward to it or enjoyed it much when we were there. He did keep house pretty well and it was a great credit to him the way he brought up Thomas. But believe me, Katrin, we were so relieved when he married you. Things were much better after that and you mustn't be upset by Michael now. Eric's death had a funny effect on him, it seemed to throw him right back to the time when Eric left him, as he puts it, and it's as though he can't forgive him for all the years they lost and which couldn't be made up again even when you and Eric set up home together.

Katrin knows very well what it feels like to want to make up what cannot be made up, and she might have talked at length on the subject to Sheila there and then; but that – a further statement of the principle or generality – is not what she needs. Instead, walking close behind Sheila on a narrow stretch of the path, she says, Please can you recall any of the concrete details of what it was like when you visited Eric and Edna? Yes, I can, Sheila answers over her shoulder. And halting and looking back down the dale to where it narrows, darkens and moistens under the trees, she says, Edna's tone of voice for one thing. When she spoke to Eric or spoke of him to us in his company, her tone was invariably sardonic. And she addressed him not as Eric but as Swinton. So she might conclude a few remarks with, Am I right or wrong, Swinton? Or, Just like your bloody father, Swinton. I can see her face as I tell you this – very beautiful but with a sardonic cast around the lips and a bitter amusement in her eyes. She always seemed to be sitting sideways on to him, never face to face but like an onlooker, slantwise appraising him. On one occasion she wasn't there when we arrived. Eric said she'd gone shopping and wouldn't be long. And five minutes later we heard the car and in she came with bags and bags of shopping. She made three trips and loaded it all on the table in front of us. Each time she went out Eric glanced our way and shrugged. When it was all brought in she said, There now. You won't starve. Gave Eric her sardonic smile, nodded politely to Michael and me and left us, with Thomas, to our own devices for the duration of our visit, which was only the one night, needless to say. Eric would never speak about her when she wasn't there and when she was there, appraising him from the side and calling him Swinton, again and again he shrugged or made some gesture with his hands which seemed to mean, That's what I'm like. Nothing can be done about it. Her dress was rather slovenly, she wore trousers and an old shirt and jumper, but at first this was perhaps her own in fact quite chic way of setting herself at odds with him. Later it looked more and and more like an attractive woman letting herself go. In brief, Katrin, after two or three years of marriage Edna knew she was disappointed, the baby made no difference, Eric had disappointed her and that was that. And he seemed to agree – he was a disappointment to her. He shrugged, as though to ask, Well what did you expect? At bottom, I don't think it grieved him all that much. I think he felt that being disappointed was her problem not his. Had he not come to her trailing disappointments of his own? And now, if you don't mind, let's leave the subject. I do want to show you Tideswell. The church is lovely and you must also see the wells that they are already dressing for the festival.

Again the bad dreams, long interrogations in two or three languages, and whether Katrin puts the questions or refuses to answer them the feeling is the same: panic, headlong haste, the rapids. She wakes early, sits at the small desk in the window, glances in disgust at her notebook, page and after page of insect scribble. And outside all is unspoilt, it is dewy and still. She opens the window, faintly she can hear the river and heading south down the empty road there's a bright yellow truck, compact and suited to its purpose, like a well-made indestructible toy that a two-year-old would load with wooden bricks and kneel by and shove down the hall and it would never leave the house, his own children and their children would come back in turn and discover it, bright yellow, indestructible, good for the job it was made for. The yellow truck passes out of sight down the valley that is waking to chimes and cockcrow.

At breakfast Katrin tells Sheila and Michael that she will leave today and not tomorrow. She hopes they will forgive her, she has no wish to be rude. She is feeling anxious suddenly and it will be better if she goes home. They press her to stay, their concern touches her to the heart, in a rush she feels that she is denying herself chances of life and how will she ever get better if she does not gratefully seize them? Still she shakes her head. Thank you, she says, you are very kind to me, the two days have done me a lot of good, the anxiety will soon pass and the good will remain in me and be a great help.

Sheila will run her to Buxton. There are plenty of trains, she says, no hurry, we'll have coffee together. And I'll change at Stockport, Katrin says. I'll gain some time that way. It will be an easy journey home. I want to show you the top end of the garden, says Michael. Get yourself ready and come and find me up there.

The top boundary, a limestone wall, is the one straight line. Either side, the acres are hedged in sinuously, which effect – of something fluid and sentient – is enhanced by the sloping ground. The hedges accommodate themselves to the terracing, they negotiate a way up. The final terrace makes a broad platform where, on the heights overlooking Ashford and the Wye, Michael has built himself a summerhouse. That's where I write up my notes, he says, in summer, at least. Through the open door, along bare-wood shelves, Katrin sees rows of shoeboxes all labelled in Michael's neat hand. My finds, he says, that still want cataloguing. On the table, with a magnifying glass, a notebook, a handbook and three or four large-scale maps, are screwstones, corals, lamp-shells and specimens of calcite, Blue John and galena. He hands Katrin the Blue John, to hold up against the light. The vision she has is not of light coming through but being shown to be *in*. The crystals harbour their own blue-black light inside themselves. But chiefly Michael wants to show her his way out of the garden through the wall. It is an old iron gate, painted dark green. I like this gate, he says. In fact, I'm rather proud of it. In all the mist and rain I've kept it from rusting. And listen – he pushes it open – not a sound. Sometimes, he says, when I push through, especially in the early morning or late evening, I feel like a sleepwalker. I feel I don't make a disturbance. And now come and see. He ushers her ahead of him and follows. The hill rises gently and unenclosed, the bones of it, the limestone, showing through. He has the country of the blood-red cranesbill, the thyme, and the dewberry, curlew, hare and peewit, for him to enter from his upper threshold. There's a dip further up, he says, which becomes a shallow lake for a while after heavy rain, quite an extent really, in a lovely shape, and would you believe it: when the sky clears, that ordinary rainwater biding there on the green fields looks blue. And just beyond that there's a view north to the Kinder Dome. Anyway, this is my way out that I wanted to show you and that's where I go looking for the things that I like to find and study and learn more and more about. We never minded the children going through this gate on their own and now they don't mind their children doing the same.

At Chapel-en-le-Frith the railway and the A6 run close side by side. Katrin had thought she would perhaps get off there and look around for a stoneyard that might be the one Eric's truck belonged to, but she closes her eyes and carries on through. She is coming to the conclusion that other people's fullness of life will not restore her, be those people alive or dead. Neither their living present nor their resurrected past will serve her as an elixir of life. She is an emptiness into which a multitude of lives might pour for ever and vanish without a trace of good. Loneliness is an appetite that feeds and feeds and cannot get nourishment. She will make her way back to the home that is not a home, changing at Stockport and Birmingham among strangers, on and on, all that long way. She presses the dull pain in her left side under the ribs. Unlikely that it will kill her. More likely it will live in her for ever, dully.

# 10

ARRIVING HOME, KATRIN climbs at once to her workroom and emails Thomas. Please could you send me a recent photograph of your Mum? She writes that; then around it forces herself to compose the semblance of a more general human interest. She has just come back from a couple of days with Sheila and Michael... Their beautiful house... How kind they were to her... And how is he getting on?... She has been thinking about Edna lately... Has he heard from her?... Then a couple of sentences about herself, the weather... And to finish, do keep in touch, it would be very nice to meet. The one sentence that matters is embedded almost discreetly pretty well in the middle. Good. She clicks on Send. She scrolls down her Inbox, deleting, deleting. There is one from Daniel, she saves it. And another from an old man who was Eric's form prefect and who since the funeral has been sending her long reminiscences of his own schooldays which were indeed, he says, the happiest days of his life. Katrin glances through, sees no mention of Eric. She replies, thanking, and deletes it.

She unpacks, makes tea, opens a carton of soup. The house is hard to be in but where else should she go? She clears aside her supper things and writes a thank-you letter to Sheila and Michael, and having signed off, after a few moments absence or abstraction, she adds: You helped me. Looking at this statement Katrin concedes that it may not be true. But perhaps it has in it the possibility of becoming true? I say it. Now you become it! She goes out to post the letter and continues on her usual walk along the riverbank. The evening extends warmly and cheerfully towards darkness. There are still people on the water, serious scullers, families in easy rowing boats, the towpath is crowded, the pubs have spread their drinkers out of doors. Katrin has no part in any of it, she passes through, but with some resolution. Either her state is beyond her power to alter it and it will last for ever; or it isn't and it won't. If the latter, she must exert herself constantly, overriding the lapses. Better to assume possibility than impossibility. So she will go on with her life-writing. It is the only thing that engages her. It engages her because it keeps him near her. Is that good or bad? She cannot say. But good or bad, it is the only thing she desires to do, so she will do it. If it helps, good. If it doesn't, too bad.

She phones Daniel and puts this reasoning to him. He has his doubts but cannot answer her question, What else should I do? OK then, he says. And mutters something she doesn't catch. What was that? she asks. *Pecca fortiter*, he answers. Luther. Sin hard. Yes, I know what it means and I know who said it now you've said it clearly, she says. But I'm not sinning, am I? No, he answers, not exactly. But you know what I mean. Do it, carry on doing it, heart and soul. Only not for ever. No, not for ever, she answers. I know how far I want to go. I know where I want to stop. Thank you for your email. It will be very useful a bit later. But now I have to write about the winter of 1962-63. In a way it's against Michael. He told me he hates all that. Understandably, says Daniel. I suppose so, says Katrin. But I have to write from my point of view, don't I? – Of course you do. – I mean, I'm not interested in balance, I'm not trying to be omniscient. Eric's not a public figure I have to be fair about. – Of course he isn't. – I have to write what helps. – Yes, of course you do, says Daniel. If you can be sure it helps. – I can't be sure but I can't think what else to do. – Do it then, says Daniel. I'll watch your back. Katrin smiles at this. He will do nothing of the sort. He is her accomplice, he feeds her what she needs, more and more of it, whenever she asks. He was there. He wants to see what she will make of it.

Katrin writes: Michaelmas 1962. He was distracted. They both were. Daniel had stayed too long in the mountains and came home haunted and solitary. Soon – in a college of public-school boys – he was lonely too. He wanted to be back among the glaciers, breathing thinner air. But after two or three weeks moping (his word), hating and despising his fellow-students, he decided that his form of revolt, for now, should be work. So he worked, with a cold passion, at whatever he was set to do and, beyond that, at whatever he set himself to do. He got used to being disliked by most people. He knew they ridiculed him. But at least, Katrin writes, he concentrated on being where he actually was. He saw that the place was rich and that he could use it. Eric, however, remained distracted. He wrote to Monique. Laboriously, he even contrived to telephone her at the café, but he suffered so much – he could hear them laughing in the background – he never did it again. Soon after that, according to Daniel, he hitched to London, walked to Victoria, and watched the night train leave for Paris. Then he hitched back, for a tutorial that morning. One refrain in Monique's letters was that if he really loved her he would come to Paris and live with her, they would manage, he could teach English. According to Daniel's philosophy, everyone must make their own choices and couldn't be directed among them by anyone else. So he would not urge one course of action or another on his best friend. The most he would say was that limbo (dithering around) was not much better than hell (living in bad faith). Eric knew what he meant but couldn't act on it. From home, from his father, he had letters in which he was already being cast as the disappointer; and before long, no doubt, if he carried on in his folly and wildness, he would be worse: a downright disgrace. It became a leitmotif in these letters that sooner or later he, Eric, the son they had been so proud of, would get 'some girl' pregnant, and that would be that. It would kill your mother, the father wrote. No it wouldn't, Eric said to Daniel. And wonderingly he repeated the words 'some girl'. But he did feel keenly, says Daniel, that his family had no joy in him. He carried their anxiety and disappointment on his back, and in his heart of hearts he agreed with them that they had every right to feel anxious and disappointed. But he also felt it was his own life to fashion the best he could. He never wrote back, or only a card now and then to say they needn't worry, he would sort himself out. The stupidest thing – says Daniel – was that he had landed in a congenial college, his tutors were good, many of his fellow-students were from northern grammar schools. All that was asked of him was that in friendly company he should study the literature he loved. And he couldn't do it. He was distracted. He saw her sauntering naked through the flat. He saw her standing naked at the open window viewing the roof-top world in the grey-silver morning light. And he heard her saying over her shoulder, The swifts have gone. I didn't tell you my mother has a house in Marrakech. We can go there whenever we like and make love on the roof and sleep under a blanket of many colours under the stars and make love in the morning when the world wakes up and goes about its business having less fun than us. But if that tormented him, worse by far was the feeling that he could never be sure of her, he felt that she, being happy in her world and dismissive of his, had the advantage over him and that he was at her mercy. Daniel said it surprised him to see Eric so incapable of countering Monique. Oxford meant nothing to her and now, after all the effort of getting there and his family's aspirations riding on his back, it had begun to be nothing to him. Well, not nothing – clearly, it was something; but he could not attend to it, he was in love and could not concentrate on anything else. Did Daniel blame Monique? Daniel was not sure that, in those days, he ever blamed anyone for anything. He liked or disliked people, respected them or despised them, and always according to the very rough measure of whether they were living in truth or not. Those who, so far as he could judge, were not, he declared them to be in hell, and in the deepest circle of hell if they did not know it. In his view, Monique and Eric, both in love, were living in truth and to Daniel that mattered far more than whether they were conventionally happy or not. He could not blame Monique for how she acted towards Eric. It was up to Eric to act in assertion of himself, against her if need be. The most Daniel would say against his friend was that he risked becoming blameworthy if he dithered much longer in mere distraction. But Daniel never did blame Eric. He was his friend, he loved him. In fact he continued as he had been at school, rather in awe of him. On the hill outside Vizille when Eric recounted his journey and, for its culmination, tipped the small hoard of silver into Daniel's cupped hands, the admiration and wonderment had been increased and in the mountains his friend felt very present to him in those feelings. Then Monique – she only enhanced Eric's aura in Daniel's eyes. He, Daniel, said yes to it all. It was glorious to be in love like that. Himself he never would be, he felt sure. The books came alive. Daniel was reading them and watched them living in Eric. The poets were right. Eric, his friend, proved them right.

Katrin writes: I've found ten letters and two postcards from Monique in that Michaelmas term. I doubt if any have gone missing. When I read them, translated and transcribed them, I didn't feel there were any gaps. It's a proper correspondence. They answer one another. Daniel says Eric never again conducted a correspondence at all like that. Not even with him. When they parted company – Eric leaving Oxford, marrying Edna, moving to Surrey – some letters were exchanged (I've probably got them all), but it soon lapsed, and thereafter they wrote only occasionally and met now and then. (When Eric and I met, at the very beginning I was away from him for a fortnight, we wrote three times each and I've got those, of course. After that we were scarcely ever apart, and then only for a night or two, so we didn't write and I have no letters for our twenty-two years together.) If Eric were somebody famous and I had a contract to write his biography I should certainly by now have written to Monique to ask could I come to Paris and interview her. And if she allowed me that much, I should have tried to win her confidence and one day – I imagine us meeting half a dozen times over a period of a week or so, I'd be staying in the Hôtel Malebranche and at the agreed hour I should walk the short distance to where she lives now – one day I'd ask her did she feel she'd ever be willing to let me see and make copies of the letters he wrote her between the end of September 1962 and the end of March 1963. But for that, it seems to me, I should have to be someone else and not his widowed wife, which is something I cannot bear even to imagine. So what if I wrote to her and visited her and made my request to her in my own person, in my own grief, as the woman who welcomed her in out of the cold and the dark that evening of the funeral only four months ago and felt for her when she stood there crying like a six-year-old and her make-up smirched her face?

Katrin halts. She sees Monique's face as it looked on that occasion, it is for a moment as present as the photo of her undressing in Jean-Luc's studio. And for the first time in all these weeks of writing and reflecting Katrin, with a pang of shame, thinks of Monique as a woman like herself, grieving. She said she had dreamed of him, she wept, she gave me the bowl that she had made herself back then. Could I go to her and ask her to let me read what my dead husband, her youthful dead lover, wrote to her so many years ago? Doubtful. I wonder if she wonders what I'm doing now. I wonder if she asks Daniel and he tells her. I wonder would she like her letters back, to marry them up with the ones her more and more unhappy lover wrote to her. I wonder could she bear to know that of the last fifteen she wrote to him he never read, he never even opened, one. And they came to me, and I read them, wrote them out in her French in my own hand, translated them in my own hand into my husband's tongue in which I am so naturalised my mother tongue has slipped and slid and lost its edge and virtue in the telling of the truth.

That night Katrin phones Daniel. I've been thinking more about Monique, she says. Ah, yes, he answers, Monique. You know when you came here a few days before Eric died, Katrin continues, did he talk to you then about Monique? A little, says Daniel, among other things. But he was very weak, you remember. I remember I went out for two hours, says Katrin, the longest I was away from him in all that time. I took a bus out to the estuary and sat there for a while. Then I caught the same bus back. I knew he would be safe with you. I thought you would want to talk. We did, says Daniel, as much as he was able. – And about Monique? – Yes, a little about Monique. He said he would ask you to invite her to the funeral. It was part of his not wanting to be at odds with anyone, you remember. Yes, says Katrin, I do remember that. I believe he mentioned Edna to me at the same time, after you had gone. But about her and the funeral he said, It's up to you. And you did invite her, says Daniel. And everyone said that was very generous of you. But Monique, says Katrin, he didn't leave her up to me, he did definitely want her to be there, and she came. Yes, says Daniel. Daniel, says Katrin, I've been thinking how she stood in the hall and cried like a little girl. I've been thinking I haven't thought about her anywhere near enough. She said she had dreamed about him the day he died. Did she tell you her dream? Yes, she did, says Daniel, when we left your house and we were walking along together she told me what she had dreamed. Katrin senses a discomfort in Eric's friend. He is sparing me, she thinks. Or perhaps I am making him suffer all over again and undoing any good the last few months may have done. Tell me, will you, she says. Tell me what Monique dreamed. Shall I? he asks. His tone is rather that of, Must I? Not if you don't want to, says Katrin, who now feels certain that he does not want to. No, no, he says, of course I'll tell you if you want to hear it. Only it's very Monique, a bit ridiculous really. She never changed, she always loved the great solemnities – 'solemnities not easy to withstand' – if you know what I mean, and she still loves them, she is forever encountering them. A bit ridiculous perhaps. – Tell me her dream, Daniel. – Well then, she was in a large park or garden, like the Luxembourg, she said, but much bigger, in a mist, and there were no other people, only trees, as she advanced she saw winter trees and classical statues, the nymphs and dryads, Venus and Pan, the whole company one by one appearing and disappearing in the mist. And she was walking down a long allée, on the gravel, all she could hear was her own feet on the gravel. But she walked with a purpose in a terrible cold loneliness straight down the long allée until she came to the ornamental lake, which was vast and lightly frozen over and on the surface, pushing through the thin ice, were two swans, they were pushing slowly away from her across the lake, leaving behind them a wake of open water that would soon close again under the re-forming ice. Then ahead and above her the mist began to lighten, she had the very strong feeling that the sky was opening, the swans moved more quickly now, side by side, and as the mist opened, with a loud beating and splashing, by a great and yet graceful exertion, they lifted themselves clear of the freezing water and in a steepening diagonal rose through the mist and vanished. For a little while she could still hear the clouts of their wings. Then in silence the gap in the mist closed, the air itself closed in again grey-white, rapidly the ice hardened and thickened over the whole extent of the lake and she was left standing at the encircling stone rim absolutely alone, very cold, and without the least sense of any direction home.

That's not ridiculous, Daniel, says Katrin after a long silence. You don't have to defend Monique. She is not at all ridiculous. And now tell me did she say anything else to you as you walked along together, anything about Eric that might explain her dream. Yes, says Daniel in a flat voice, she said that Eric was the one true passionate love of her life, she said she forfeited her happiness with him, lost him, through her own folly, and had grieved ever since and his death had only deepened that grief. Oh, says Katrin. And to be honest, says Daniel in the same flat voice, I do find that more than a bit ridiculous. It's just a story. She has made up a story. Of course she has, says Katrin angrily. What else should she do? What else can any of us do? And who are you to object to other people's stories? OK, says Daniel, OK. And now one last thing, please, then I'll let you go to bed, and I will too, not that I'll sleep, but one last thing will be enough for me tonight. When I went away for two hours, out to the estuary, and you had your last talk with Eric, did he say anything to you at all like what you just told me Monique said to you as you walked along together after his funeral? Tell me honestly, Daniel, I have to know, I'll never get better unless I can be certain there won't be harder things I'll have to face up to one day that I haven't faced up to now. No, says Daniel, he said nothing at all like that. We did speak about *then*, and a little about her, but it was long long ago and far far away, he said, and all he asked was that she should be invited to his funeral.

Katrin sleeps at once. Her consciousness, overladen, shuts down, as it were mechanically. But then, a long way from daylight, she wakes, and this too, this sudden waking, is like a mechanism. Overburdened, the machine shuts down. Sufficiently recharged, it starts up again. But as the housing of the machine and as the ghost in it, Katrin feels not in the least rested. It, beyond her volition and having nothing to do with her wellbeing, merely starts up again, and she resumes her thinking.

The mind coming awake in that watch of the night proceeds in ways the daylight hours will hardly tolerate. It engages with a vengeance in self-harm. All the malign arguments assemble, they fall into line, one by one they fit into the syntax of a harmful and compelling fiction. Then it seems that in daylight you resist and won't accept this version of the world only because you can, in daylight, more easily distract yourself and find excuses. But in the dark before there is any glimmer of dawn or murmur of birdsong and human traffic, you are obliged to concentrate and soon you will concede: this is the truth.

Katrin puts on a dressing-gown and goes upstairs to her workroom. Seeing that place – her small table against the lefthand wall, Eric's jacket over the chairback, the neat piles and orderly lines of documentation by now commanding much of the floor – she feels sick and defeated and the idea that woke her or that she woke into and that developed itself swiftly to its logical end, that idea sets hard now into an annihilating conviction. She crosses to her desk in the window, switches on the computer, waits, not impatiently but resignedly, till it reactivates and puts at her disposal all its vast capacity to recall, sort, order and compose; then she emails Daniel.

You said that when you spoke to Eric last he said nothing to you at all like Monique's 'it was my *grande passion*', and I believe you. And when he said he wanted her at his funeral as a part of his wish to forgive and be forgiven at the end, I'm sure he meant it. But now I have realised a blindingly obvious thing. His last big effort at speech with me, after you left and the day before he died, was to begin the account of his journey to meet you in France. As I have told you, he got no further than the place the postman dropped him on the

Dover road. That far, no further, and it wore him out, he used up his last strength getting himself that far. I hope I'll never again see anyone so desperate to say more and not being able to because his strength gave out. Well, as you know, mostly through you – ask Daniel, he said, and gripped my hand so tight it hurt – but also with other bits of evidence and by the power of my own complicit imagination I got him not only to the meeting place in the Café Elsa in Vizille and to the couple of nights on the hill outside talking to you under the stars, I got him beyond that all the way back to Paris and to Monique's, which was the accommodation you set up for him, and so into her bed. Daniel, it seems to me now that with your help, with your aiding and abetting me, I have accomplished his last wish and got him to where at the very end of his life he again desired to be: back to her, his *grand amour*, his *grande passion*, whether or not he used those words or hinted at the fact itself in his last talk with you. You helped him *back then*. You sent him a telegram poste restante Nemours: YES GO TO MONIQUE, and you helped me return him to her, into her bed, fifty years later, now. Tell me, Daniel, is that a fair way of looking at what you and I have done?

I have more, much more, to write about her and him, it is already present and marshalled in my head, it has been assembling itself out of conversations with you and out of the papers and the photographs on the floor and on the table in this terrible room and in my head it is so pressing I shall have to write it out and say how wildly happy and outrageously in love they were that winter, the coldest in living memory, at the turn of the year. I shall have to write it and then perhaps what was asked of me will be done. Perhaps that was all the commission I had from him: to show him and her as the exemplars for ever of what it feels and looks like being that much in love. And all the rest – Edna, me – is only the long fag-end of it, the loss, the sorrow, the errors, the resignation, the long, long dismal remainder of a life, till it comes to now and to me, his widow and biographer, writing up the best for him because he could not say himself how good it was, so good, but had to leave himself on the Dover road and left it to me to convey him on through you to her. Can that be right, Daniel?

Katrin reads it over, corrects a few typos, improves the expression here and there. Then she looks up, through the window, east. Over the invisible moors there is a grey-white misty parting, daylight is seeping irresistibly through and will soon command the attention of the waking world that wants or is obliged to live, that has its duties and its pleasures and its troubles to attend to on this day as on every other day and cannot be doing with the insights you arrive at waking in sorrow on your own, they are not serviceable, they will not help, they will only hamper and erode you. Katrin clicks on Send, shuts down the machine, switches off the lights, returns to the bed that is too big for her and curls herself up small in it much as she did the night after the funeral guests had gone.

Katrin sleeps late. This novelty occasions another: she leaves the house at once and walks quickly to the café on the busy street where, some weeks ago, she sat without panic for twenty minutes. She finds the same seat in the window, orders coffee and a croissant. The waitress recognises her, smiles. The place is friendly. Most there, reading, working at very neat laptops, are younger than Katrin. They seem to her accustomed and self-possessed.

Katrin's idea, conceived and uttered in the worst hour of the night, has come through with her and, she ascertains, is proof against the daylight. She sees also that it is capable of being turned and looked at from different angles. She feels a sudden love and pity for Eric and Monique equally, tears fill her eyes, so that when the waitress comes back with her order she can only nod, smile downwards and then look away outside at the mid-morning traffic. The place is kind. Why should she not come here and become a familiar person among other people? She could read here, and write. And why on earth should it annihilate her to write as well as she can about her dead husband in love with a woman who, in old age, remembers him passionately? Now she likes the thought of its being her commission. So she will carry on doing what she has been doing since she first got herself out of the paralysis of grief by going like a sleepwalker into the loft and rediscovering his letters. But now, to her at least – which is the view of it that matters – the same thing will have a different slant and a different light. She will write to say as best she can how good their life was, how youthful and courageous and fit to be looked at by all the guardian and recording angels. And she will do this not for herself, to recover her own life, but for theirs, then, as a tribute to its beauty.

Back home Katrin has emails from Daniel and Thomas, and a long letter from Michael. She considers all three in the light of her new resolve. None disturbs her. In their different ways, all fit.

Daniel writes – she notes with alarm that he replied only half an hour after she wrote to him – first that he is sorry he called Monique ridiculous and used the word 'story' dismissively. Between her and Katrin he felt uneasy, loving both and wishing to protect them both. Katrin's own story – as she told it to him in her email – is lucid, beautiful and terrible. Then he turns it much as she did herself in the café, which gladdens her. Yes, she has a sort of commission to carry Eric's story through to Paris and to Oxford in the cold winter. So she must do it, and he says again – and this time it touches her and she believes him – that he will watch her back. And he thinks that in the end, even if (or perhaps especially if) this is not her intention, she will come to see herself as he, Daniel, always has seen her, since she married Eric. So they are not at odds. Only she must ask more of him, let him help her more, since she is his friend.

Thomas seems touched that Katrin has asked after his mother, and she recalls with a little start of shame how *interestedly* she wrote to him. *Déformation professionelle*, she says to herself. Can't be helped. Thomas writes to Katrin that Edna worries him, he doesn't know what to do for the best, she seems set on making her life as miserable as possible. She complains to him that she is short of money now that she no longer gets maintenance from Eric. But if she is, she has only herself to blame and he, Thomas, helps her where he can. But she seems bent on making an enemy of him, her son, her only close family, too. She can't get at Dad, he says. So she is taking it out on me. He attaches a photograph, not all that recent, eighteen months ago, if he remembers rightly, they haven't seen much of one another lately and not at all on occasions when you might have taken a photo. Katrin opens the attachment. The picture shocks her. She hasn't seen Edna for many years, ten at least, and the images of her she has lived with since Eric died have all been black and white from half a century ago. She fetches one: Edna in a short summer dress on the river in the bows of a punt, full on and close to the camera, laughing, confident in her beauty, her hair is black and long, she has an arcade of willows behind her into which she is being conveyed. Against that, the woman now, smiling not in a way to counter the bitterness around her mouth and in her eyes, but to point it up, as though to say, See what I have become – with the subtone, See what you have done to me. Katrin sees that it is not a question of age. It is not even a question of suffering. Monique in her duffle coat, red stockings and black cloche hat could stand side by side with the girl undressing in Jean-Luc's studio, the years would be shown to have been cruel, but there is nothing of bitterness in her face and bearing, she does not say to the world, I blame you for how I look now.

Beginning Michael's letter, Katrin at once thinks of the gate at the top of his garden in Ashford, the iron gate he is so proud of because he got it to open easily and silently on to the unenclosed hillside. She feels his letter to be a similar opening out. And she regrets leaving a day early. He wanted to tell me more about himself and Sheila and Eric, she thinks, and I didn't let him, I didn't ask even the ordinary polite questions, I only asked and listened to what I thought I needed to know.

Michael writes about his job. All my working life, he says, I've dealt with people in trouble – hundreds of lives, many hundreds of reports on them, so much writing and talking about them and on their behalf. And I think I haven't forgotten a single one. I think if you said a name a face would come back to me and then the life I had to do with under that name. I don't mean everything would come back in every case, of course not, but certainly some bits and pieces, a tone of voice, a look, a phrase or two, a gesture, fragments of a particular story, its continuation until it stopped being my business. And then, of course, quite often, far too often, the whole thing, the whole file, the whole failure, would get sent back to me, to try again. All the life-stories, bits of which he remembers, some of them haunt him, the loss, the waste, and the feeling, that comes with the job, that he could have done more. There's no end to the help some people need, he writes. The worst are like bottomless pits, black holes that suck in every life around them and still can't get enough. All the life-stories, all different of course, no one suffers quite like anyone else, the bits and pieces he remembers are very particular, they could only belong to this or that person in their particular time and place. But in all the welter of these telling fragments, he admits there are repeated sets of circumstances, the same patterns and structures again and again and again, and in them the new characters struggling and losing. And that's what is so disheartening on a bad day or during a bad period of your working life: the feeling that it's all much the same, that in the end, when you weigh up, there aren't many stories. Some days, to be honest, it seemed to him there was only one: the deal at the outset, the fall of events, the struggle, the losing, the long and repetitive end-game. Variations of that one plot. Mostly, he writes, it's settled for you by the age of three, the lots have been dealt and have fallen well or ill for you conclusively by the age of three. I could show you on maps of Manchester or Derby pretty well street by street what the odds are for or against you at the start. Sheila and I had quite a few boys and girls, young men and women, in common. She knew them early, I knew them a few years later. And there seems to come a point when such people accept (or decide) that the management of their life is not, after all, their business, it will be assumed for good or ill by somebody else, by one office, agency, department, institution or another. And this may be the inevitability surfacing that was there all along, born where you were, into that family at that time on that street, and once it has risen up and stopped you in your tracks or marshalled you a way you did not want to go, after that you bow to it, you acquiesce. The structure of the story is very simple, Michael says. I've listened to countless life-stories that proceed to some commonplace bad event – a mother dies, the sister you were living with gets married, a stepfather moves in – and having told the tale so far next thing the teller says is, So I.... Or, worse: So obviously I... So I started drinking... So obviously I hit him... In essence, says Michael, the structure is: This happened, and that was that. What else could I have done? Nothing. That was that. Listening, says Michael, I was always waiting for the words, So I... So obviously I... 'Obviously', used like that, is a word that would break your heart if you let it. The life-stories, endlessly trotted out to anyone who would listen. And much of my job consisted in halting the storyteller at the point of the life-excuse, and getting him at least to imagine a different continuation. But many would carry on for the rest of their lives in the same old version that exculpated them.

Life-stories, Michael says, the life-chances. And how fragile any life is, even if you're dealt a good hand and are doing pretty well, shaping a life into something fit to be looked at. From one day to the next, as drastically and finally as smashing a precious vase, that life may be all in bits. The people that happens to, they don't say, So obviously I…, they say, Why on earth did I…? And they spend the rest of their allotted time wondering over the wreckage. They are the ones who, in a bad sense, 'never knew they had it in them'. They did a thing they never dreamed of doing. Either that, or the whole structure was all along, unbeknownst to them, a very precarious thing. Say the wrong word, put a foot wrong, it collapses, almost innocently you destroy it, you inhabit the ruins ever after and nothing you do will make it right again. That was the very worst, says Michael, dealing with people who had, so to speak, crossed over and would have behind them, for ever more, the irreparable.

Katrin halts in her reading. Then she writes, Things are what they are by virtue of other things – *in relation*, always and only in relation. Michael is writing about himself, about himself and Sheila, perhaps because I didn't ask when I was there. But knowingly or not he is doing it so that I will give more thought to Eric, whom he hasn't mentioned yet, as the brother of a man living very differently. Michael's apologia for his life, so that I shall see Eric differently. Eric as a *case*? Well, I won't see him like that. But when he gets Edna pregnant and he needs money for the abortion and then the abortion itself – suppose she had died? – around then he might have been on the way to becoming a case and perhaps in Michael's own life-story he figured as a warning? (I don't know exactly what Michael knows about it all – about the worst things. And if he does know, even some of it, he must wonder how much and exactly what do *I* know.)

Michael's letter continues: Sheila tells me you didn't rightly understand what I meant by saying Eric deserted me. But that is what it felt like back then and does still, or again, now he's dead and I'm missing him. On the other hand, I have to admit that but for Eric we might not be living in Ashford in this house with the terraced garden and the gate that lets me out on to the hill. So if I feel it to be true that he abandoned me it's also true, in a way, that he left me with a local habitation I love so much the love will fill all the remaining days of my life and whoever has the place after us will feel it to be haunted by very benevolent ghosts. You see, the limestone was Eric's passion first, I caught it from him, he gave it me. He loved the gritstone too, of course he did, and that was where we mostly went because it was easier to get there and back in the day, most often a Sunday, on Saturdays we were playing rugby or we had a job. That was a thing, Katrin, to be in Manchester very early on a Sunday morning and nobody on the dirty streets except the hikers heading for the stations to get out for the day, tramp, tramp, tramp, when I think of it now the city was entirely silent, no traffic, only the hikers making for the stations, in silence, only the tramp of boots on concrete, the boots that wanted the grass, the mud, the bog, the bare stone under them, hundreds of people heading off out of the quiet Sunday-morning city, hundreds of us, congregating on the platforms, shoving into the trains to go out to the margins where we dispersed into solitudes, into wilderness, that was a thing, Katrin, and my big brother gave me that, he took me with him just as soon as Mother and Father would let him and I never once felt he didn't want me there and that I was only tagging along. The gritstone was nearest – Hayfield to the Downfall and across to Edale, to and fro we went over Kinder, time and again, through the cottongrass and the bilberries, in sun or rain or fog or snow, down the deep black groughs along the little clear waterways that don't rightly know which way to turn to ever get off the dome into a stream or a river with a name.

You'll have heard of Mam Tor, the Shivering Mountain, it's an outpost of the gritstone, shale and sandstone, outpost and vantage point over the limestone, the caverns, potholes and Blue John. And it's collapsing, it's on the slide, one vast terrain is sliding down into the other. Often enough we stood up there, Eric and me. I love a threshold. And I don't mean we stood there looking down on impossibilities. Not in the least. We stood there seeing where we'd like to go, how long we'd need, which paths we'd take, one day. It was more and more we were after, and we stood up there on the Shivering Mountain and worked out how we'd get it. This is important, Katrin. This is what I most want to get across to you. I'm not talking about fairyland and places you only ever long for and never reach. I'm talking about places we saw ahead of us and worked out the way to and actually got there and were not disappointed. It's as simple as that. Again and again he took me to places that did not disappoint either him or me.

One Sunday, before Mother and Father were up, I suppose I must have been eleven or twelve, we slipped out with a map, a compass and a bite to eat across Leicester Road uphill to Clowes Park. Of course, that early it was all shut up but either side the gate the railings were still missing, from the War, and we got in there. At the fishpond he lined up our route, north-north-east, by the spire of St George's Church, and at the far end, again he knew a gap in the railings. Then we were on Bury Old Road, heading for Heaton Park, climbing. That's a thing in the big city, Katrin: from our own front door we were climbing, we were heading north, up and out. We got into Heaton Park by a way he'd reconnoitred the week before, avoiding the lodge. And that's something else, Katrin: he taught me trespassing, he showed me the ways into the public parks that were still shut up very early on a Sunday morning, so that we saw the swings, the bowling green, the boating lake, the pitch and putt, the museum, the hothouses, as though we were visitants from another planet, all so eerie and untouched as we passed through. But that particular Sunday, and that park being so vast, we kept on the open ground, across the great open space, already quite high up, only us two and the rabbits, and the northern world opening up. He said it was here that Grandad came with the 17th Manchesters, in September 1914, before he went off to be blown to bits in France, and after that war Mam and Dad did their courting here, he said, in a wonder at the place and those stories in it. But we headed on through, over the big hill and down into the trees by the reservoir, to the brick wall around the perimeter. Along this wall there was a sort of ledge, half way up, but he said we needed a tree as well, growing close, to help us, and he soon found one, just right. He put his hands together, and I stood on that clasp and he heaved me on to the ledge and by a branch I got up on top and astride. Then he followed. He dropped first into the dead leaves on the other side, I hung down after, my arms' whole length, and he reached up, held me at the hips and let me down safe. After that we went due north, where there were still farms and streams, but with the city hemming them in on either side and works of one sort or another, small mills and factories, you could smell them, more than a hundred years of it, wherever there was water that could be put to use, there were fumes drifting off it in places. But still it was rural. The first human being we saw was a farmer bringing in his cows. Last thing, we hit on an old cobbled road, heading due north, between hedges of hawthorn and elder, I remember the smell, or I've smelled it often since, hedges of elder and hawthorn in early summer, and I'm back on that cobbled way north. The suddenly Eric said, Best go home now. But look, that's what I wanted to show you, up there, Harden Moor, Knowl Moor, Whittle Hill. Once you're up there, you can walk for ever. We'll go up there one day. I promise you. That was the farthest I'd ever walked with him then, our first long outing, from our own front door. And at the limit of it, on a Sunday morning, still early, he showed me the uplands, the way you would climb to get on to the backbone of the land. When I remember it now, I feel silence and stillness and far ahead, but not impossibly far ahead, I see the high, clean, empty moorland, shining.

One thing more, Katrin, and then I'll stop. The summer he went to France, before he started at Kelloggs, we took the whole weekend and climbed the Dane out of Cheshire, out of the flatlands, on to the moors. We slept Friday night in Wincle. The Vicar saw us eating oranges on a gravestone and said we could sleep in his barn, if we liked. We left very early, we were at Lud's Church by six, we squeezed through the length of it and down a few side-tunnels too, that green slit, all dripping, all hung with ferns, and twisted trees sprouting up out of the cracks for the daylight, and we were deep below, wriggling through. After that we stopped at the pool where the three shires meet, it was warm, we stripped off and larked around in the waterfalls for a while. I've climbed scores of streams since then, it became a passion of mine, something I tried to do at least once a year, a new stream, or go back to an old one and climb into the memory and the novelty of it again. I made a rule that I had to keep as close as humanly possible to the water itself, from rock to rock, or in it if necessary, under its foliage, and when there was a falls getting up it by tree-roots and digging my fingers into the moss and ferns, quite perilous really. And I think I got that from Eric, from climbing the Dane with him, coming out on to Axe Edge Moor, tracking the source. And when we were up there so pleased with ourselves a mist blew over very suddenly, very dense, white and clammy, every shape and faint sound was distorted, you couldn't say were they near or far. We got across by dead reckoning, twenty paces at a time, from one nondescript stone or tussock to the next. We'd tracked over Kinder often before, but Axe Edge was special. I remember how solemn we were, we checked every setting umpteen times, he made me his equal and necessary comrade in getting across the moor, we lined up the route, twenty paces, he went first, I followed on his heels. Axe Edge was special. We got it pretty well dead right, we got over the gritstone moor, the heather and cotton grass land, and the mist drifted nonchalantly away and there below us, in sunlight, just where it belonged to be, was the limestone country, green fields, white rock.

# 11

AT THE END of that first term in Oxford Eric was summoned to see his tutors. They told him, not unkindly, that unless he mended his ways he would fail his Prelims, would have to resit them, and if he failed them again he would be sent down. His tutor in French added that they were puzzled by him. He had been expected to do very well and they didn't understand why he wasn't. And they waited, not in the least unkindly, for an explanation. But he had none, or none he could utter. Leaving them, he collected his post, which was a letter from Monique and one from his mother saying how much they were looking forward to having him home for Christmas, with a PS from his father, saying that, either side of the job on Christmas post, they were taking on casuals at Dulux paints so he should hurry home and get in there quick. Eric went to the post-office and sent a telegram to Monique; then to the bank, and emptied his account; then, packing as little as possible, he hitched to London and caught the night-train to Paris.

Katrin understands this moment in Eric's life as a radical simplification. He knows wholeheartedly what he wants and he goes after it, leaving all else behind him or to one side. Perhaps he thinks such other matters can wait, he will attend to them when he has settled the one thing that cannot wait. She, of course, sees perfectly well that this thing that cannot wait, cannot and will not ever be settled either. He will want more; never again, she believes, will he want anything so consumingly; and the more he feeds, the more he will hunger. But she does share his sense that after weeks of distraction now at last his life has concentrated on what it most desires.

The boat-train got in early. Eric ran for the métro, the 4 to Châtelet, down the long corridors he ran, caught a 7 just leaving. He surfaced in the Place Monge, into the city aiding the weak daylight with lamplight, and among people opening their shops or going to work or to their studies and past the damp *clochards* on the métro vents, he ran to 7 rue Tournefort and halted there, heart pounding.

Across the street, from the Café Amyot, Maurice saluted him. Two or three of the others were already there. They also raised a hand in friendly greeting. Good, said Eric to himself. Let them see. Let it be known in the *quartier* that I love her helplessly. The house door was open, he climbed the five flights, the light went off half way up, he climbed the rest in darkness and only switched on again at her door to which she had pinned a note: Je suis au lit. He removed this document and folded it away between two pages of his passport. Then he went in, locking her door behind him.

He crossed the big room to the window and drew back the curtains. Hesitantly in a pearl-grey light the roof-top world was appearing. He opened the window a little, took in the smell of that zone above the streets. Then shut out the cold of it, in a hurry undressed, felt his way along the corridor to her cluttered and lightless bathroom, pissed as quietly as he could; then slid without a word into her bed. Neither did she say a word – only reached for him, felt for his mouth with hers, felt in for his tongue with hers, shared breath with him, and for a while they lay so, mouth to mouth as though that were the cave of night and sleep and the antechamber, sweet to linger in, before their hands reached down to begin the union that is as thorough as becoming one blood. At that threshold he made some gesture towards the box on the bedside table but she shook her head, C'est bon, she said. If the spirit can shrug, his shrugged. Whatever she meant, he agreed to it. He wanted whatever she wanted. His life had simplified.

They stayed in bed, idling, still not speaking much, recovering the feel of one another from top to toe, fitting again. When he fell asleep, she let him be for a while, but only for a while. Too wakeful herself, she wanted him back. She went and made coffee, brought it in on a tray with a pot of jam, a spoon and some bits of the day before's bread. She woke him, they sat up in the bed, drank, ate, their eyes all the while feasting on one another in the silvery light cast upon them from the sky through the window in the roof. The shock of her, having entered him again, settled now into a condition, his state of life. He felt wonderfully gifted, all of him, eyes, mouth, hands and the flesh stirring again between his legs, all felt made for the noble purpose of admiring her. How beautiful she is, black hair cut short like a boy's, her tilted head, the sex-light in her eyes, slim shoulders, her small breasts, and how I love her. He was glad of his body, that it was thin and strong and quick to learn what she wanted of it, and he was near to saying aloud, because it was so and he could say it truthfully, With my body I thee worship. Then she took the tray and, leaning down out of the bed with it, set it on the floor. And lay back, pulling him and the wrangled sheet up over her.

When they woke it was mid-afternoon, already drifting towards darkness. They were hungry, there was little or nothing in the flat to eat. He went down into the streets, his delight was ferocious, he shopped with a keen foretaste of everything he bought and of the happiness that would come to life from these purchased things when he laid them before her and they ate and drank together.

Katrin, writing, lives in it, and foreknows the power it will exert against her in the days and nights that will surely come when the present cannot hold and the desire to live abandons her.

When they began to speak, out of tact or fear or truly because they were heedless of it, they said nothing of the future, their story to date, up to now, was their only subject. Already they felt themselves to be legendary. Over certain episodes – her fetching him into her bed, for example, or their trek to Père Lachaise, the roots in there that tilted the colossal family tombs, the spikes along the walls festooned with old man's beard – over such passages of their life they dwelled in wonder, turning them this way and that, adding more details, shaping them ever more pleasingly. And all without elegy or nostalgia. Every day, effortlessly they matched the past, they wove another *geste*. Her bed under the skylight, under the winter moon, the winter stars, the faint and poignant winter sunshine, the many kinds of rain, this bed under the slant glass was the centre of their fairyland. They resorted to it and quitted it just as they pleased, with no regard to the clocks of everyday. So to their amazement they might find nothing open on the rue Tournefort when it entered their heads to want something to eat. Then they strolled down to the river, saluting the homeless, the drunks, the streetwalkers and the sleepwalkers. The river was fast, black, flecked with lights, they stood on the bridge and watched a barge pass silently under them so vast it could have carried to burial a whole company of young men. They ate among the blood-smeared meat-haulers in the belly of the city and wondered at the labours, the hurry, the unsleeping busyness of the world. Themselves they had nothing to do, only be, only be as they liked, hand in hand, wandering the streets. It was her city, she conducted him to places she loved so that he would love them too and the common territory of their passion would be extended.

Continually she surprised him, not by forethought, but by sudden impulses, spur-of-the-moment desires that she acted on, so that he supposed she must continually surprise herself. He woke one afternoon and saw her standing over him, dressed to go out. Hurry, she said, and stood at the window, facing away and drumming with the backs of her fingers on the glass. As they left, she gave him some chocolate, 'to wake him up', and set off so fast – Thouin, Descartes, Montagne Sainte Geneviève – he had to run after her, like a child. She made no halt until they reached the Flower Market. Go and get some bread, she said to him. And some cheese if we can afford it. See you back here in ten minutes. He was quick, when he found her again, not quite where he had left her, she was clutching a bunch of red carnations. They were thrown away, she said. I know a stall where they throw good things away. He broke the loaf, opened her half, squashed the camembert inside. She nodded, T'as bien fait. Je t'aime. They stood still for five minutes, watching the market. Lamps were already burning. There was an aura around them, a damp, like visible scent. Then abruptly, stuffing the uneaten end into her coat pocket, she set off again, fast, and he kept pace.

They walked half an hour, forty minutes, bearing north then east. He thought they might be heading for Père Lachaise again but didn't like to ask. She said not a word, only kept to her purpose, through the scores of streets that intersected, joined, swelled into squares, thinned back into streets, intently she pursued her course; and although they were side by side, when he glanced at her, he saw with wonderment and pain how entirely set on her own intent she was, with all the city around her, in the midst of its countless possibilities, she had her own objective and went her way towards it and he, ignorant, enthralled, accompanied her because she wished him to.

She walked faster; and it seemed now that she was hurrying not just to arrive at the place that would surprise him but also, and more, to carry through a decision before her resolution failed. He glanced around for landmarks, saw none, the *quartier* was new to him, and again and again his eyes went back to her, to her set, fearful, determined face. As so often, he was given up to her, in her hands, waiting for another revelation of herself. Then quite suddenly, with a long and helpless sob, she halted. We're here, she said. This is it. They were at a place where a railway line crossed under the road. On the bridge, on its wall, was a plaque. The date: 23 August 1944; the action: the ambushing of a Nazi train; and five names: the French dead. That's him, said Monique – the last, the youngest, only twenty-five. I was six weeks old. He never saw me. I was with my mother in Nevers. Eric looked over the parapet. The tracks curved away through an urban lost terrain. There's a tunnel further up, Monique said. They ambushed the train in there, it was full of soldiers, they smoked them out. She threw the carnations on to the pavement under the inscription. I come here with my mother once a year, she said. But never with anyone else. It was getting dark, the street lamps were hazy in a freezing drizzle. Now we'll go home, she said and took his arm. We'll walk slowly. We'll cook a nice meal and go back to bed.

On the streets of Paris he only once saw her disconcerted. They were somewhere in Montparnasse, long past midnight, on a street of high wealthy tenements, and she halted, lost. The street was softly lit, and silent, and it ended in a broad marble staircase, lamplit, curving out of sight. She let go his hand. More than once, knowingly, she had led him into streets that had no exit – Impasse des Jardiniers, Impasse des Anglais – to show him how secretly it was possible to live, even at ground level, in the teeming city. But this was different: the street became a staircase, its continuation and connections were somewhere higher up and out of view. Eric made a move to proceed, but she shook her head, which surprised him. She had walked him over sluice-gates and through the orbits of murderous traffic across Étoile, charming his life with hers, but on this street where she had never been before, viewing its beautiful transformation and disappearance, he saw her halted and her spirit frightened. Again she shook her head. He shrugged, there were plenty of other wonders. Then she turned and walked quickly away, not looking back, quickening her pace into a run, and he ran after her and their haste sounded loud on the opulent sleeping street.

They never talked about that night. Eric knew she did not like to be at a loss in her own city, she liked to be the guide, conducting him; and perhaps also the staircase itself, by its grandeur and white aloofness, had dismayed her. And though she soon resumed her boldness, daring him to follow, something had shifted in their way of being with one another, he had seen her fearful, she had run away, and this moved him deeply, it gave him the hope, which no one in love wants to do without, that he might after all be allowed and be able to cherish her, to aid her with strengths of his own; in a word, that she might need him.

In the Café Amyot, that since his first arrival at her door he had felt, often painfully, to be almost as much her territory as the flat itself, there too he sensed a change in her feelings. She was quieter; often in full view of the others she took his hand; and Eric saw her as they must be seeing her – as a young woman in love and made vulnerable by it. Himself he felt easier there. The company was good-natured, the teasing was friendly, he could hold his own in fluent and colloquial French. Jean-Luc came in now and then and stood at the bar, saying very little. Monique went over and kissed him, Eric smiled and nodded to him across the room. He was perhaps in his mid-thirties, on some occasions he looked aloof, on others forlorn. Always when Monique returned to Eric she sat so close they were touching. Eric, after the photo, the letter, the postcard of the Bonnard nude, never mentioned Jean-Luc. He felt forbidden to, as much by himself as by her. And his fear of learning facts that would torment him was less, far less, than his fear of losing her by any bid to possess her entirely. Besides, glancing across, he liked the man, he admired and was drawn by the look of him. So he tried to fashion and deserve a generous idea of himself. Her hand touched his on the table. He would let her be. He would love her and she him, each in freedom. Then he drank his glass quickly, and bowed his head under a happiness so great he felt abashed by it, in confusion and shyness he hid his face from her, surely to the whole company he must look foolish, chosen, holy. He stared at the table top and exulted that he was who he was, here, now, in a foreign and lively establishment which they would leave at once when either of them wished to and go back to bed or walk the city from end to end observing the lives and manners of thousands of strangers.

They stood at her window naked, looking down. Our café, she said, don't you ever forget it, our café is a famous and heroic place. The old *patronne* hid the parachutists in there, though the Gestapo had an office right next door and her own husband was a prisoner of war. I shan't forget, Eric said. I promise you.

In their last night finally they broached at least some of the subjects they had kept clear of. He told her how things stood at home and in college. His father moaned at him, they were all worried sick on his account. He seemed to have cast them out of his heart. And he couldn't study, he couldn't concentrate, for wanting to be with her. In truth that was all he wanted: to be with her. But he must go back and make an effort at the other things. Also he had no money now till the next instalment of his grant. So after Christmas he would have to get a job, which meant he wouldn't read what he should have read long ago, which meant etc etc. He half expected her to be glad and to say, as she had often in her letters, that he should give it all up and come and live with her, they would live on love, what else did they need? But she didn't say that. She said nothing. And he felt he was burdening her and both of them with a great trouble. She took it in, it would diminish her joy in life. Then in a voice he hardly recognised, a voice your soul might speak in at its most alone and distressed, she said, into the darkness, that it was much the same for her, she couldn't work, she had hardly sketched, drawn or painted a thing and made no pots whatsoever, she was all at sea for love of him, wanted nothing else, cared nothing for anything else. And, of course, she had no money and no prospect of any unless she borrowed from her mother who didn't like her being in Paris and wished she would come back and live in Nevers and get a job there as anyone sensible would.

At the mention of Nevers, Eric slipped back into *that* world, really into a different dimension, and said aloud, J'étais le plus jeune de toute ma vie à Nevers. To which Monique answered that she at least had never felt younger than now, with him, in bed, and to hell with all their worries, what mattered was this – and sat up across him with the sheet around her shoulders against the cold. He agreed. Their conversation after that was of a different kind, the sleepy kind. He began to tell her about the country he loved, the gritstone and the limestone country, and how close it was. And that reminded him of the morning very early when he had left home with his brother Michael and walked with him, who was only eleven or so then, to within sight of the uplands, how they lay high up in the sunlight between and above the mill towns. He should love to do that walk with her, only go on further, up on to the moors which were the backbone of England where you could walk for miles, day after day, as free as birds. Would she come up there with him? Would she promise? He had worked out a way almost from his own front door, it led through the parks at dawn before the gates were open, you got through the railings and trespassed over the lawns before anyone else was up. Would she come and do that with him? Did she like the idea of trespassing through the urban parks? But Monique was almost asleep. All she murmured was that Jean-Luc knew a way into the Catacombs through the church of Saint-Sulpice, you could walk for miles down there, along tunnels lined with bones, miles and miles under the busy streets. People even lived down there, people with nowhere else to live or who were afraid of being seen on the streets in daylight. Jean-Luc said he would take her down and show her whenever she liked and surely he'd take Eric too, since they were friends. That was sleepy talk, she slept. Eric lay awake for a while, wondering and anxious, his world, the best he could offer, seeming a poor thing set next to what she already owned. But then he turned and curled around her, pressing his forehead, behind which the bad thoughts bred, against the nape of her neck and cupping her left breast in his right hand. Slept.

Next morning, without being asked, she said she would come and see him in Oxford after Christmas. Good, he said, my grant will pay for it. Till then we work. They got up late, wandered the streets, at a bric-a-brac market, place d'Aligre, he bought her a necklace of cherry amber, his last sous went on a glass of wine each at the Gare du Nord. She stood crying like a child at the barrier. Not looking back, head down, he hurried for the train. Spent his few English coins on the tube to Mill Hill East. Hitched home from there, arriving late on the 23rd. He had to borrow money from Michael for the four necessary Christmas presents. Between Christmas and New Year, when things re-opened, he cycled to Trafford Park, asked at every gate there for work and got two weeks at Mather and Platts, on nights, cleaning machinery.

# 12

THE SURGERY PHONES. Katrin should make an appointment to see Dr Gracie. Nothing to worry about. They offer 11.30. Good. She sets off at once, she will have an hour in the café on the way. By now she is a regular there. She feels they like her. In her solitariness, apart among younger people, they let her be. Whenever possible she sits in the window and on either side of the pane of glass life pleases her. Not once has any passer-by or coffee-drinker recognised her for who she is. Nobody asks her how she is bearing up, managing without him, whether it has got any easier. Several at other tables amidst the comings and goings, talk and background music, are working at things that need some concentration. So when her order has arrived, Katrin opens her notebook, reads over what she wrote last and considers what she must struggle with next. In this place she found for herself, whose only connnection with Eric resides in her, the commission, as she calls it, is peculiarly clear. The house, her workroom on the top floor, her table that faces the wall, his jacket over the chair, her computer on the desk in the window, the mass of ordered and not-yet-ordered documents, all this is hard to return to; and the cheerful café, being among, even solitary among, other people, helps. Her stratagem, which most often works, is to clarify the day's passage of writing, its line of feeling, the shape of its progression; and then go home and write it. Some days she allows herself to feel proud that she has developed this necessary ability: there among people, looking up and out through the window at the world of traffic and people, to be able to collect and hold her narrative for the day, hold it steady, keep it clearly in her vision and carry it, the makings, home. But today she must first visit Dr Gracie. She presses her left side. The pain is still there. But Dr Gracie has said it is nothing to worry about.

The room is as Katrin will always remember it: sunny, airy, its pictures, photographs, flowers (they are bronze chrysanthemums) all in place, and the tree in the garden, that she saw blossoming and heard the singing of its blackbird, shines now with golden apples. But Katrin, entering, sees at once in Dr Gracie's face the look she had to live with in Eric's: the look of having been claimed for elsewhere, of beginning to not belong here any more, the helpless sad remoteness. Dr Gracie has begun dying. It quickens in Katrin the horror of last year's Christmas, of the turn of the year in a cold winter towards a spring he would not live to enjoy, and she sees in Dr Gracie's face the weary sympathy that she, the doctor, feels for every newcomer into the fact that soon she will die. So much goes between the two women in their exchange of looks. Katrin sees that her doctor is sorry for her, that she does not wish to increase the harm death has already done to her, that she is a physician, there to heal and encourage the sick back into health and the love of life, and that the shadow of death over her features will vitiate her will and power to help. She will leave. Death will evict her from her sunny room and cancel the tenancy of her vocation.

Dr Gracie shakes her head and says briskly, The scan shows nothing you need worry about. There is some inflammation where you feel that pain, which will get worse only if you encourage it – in fact, only if you want it to. I'll give you some tablets that will ease it, and while they are working, do your best to forget it, and with any luck it really will have gone when you stop the medication. So that's that. Now tell me, How was Ashford-in-the-water?

For a while Katrin cannot answer. She is entirely possessed by the knowledge that Dr Gracie will die and she feels again the fact of approaching death as it manifested itself to her in Eric. Will it always be so? Death upon death upon death, a cumulative dread and grief? She thinks of the woman's husband, her two children, the hundreds of people who love and revere her, who were helped by her, the many who are alive with their husbands, wives, children, friends, only thanks to her. What cold circles of sorrow will spread out from the centre of this woman's death! Look, Katrin, says Dr Gracie, I'm not here to upset you. Truly I want to know how you got on in Ashford. Prompted by you, I did as I said I would and booked a house for us all above Cressbrook Dale and with any luck I shan't have to cancel it. Did you go to Cressbrook? Think of me there with my family in two weeks time. Cressbrook is a lovely name, says Katrin. I went there with Sheila, Eric's sister-in-law. Yes, they were very kind to me in Ashford. And when I got home I wrote and told them that it had helped. To be honest, I didn't quite believe it when I wrote it. But I sent the letter and vowed I would do my best to make it true. That sounds like a good way of going about things, says Dr Gracie. Then she asks, And your life-writing? Grief is very hard to live through, people try all sorts of ways, but I haven't met anyone doing quite what you are doing. Is it helping you? I hope it is. In a rush, staring into Dr Gracie's face but conscious also of the garden and the apple tree behind her, Katrin tells her what she has written about Eric and Monique and how she understands that writing, as a commission to say what being in love to that degree is like. And next, she says, I must write about Monique's visit to Oxford in January 1963, in that terrible winter, how it moves me, she says, to imagine them together in the hardest cold since records began. Fast as her mind runs, fast as the images form and clarify, still the words for them rise at her disposal, she feels she could there and then express the entirety of it, the glory, the dance on the crest before the fall – but she halts,

sick in the stomach, winded, silenced by the cast over her
doctor's face through which, distantly, a school-girlish
seriousness and innocence still peers. Dr Gracie smiles. My
little sister Brigit was born just about then, she says. It is my
earliest memory. We were living outside Bodmin, under the
moor, she came early and Mother and Father couldn't get to
the hospital because of the deep snow. They had to fend for
themselves. It was two days before the doctor could reach
them. My first memory is of my mother in bed with the baby
at her breast. They thought she might not live, but she did,
lives still, is well and happy and does much good in the world.
I wish you luck, Katrin. Be kinder on yourself. Don't blind
your own life out of the picture by the brilliance of anybody
else's. And now I'm afraid this will have to be our last
appointment. But Dr Jefferson will see you whenever you
wish. You'll like her, she's a good doctor. Think of me, will
you, in Cressbrook Dale, in two weeks time.

Katrin stands on the street. Inside and outside her head there
is an obscure noise, getting louder. She will lose her shape in
the world, become a condition, a mere noise, the noise of fear.
She presses the place under her ribs where the pain should
be, Eric's effective pain, her phantom nonsense of a pain,
presses and presses until it hurts. But that proves nothing.
Being able to feel a make-believe pain does not prove you
inhabit a self with a shape, certainly not one that will hold
against the general, indeed absolute, condition of dreadful
noise. She begins to whimper, there on the street, and to
make little sallies of a few yards duration, this way and that.
But in no direction is there any hope of lessening the noise
of dread, nor of shaping herself against it. Herself at the table
in the window of the friendly café, herself fashioning a story
that might help, herself attending to others in the world, these
possibilities, proven possibilities, of life, wither and disperse in
the tumult of her panic. After all, there was not enough life in
her to hold on to them.

But then around the pain, which is nothing to worry about, something does materialise upon which the noise can swarm and batten. The horror in her focusses. Worse than death, anyone's death, is the horror of her workroom, its materials, her purpose with them, her commission. And the documentation of Eric's life mixes with her father's hundreds upon hundreds of books, it becomes all one, a leaden poison, filling every room of the house she called her home. How shall she ever live there?

And if not there, where else on earth could she bear to enter, make a meal, undress, lie down, go to sleep? Nowhere. She whimpers, she runs to and fro, clutching at her left side, clenching the fingers of her left hand up under the ribs.

Then a man addresses her, a big man with a big outdoor honestly simple face, he blocks her little scurries to and fro. Excuse me, he says, I saw you in there when you came out, I was at reception, you wouldn't have noticed me, I was asking after Dr Gracie, but they wouldn't tell me anything, they have to be discreet, of course, but I did want to know, I heard from a friend that it's come back again and that this time there's nothing any doctor in the world can do about it, not even her. And my friend says she knows that, of course, and this time she is refusing treatment, she wants to be as well as possible for however long she's got and not be sick all the time and her lovely hair falling out. He doesn't know what he'll do, my friend, now she's not taking any more appointments, and by the look of you when you came out and passed me in reception, you don't know what you will do either. Katrin regards him. His big face is quite bewildered. But he looks as strong as an ox. He wears the clothes an old-fashioned farmer might put on for coming into town to see a doctor, a clergyman or a solicitor. He looks strong enough to do any work, to gather up children and grandchildren in his arms, to make, build, encompass, protect and cherish, strong enough anywhere and everywhere to be a present help. And he looks in bewilderment at Katrin and says, That lady saved my wife, she gave her back to me, if you saw my home you would say it is a very blessed place and you'd be right, and why? Because of that lady doctor who won't see another Christmas.

The big man in his trouble steadies Katrin. Which way were you going? she asks. Do you mind if I walk with you a little while? They walk along. Now and then he glances at her and shakes his head. Is your wife quite better? she asks. You're never *quite* better with that sort of thing, he answers. And this with Dr Gracie I've no doubt will set her back. But she manages, we manage very well, and for months at a time it goes away altogether. But I was losing her, she couldn't help it, she was drifting away from me, she had bad thoughts, very bad. And Dr Gracie showed her what she could do about it. Katrin halts. I go this way now, she says. She will never forget the big man's face, the helpless candour of it. My husband died not quite seven months ago, she says. That's why I'm like I am at present. Please tell your wife you met me, and say I said that you were very kind to me, and that Dr Gracie helped me too and I do hope she, your wife, will continue well.

# 13

KATRIN WRITES: LONG before it ended, that winter, the Big Freeze, had become legendary. Every day brought new stories, heroic, romantic, tragic. It lasted so long, people almost settled into a life of difficulty, hardship, surprises, bravery, resourcefulness and phenomenal beauty. This will be remembered, they said, and they aided memory with scrapbooks of cuttings, personal writings and photographs, for the children and the children's children.

Eric's alarm woke him. He dressed quickly and as though for the moors. The two bars of the electric fire and the kettle for his coffee made a brief and very local heat. Then he left his room and descended the many creaking stairs into the back quad. It had snowed again. His footsteps past the library, the hall, the chapel, into the garden and under the bare branches of the gigantic beech tree, were the first. His illicit route would be obvious. He climbed out, on South Parks Road he saw two foxes – they had taken to hunting in pairs, for cats – and on the Broad his first fellow-humans, trudging to their work. He caught the milk-train and at Victoria, arriving two hours early, he learned that Monique's train would be two hours late.

Eric sat in the tea-room trying to read one of his set texts, an obscure novel by Balzac which had, he thought, nothing to recommend it except its being written in Monique's mother tongue. He was the least patient among the many waiting for an arrival or their own departure. Still half an hour too soon, he bought a platform ticket and walked to the far end of Platform 2, then back again to the barrier, then again out to the limit. At last, very slowly, the train came into view. He waited till he was certain that the points and the track would direct it correctly, that it would indeed be her train, his train, the long slow and heroic train in a cape of snow. Then he ran back to the barrier, to face the whole length and watch for every passenger from every opening door.

The first sight of her was like a bolt of ice into his heart. He saw the peril he was in, clear, cold, sharp, hard as ice he saw that his life was a ruin if she did not love him as he loved her. How at her mercy he was, how given up without security. And what promise, bond, proof could ever be enough? He saw her for perhaps three seconds before she saw him. She wore a fur coat and a red woollen hat, red gloves, jeans, red leather boots, and all her luggage was a shopping bag and a military-looking haversack slung over her left shoulder. And for that brief space of time, searching for him, she looked small and lost, so that the hope he had first felt in Paris before Christmas, that she might need him, stirred again, but as a frail thing, an insufficient resource, under the overwhelming certainty that he could not live his life without her.

Then, seeing him, Monique ran to him, dropped her bag, her haversack slid off and soon after it, as she lifted up her mouth for his, so also did her hat. And almost before she had done kissing him, her account began, pell-mell, the talk breaking through her laughter and little cries of delight and pride in herself, that she had crossed from capital to capital, from coast to coast, through snow and ice, over a night sea black as jet, and seen the white cliffs in a dawning winter sun risen up like banshees, was she not brave, did he not adore her for being so intrepid, did she not look wonderful in her fur coat? It's my mother's, she said. I was back in Nevers. I told her I had met an English boy and he wanted me to visit him in Oxford and that it would be good for my art to see Oxford in the snow. And what did she say to that? Eric asked. She said be careful, Monique answered. And she lent me some money and her coat that my father bought her in the winter before he got killed.

It was snowing, the traffic proceeded cautiously, almost in a hush. They walked along Grosvenor Place. Eric knew nothing of London except his first crossings of it and to and from Victoria since, all of which had to do with Monique. The Queen lives over there, he said, nodding at the ugly wall. I think. When they reached Hyde Park he took out a crumpled map and devised a way through. The snow came on thicker. Grass, asphalt, the waters of the Serpentine all lay under a level and equal white. The fowl looked forlorn; the trees, stark black, were softened and blurred by the snow. The park was a vast quietness. A few other foot-travellers, crossing their path, greeted them with solemn courtesy; and a horse and rider, like one creature, stately, dark and huge, passing very close to them, the rider saluted and from off the animal they felt an aura of warmth.

Eric was pleased with himself. They hit the Bayswater Road pretty well where he hoped. Paddington was damp, mucky underfoot, heaving with people anxious to get home. Eric had planned ahead. They boarded a stopping-train before it filled up. In his rucksack he carried oranges, chocolate and – saved for this occasion – some of his mother's Christmas cake. So he made provision. He watched Monique, fearful she would think him absurd, ready to shrug at himself and agree. But she ate – so it seemed to him – without any thought, just as though these things came to her by right and by magic. But later, when they were moving and the suburbs, the commuter villages and the surviving fields appeared on either side estranged by snow into beauty, he produced a bottle of brandy and nipping at that with the last of the cake she did then look at him almost as though she had not yet quite given him his due.

The snow ceased as they came into Oxford, though the sky looked bruised by it. Arriving with Monique, Eric saw the city entirely afresh. He had not felt at home there. He had always wanted to be elsewhere, anywhere with her. But now everything famously beautiful was shifted into further degrees of beauty by the snow. The verticals of bare stone, the domes, curves, slopes, crevices and horizontals of white transformation, the usual traffic continuing with unwonted slowness and almost in silence, all was strange and a wonder to him, and she, the foreign girl at his side, he felt her to be the new spirit of the place, the maker of the change, and all its beauties hers to give or withhold. He said nothing, neither did she. Only at the college gate he said, Walk through fast. Which they did: front quad, back quad, far right-hand corner to the skewed and rickety staircase, higher, higher, to the creaking top landing and his room. She stood at the gable window looking out over roof-tops, their leads, shingle tiles, copings under snow, and the spires, towers, domes assembled in a distinct zone, as it were above the canopy under which the streets threaded. He switched on the meagre fire, plugged in the kettle. When she turned, he saw that her face was almost fearful, something in her seemed to be cowering away. And that's your bed? He smiled. Yes. It's a good job we're not fat. We'll be warm enough under your mother's coat. Their nakedness between his sheets, under the many-coloured bedspread his grandmother had knitted for him, under the coat from the war, under the sloped ceiling, in one another's arms, Katrin writes, they will be warm enough.

Eric went out for food and wine. When he came back, she was asleep fully clothed under the bedspread. His room had one small cupboard with a broken door, a stained and battered desk, an uncertain chair, a plywood bookcase, coathangers behind a curtain, not much else. He laid out the food on its papers on the floor, and the bottle by it, with the one glass. She had woken and lay watching him. *À table*, he said. They sat on the rug – from home – close to the ugly hot bars. It's not like you thought it would be, is it? said Eric. I mean, it's not very grand. They ate and drank, and he explained that if she were discovered in his room he would get sent down. Which would save me worrying about the exams. She stared. He told her a few more things and in the telling, viewing her incredulity, this place he had striven for and attained but, because of her, till now had lodged in only marginally, he felt it to be as weird as Gormenghast, locus of ritual, rigmarole and bizarre lore, but in which, with luck and cunning, you might follow your own bent, warp the way you chose and fashion an earthly happiness you could call your own. And a new hope started up in him. Why should he forfeit this advantageous situation? Why should he not entrance her into it, so that on either side of the Channel they would have a home, and endure brief partings for assured reunions, until he was done here and they could go and sojourn where they pleased? There she sat now in a small warmth on a rag hearth rug from Salford listening in astonishment to his wonder-tales while beyond the ill-fitting windows and the thin roof a cold extended that not all the human lives there had ever been or ever would be and all their stories and desires would ever in a billion years make one jot warmer.

Eric took a sheet of notepaper and wrote in big red capitals: WORKED LATE. PLEASE DO NOT DISTURB. For Joyce, he said. So she won't come in. He opened the door and affixed the note with drawing pins stuck in the wood already for just such a purpose. The cold entered, as though it had stood there, like a bodied ghost, waiting. Won't be a minute, Eric said, closing the door. The landing sloped like a ship's deck and every board of it creaked. Returning, he said, We're lucky, the water's quite hot. My towel's the blue one, and it's OK. Monique put her coat on and rummaged in the haversack for her wash things. Eric moved the remains of supper to the desk and looked out. The sky had cleared, there was a sickle of moon, the cold had absolute dominion. He heard noises on the landing, one door, then another, footsteps, and Monique's clear voice: Bonsoir! Then she came in, clutching all her clothes in a bundle against her coat, backing the door shut. I frightened your neighbour, she said. – Hassan? – I think he hadn't ever seen a female before. – Well not close up, said Eric. Except Joyce.

Monique flung her clothes down and knelt on the rug, letting the coat come open, to warm herself. Eric saw that she had put on her cherry amber necklace. He fitted the chair, tilted, under the door handle. Just to be sure, he said. You seem to know what to do, Monique said. He shrugged, and stood there hesitantly. And next, she said, turning to look up at him, you have to get into bed and warm it before I come in. He nodded. Fair enough. He switched off the main light, left the reading lamp on, undressed very swiftly and slid between the cold sheets. That's what men are for, she said. And then: I suppose I'm not the first who's been here for a night. He recognised the expression on her face and the tone of her voice as though he had himself looked across the room and spoken; and between pity for her self-revelation and gladness that she suffered and that he could stop her suffering, he said, Monique, you're the only one. I know what to do, and also that Joyce will know what the note means and will expect some hush-money, from listening to the others talk. Come in now. I think it's warm enough. Switch off the fire, we'll be OK. She stood by the bed, opened the fur coat for him to look at her, slipped it off, laid it over the bedspread and slid into the body-length and body-width that he had warmed. He reached across her for the lamp-switch. Rapidly in the dark the air around them cooled.

They were woken by Joyce. They heard her clattering about on the landing, knocking, flinging open a door, shouting, Good morning, Mr Das, freezing again, worse than ever, I'd say, must be terrible for you coming from a hot country, stay where you are, I should, Mr Swinton is, working late, he was, bed's the best place on a day like this, I'll just switch the fire on and shall I make you a nice cup of tea? Eric touched Monique's nose with the back of his middle finger. The shock to it was great. Is she your servant? Monique murmured. She's my scout, Eric answered in a flat voice. She's supposed to check I'm here and still alive. And if I am, am I alone? I don't mind her doing that – except now, of course – but everything else – washing my two cups, cleaning the room, making my bed – I don't like her doing that because it embarrasses me. So I make her a nice cup of tea and she tells me her troubles, which are legion. Her husband thumps her when he's not in jail for thumping someone else, her son takes after him, her only hope's her daughter, Avril, who is eleven and very bright and deserves to go to the grammar school, she says, and get off the estate. She has a pantry at the bottom of the stairs. She sits in there when she's done climbing up and down and smokes a lot and drinks sweet tea and eats a lot of custard creams. She knitted Hassan a big red scarf for Christmas because he's always cold and he couldn't afford to go back to his hot country. I wanted to call her Mrs Parker but she wouldn't let me. I'm Joyce, she said. So I wanted her to call me Eric, but she wouldn't do that. You're Mr Swinton, she said. Christ, I hate this place.

Eric got out of bed, switched on the kettle and the fire, dressed fast, and drew the curtains. Over the window glass the cold had leafed and flowered, harshly embossing every pane. We're in a wood, he said. It's sprung up while we slept. Arden or Brocéliande. We can't see out. Perhaps the whole town has become a frost forest. Here's your coffee, Monique. The milk's frozen. Frozen is better than off. He fished in his pocket and found a ha'penny, warmed it as hot as he could bear at the bars of the fire, then applied it to the foliage on the window pane. It made a neat round spyhole, through which he peered. Alas, he said, Oxford is still there.

Katrin halts, and views with distaste the double page her ink has dried across. Drying, it sets. The letters, the words, the sentences inch by inch advance their claim to be the account of how it was. Three full exercise books already, an accumulating deposition. Worse would be to transfer it to the screen and read it in the assumed authority of one of a hundred possible fonts. Worst of all, to print it into a pile of A4 sheets. Katrin has a sudden longing for Daniel's voice, soft, rapid, close to Eric's, as it was that night, so fleeting, when she listened sleepily, dozing in and out of the feeling of the story, the line itself unravelling. But that won't do either. She closes her notebook, flings off Eric's jacket, and hurries from the house.

October has begun, and with it a new university term, but weeks ago she converted her sick leave into a permanent absence from the place. Now she is not part of the year beginning. She has no job, she has enough money and nothing to do except this thing she lays upon herself, the commission, on which, she believes, rides her only hope of fashioning a life. Dr Gracie will be in Cressbrook Dale by now, if she is well enough. Katrin has made no appointment with Dr Jefferson. She is trying not to need to. On the street again the terrible nervousness possesses her. Does it rise within, from the heart, to be driven all round her body? Or settle upon her from outside like a swarm? There are times when it seems to be the air itself, and she has no choice but to breathe it in. She arrives at the café. This is not her accustomed time. But the seat in the window is vacant, the waitress is the one she likes best, she recognises people at other tables who perhaps sit there all day doing whatever they do and the world goes on much the same. She has no book or pen and paper with her. She sits still, looking out, and very slowly the nervousness transforms itself into a different state, a sort of collected excitement. Her spirits lift. What has to be done is surely do-able. Are they not passionately present to her, Eric and Monique fifty years ago? Not another living soul do they inhabit as they do her. She feels no one else on earth can be their advocate. She sips her coffee, she lays her hands flat and still on the table top and through the window watches people going about their lives. How present they are, and how she attends to them. Yet present also and even more intensely in her vision are her two lovers back then, back there, in the cold, so cold the watery city's veins and arteries slowed, halted, froze, took on the character of paths and lanes so that for trespassers a new world opened up.

They don't leave college till mid-morning, by which time females might well be there legally. They head for Brown's in the market, take the Full English in a fug of cooking, steam off tea, condensing cold and cigarette smoke. Then he hurries her. It is on the hour. Wrapped in gowns, flapping like clipped crows, his fellow-students slither through the snow to be lectured at in halls whose heating will be chiefly their own body-heat. He stands aside for them. Their garb and purpose are as strange to him as they are to her. She glances at him. He shakes his head. On the bridge he halts and shows her the meadow twenty feet below. He explains that because of the snow and ice it might be dangerous to climb down ledge by ledge. Instead, he says, we use that sycamore. I practised it last week. He positions her. After you, he says. She climbs over the parapet, lowers herself on to the first ledge. He steadies her, she turns, he holds her safe, she leans out, grasps the sprung-up sapling, ladders swiftly down. He waits a while, for love of the beauty of her upturned face. Then he follows. All the city's traffic is above and behind them now. From here I've only imagined it, he says. The river's that way. In a long diagonal they make the first deep footsteps across the Angel's snow.

Katrin fears for them. Crossing, they have the appearance of small and reckless animals, so visible under the predatory heavens. She is glad when her imagination ushers them into the cover of the riverbank. There the cold will allow them to walk on water. The trees are silver-grey, draggled and dangling with old man's beard, itself cobwebbed with hoarfrost. The sun has veiled over. Neither says a word. He steps on to the ice, takes a few stamping paces. Not a creak, no splintering. He hands her down. In her fur and dashes of red she looks not at all urbane. She looks sylvan, in the sense of savage. On the ice with him, in the tunnel of shrouded trees, she is a creature the ancient domain has never seen before. And like the beings Mandeville met who lived solely on the scent of apples, he feels he could live on her visible breath and the aura of cold around her face. But he is so much better off than the Gangines! He has a mouth, and they did not, he has a tongue and lips and teeth, he can lap at and nibble her, he knows how she tastes. Pity the merely fabulous. He leaves her lips, he lets go her hand, they walk side by side, saying nothing, on a sheet of ice under which runs the blackest imaginable sluggish water over the coldest blackest imaginable bed of mud. How warm they are in their clothing. They see many dead birds, lying on the snow, who day after day in the few hours between dawn and dusk hunted for their own bodyweight of food and found less and less of it till the night came that killed them. Now and then a wall or a fence comes in from either side with half a wheel of spikes around each end so that no one shall walk further up or down the river along its banks. And they walk through. The ice allows it. A jay flies ahead of them, screeching, frost and snow powders down upon their heads and where the trees hang lower and they have to stoop this grey extends over their shoulders too like a pantomime costume of venerable age. Later they enter parkland, still not a soul; they pass along a frontage, where a rowing boat and punt are frozen tight and a large sign says PRIVATE KEEP OUT; then a sports field, rugby posts, a pavilion; then meadows, traces of ditches, little bridges, lines of hedge – all this and more they view oddly, passing through, walking on frozen water.

Quietly, purposefully, it begins to snow. They walk into a tunnel of willows overhanging from the banks, the long branch-tresses leafless, the leaf in them hidden, suspended, biding its time in the snow over the vanished water. When they come out into the open, the snow is copious underfoot. She takes his arm. Everything is hushed. The way is not in doubt, they walk between the banks in that decided direction, and under their feet, in darkness, the water that can still move, does so, against them, very slowly towards the frozen Thames which, under ice, still feels for the distant and sheeted estuary. Making upstream with no sense of climbing, through snowfields that in their seasons will flood or flower, they do have a course, the river's, they have a counter-course, but no sense at all of being or going anywhere in particular. Ahead there are no markers on the snow and behind them their tracks are soon obliterated. The sky itself is in the process of undoing. Without haste, quite gently, in soft morsels, it disintegrates. There is not a breath of wind, not a fluster, and their own breaths survive in a visible form barely one inch, barely two seconds, outside their mouths. Pressing Monique's arm against his ribs, Eric has an intense feeling of her warmth and of his own, it seems to him a triumph in itself that they are upright, going forward in silence, on ice, in snow, and that through and through they are warm, their two hearts beat, their blood does its rounds, they employ their legs against the natural inclination of the buried water. We shan't walk for ever, he says. There's a pub somewhere soon, on the right. Watch out for the landing stage. She looks at him, and in her look, amazed, on the brink of fear, he sees the strangeness of the sounds he has made, the words in sequence, in a language, meaning something. And he thinks, Suppose you walked all day like this, and all night and into another day, and your heart and your blood and your legs permitted it, and the ice permitted it, you continued being allowed to walk on water, would you stop speaking altogether or if you did speak would either of you understand what the other said? Perhaps in snow, climbing a river you can't see or hear, you would walk yourselves out of your human selves and not speak in words any more and would love one another more like animals, like creatures that did live once but became extinct when conditions on earth turned against them.

Monique halted him. C'est là ton pub? A landing stage, disguised by the snow; and between it and a line of posts that came up out of the mud through the ice and snow, a dozen punts were fixed in the ice in chains, their long muffled shapes lying side by side in two blocks, between which there was a way through to the bank. From there a field sloped up to a large and jumbled building whose windows were curtained. That will be it, Eric said. The Ferryman.

They climbed the slope, slipping once or twice. Eric tried the door. It was locked. But light shone through the curtains. He bore left across the terrace and around the side, where he found another door, which opened. On the threshold he brushed some of the snow off Monique's fur. She stood still, like a child, letting him. Then he took her hand and they came by a flagstone corridor, through the smell of toilets and disinfectant, suddenly into a warm bright room, and stood there together, close to the bar, snow still melting on them in a sparkle, and the cheerful noise and activity of the place, men drinking, playing darts, playing billiards, conversing, all ceased at the sight of them. They stood barely a yard from the landlord, a big man in his shirtsleeves. We're shut, he said. How did you get in? Eric gestured vaguely backwards. That side door, he said. We're shut, the landlord said again. But if you're in, I suppose you're in. Snowing again, is it? Sit over there, will you – by the fire – move the dog. It won't matter if you drip a bit. They did as they were bid, crossed to the log fire, moved the dog, and hung their wet things on either end of the settle. Eric went back to the bar. The men resumed their privileged existence. Monique was the only woman. He bought her a glass of red wine and himself a pint of beer. We walked up the river, he said. There's hot pies still, said the landlord. Should you be wanting something to eat. Pies, nothing else. And he pushed a hand-written list across the bar. All but number 5, he said. Eric took the list to Monique with the drinks and explained to her, as well as he could, what they all were, these pies.

Once or twice in the café, sitting still, Katrin has felt she might walk slowly home, climb the stairs, put on his jacket and write the whole thing through in one session to the very end, put down her pen, close her last notebook, and that would be that, done with, she would be released, loving him still, living with the ghost of him, but alive and busy again in present time in a life of her own. She has not tried to prove this feeling true or false. Even the possibility that it might be true is helpful. Unkinder on herself, she would have felt obliged to prove it false. So she goes quietly along, doing what she can, which, some days, amounts to not much more than sorting out the documents for the passages which, when she feels up to it, she will write next.

And the questions: at the back of each notebook she has left a couple of pages just for questions, a list, she can always add to it. You could make up a man's life entirely out of questions, even without their answers they would point to him, draw an outline, even compose a shape of him, a space which, even without the answers, he must inhabit. At university Katrin became the sort of person who likes to begin the day by making a list of the things that have to be done; but lately she has felt less satisfaction in crossing things off, more a bleakness, a shrivelling of the spirit; and writing about Eric, needing to finish, making her lists of questions concerning him, more and more often she has felt revulsion at the very idea of ever finishing. Her lists of questions are salutary in that respect. Even when an answer comes she will not cross the question off the list. Concerning any man's life you might ask countless questions. The more you know about him the more you might want to ask. Still the countless answers will not nail him down. And year by year, even hour by hour, the questions themselves are subject to change. They change as you change, though the man you want to know about is dead.

Then – mid-October, the days continuing warm – Katrin has a card from Dr Gracie. Postmarked Tideswell, it is a picture of the way down into Cressbrook Dale, the bare, high, wide entrance narrowing and descending to where the water starts among black-green trees. It reads, Thank you! I wouldn't have come here but for you. We have had a wonderful few days, unforgettable. I do hope you are making progress. I felt confident of you last time we met. Love. Liz Gracie. Katrin turns from the writing to the picture and to the writing again. She has never seen her doctor so before, in the plain two names. It changes her, and Katrin towards her, by this small encounter they are changed towards one another. Katrin feels touched, gauche – and sorrowful that this overture is a farewell. All day it troubles her, as it might a girl, it is a sorrow but through it runs also an irrepressible joy, as over a precious new intimacy, an endearing small gift from a person you have loved at a distance. But sorrow is the stronger feeling, and all day, to combat it, Katrin busies herself with things she can do easily, about the house, sorting, cleaning, arranging, and in the late afternoon she goes to the café, only to sit there, looking out at the street, and comes home the long way, buying something for supper.

That night, fearful of sleeplessness, she fetches the duvet downstairs to the sofa, wraps herself in it and phones Daniel. Yes, he says, I was with them twice. The first time they came into the Wharf together, quite late, we were all there already, we had the back room to ourselves, with the music and the billiards, as usual, and they came in out of the snow, wide-eyed at the light and the noise, like waifs they looked or as though they were dreaming us. There was a pause – not a silence, the music carried on – but Vince and Smithy stood back from the table, the conversation ceased and even the dancers, Cath, it would be, with Bob, and Pete Simmons with Jane, they halted too, and gazed. I hadn't seen her since August, in Paris, in the heat, and now she entered from off the frozen canal, in a fur coat, red boots, red hat etc, and he stood next to her like a clown out of Shakespeare, the fool in love, come out of a frozen forest with his lady who might be a bear or a dryad for all he knew, *farouche*, they looked, like sylvan things that wouldn't survive long in a town. He was my friend, I'd known him since primary school, and there he stood, next to this snow girl, translated. The pause only lasted half a minute, then everyone unfroze, the game continued, the drinking, the conversation, if you can call it that, and Monique took off her coat, Eric fetched her a drink, and Alfie began speaking his best French with her. Soon she was dancing, Eric stood aside, watching, I thought he was OK that night, smitten, in peril, but going to be OK, it's only with hindsight that I think he wasn't. And even Monique, flirted with and dancing, when I look back from now and I see her come in, snow on her red hat and on the shoulders of her fur, looking back, knowing what I know now, I believe I can see that in her heart of hearts she was afraid. I don't mean she was shy – between dances Pete taught her billiards – but there on the threshold before joining in, I believe she felt what I often felt myself back then: that in that new music, in that way of dancing, solo, your own invention, but your eyes in the eyes of whoever danced with you, matching her, leading him on, outdoing one another, closer, backing off, closer again, touching, out of reach, close up again, in all the noise and the joy of it, something – a freedom – was opening up, lifting up, widening and deepening, such a freedom, it would engulf you and disappear you, if you let it.

We didn't leave till after midnight. Eric was explaining about the Bulldogs, how we'd have to run if we met them, but when we came out on St Giles and saw a pair stamping the snow and swigging a hip-flask by the Martyrs Memorial,

she was so amazed she halted, she stood between us, arm in
arm with us, staring and they stared back, everywhere was lit
bright by the stars and the frozen sparkling snow, and that pair
in their black bowler hats, black overcoats, black boots, stood
looking at us and we at them, and not till they made a move,
first pocketing the drink, and raised a great shout, did we leg
it, fast, down the alley by the Lamb and Flag, under the
spreading chestnut petrified, so it seemed, in the very act of
growing, bare, writhing, struck immobile, and all the verve
and the zest of life was in us three, in our blood and breath
and limbs, and we left the Bulldogs standing, down South
Parks Road we ran, to the Warden's little private gate, and
there we fell on the snow and chortled up at the constellations
who also thought it funny. She asked me in for coffee. I
glanced at Eric. He nodded. He gave her a leg-up, she
bestrode the gate, let herself over, dropped. Then I reached up,
stood one foot on the iron handle, and over. Eric followed.
The route's straightforward. You hug the wall on your left and
climb three times, in the corner, when the dividing garden
walls come in from the right. Owls and foxes – never since,
never anywhere else, have I heard them so hungry. We
climbed to Eric's lair. I pushed up the sash, let myself out on
the runnel under the gables that he called his balcony,
Monique came out too. You can make your way along, under
other people's windows, the parapet is only waist-high, the
drop fatal, the stars were pulsing over every slant and level of
roof-top glittering snow. When we came in he handed us a
mug of coffee, to share, and the brandy he'd bought to go
with his mother's Chrismas cake. I didn't stay late. I loved
them both too much and couldn't bear it, loved them my way,
lonely, they looked up at me from the hearth rug like
enchanted children, I left them to the warmth of one another
under the sloped ceiling in his narrow bed and went back out
to the owls and foxes, stood very still under the giant beech
tree for a while, till I'd seen them close, a pair of the
quadrupeds, low on the snowy lawn, slinking fast across, and

the flat white face of the bird, the downy face, the widening eyes, the beak, the swoosh of its inspection of me, close, so hungry. Then I climbed out.

And the second time, says Daniel, was in Fred's room the night before she left. Again they turned up suddenly, out of their own world, entering ours, and again there was a pause when they came in out of the snow. She was the only girl that night. We were sitting round – Jay, Vince, Smithy and the others – drinking a bit, smoking cigarettes, not much talking. It was a big room, the electric fire was useless, we had coats and scarves on, Fred had just started playing, he wore gloves he'd cut the fingers off, I remember, he was playing more or less to himself, not singing, when Eric and Monique walked in. Here's what you need to know about Fred, Katrin, should you want to put him alongside Eric, in the life. Fred's the only man I know – he's still alive, I still know him – who as an undergraduate passionately wished to be married. He said to me the first time I met him, and often thereafter, Oh I'd love to be married! He loved women, not sentimentally or lewdly, just so, as a condition, as his way of being in the world, he loved everything about them and all he asked was to be allowed to marry one as soon as possible. And he never did, all his many romances came to nothing. He told me of one girl, Ellen her name was, not in the least indecently, just as a matter of fact, he told me that when they'd made love and she started getting dressed, when she was pulling on her knickers, he begged her to take them off again because it saddened him so much to see her bottom vanishing out of his view. And all the girls' bottoms he ever saw, all did vanish, and he lives alone still, never having married, lonely, always nearly falling back into the drinking, and his fingers so arthritic he can't even play the guitar. Women, the guitar, and his third great passion was ornithology, he photographed birds, his photographs were sought after by the best magazines world-wide, his patience was legendary, he spent weeks once getting to know a particular carrion crow, day after day, same time every day, he'd visit it in on a bit of wasteland outside Hitchin, till they were familiars and he could photograph it with permission, so to speak. And hours he would sit in a likely place, on a cliff, by a river, in a wood at night, waiting for the rare bird or for the common bird as it had never been seen before, to come. But though his patience lasted, his eyesight didn't, the drinking caused him little strokes behind the eyes, he could see the space that the bird might flash across, but not the bird itself, or never clearly enough, never in time, so he had to give that up as well. And he sits in his bed-sit, trying not to drink, I phone him now and then, we talk for a while, sometimes he sings, he told me, he can't play, he can't see very well, he never married after all that loving of women, but he still sings sometimes, shuts his eyes and sings, his voice isn't wonderful, he says, but good enough for an audience of one. But that night he was playing, his fingers were quick and savvy, he was already making the music, when she came in, the girl, and with her entering came, in a rush, his choice of songs. She undid her coat, took off her hat and gloves, sat on the floor, the snow melting off her, and he sang, quietly:

Oh in my heart you are my darling
At my door you are welcome in
At my gate I'll meet you, my darling
If your love I could only win...

I'd rather be in some dark hollow
Where the sun refused to shine
Than to see you be another man's darling
And to know that you'll never be mine...

Oh in the night I'm dreaming about you
In the day I find no rest
Just the thought of you, my darling
Sends aching pains all through my breast...

We shrugged, we smiled, nobody laughed, we leaned back, smoking, drinking, Eric too, I believe, he lay back, he closed his eyes, holding her hat and gloves, and Fred sang on and on, softly, she sat cross-legged on his threadbare carpet in her mother's fur coat from the last war, I watched, she sat in a trance, her eyes on his face, his eyes through his thick glasses on her over his clever fingers and his lips moving to make the words in tune. I think he went through his entire repertoire for her, from Piaf to Gréco, Ferré, Brassens, on and on. And then he paused, nobody spoke, and into the silence she began a song of her own choosing. Eric sat up, attended, his face was more open than I could bear. She sang:

> Quand nous en serons au temps des cerises
> Et gai rossignol et merle moqueur
> Seront tous en fête
> Les belles auront la folie en tête
> Et les amoureux du soleil au cœur
> Quand nous chanterons le temps des cerises
> Sifflera bien mieux le merle moqueur...

And stopped there, bowing her head. Only then did Fred begin to play. He played, waiting. But she wouldn't sing again or even lift her head. So he sang for her:

> Mais il est bien court le temps des cerises
> Où l'on s'en va deux cueillir en rêvant
> Des pendants d'oreille...
> Cerises d'amour aux robes vermeilles
> Tombant sous la feuille en gouttes de sang...
> Mais il est bien court le temps des cerises
> Pendants de corail qu'on cueille en rêvant!
>
> Quand vous en serez au temps des cerises
> Si vous avez peur des chagrins d'amour
> Évitez les belles!

Moi qui ne crains pas les peines cruelles
Je ne vivrai pas sans souffrir un jour...
Quand vous en serez au temps des cerises
Vous aurez aussi des peines d'amour!

J'aimerai toujours le temps des cerises
C'est de ce temps-là que je garde au cœur
Une plaie ouverte!
Et Dame Fortune, en m'étant offerte
Ne pourra jamais fermer ma douleur...
J'aimerai toujours le temps des cerises
Et le souvenir que je garde au cœur!

It was gone midnight by then, the time had arrived for climbing out, for trespassing over the out-of-bounds snowy streets and climbing into wherever, alone or not, you were to be bedded down. Fred never saw Monique again, and nor, next day having gone with her to Victoria and kissed her good-bye at the barrier – her crying like a child – nor, after that, did Eric.

# 14

KATRIN PHONES THE second-hand bookshop at the estuary.
She introduces herself. My husband was one of your regular
customers, she says. He used to buy cheese next door and
then look in on you. He generally came home with three or
four cheeses and at least one book. Ah yes, says the bookseller.
He was very discerning. I was deeply sorry to hear he had
died. How are you managing? It must be hard. Katrin thanks
him. It *is* hard. But she is not doing badly. Then she asks might
he be willing to come and look at some books, a large
number of books, a whole library, in fact, not Eric's, of course,
her father's, mostly Polish and German works, the canon, and
a good deal of secondary literature? A silence. Then, politely,
he says that such things are difficult to sell locally, or indeed
anywhere, now. Might he come and look at them, Katrin asks,
all the same? Very well, he replies. To be courteous, she feels,
and out of respect for Eric. He could call by tomorrow
morning, at 10. Would that be convenient?

Katrin puts the phone down. She is trembling, from
head to foot cold and shaking. But so far so good. She climbs
to her workroom. The bookseller, after viewing the landings,
will have to walk through her materials to the loft, in which,
along with more of her father's books, stands Eric's wide-
open and still disgorging trunk. But she will hold to the
night's idea. She will clear a way through and on either side
of it cover everything else, that must not be seen, under
dustsheets. So she does, beginning with the trunk and its

spillage, then the desk and computer in the window, the small table against the wall (and the chair too, with the jacket over it), and then the floor, white sheets over a rough terrain of shoeboxes, bundles and piles of letters and photographs, miscellaneous memorabilia, leaving a narrow footpath, a diagonal, across the patterned carpet, there when they moved in, which she has never liked. Everything, all her obsession, is shrouded over. Then she must leave the room and the house. She takes a novel – one she began and never finished with Eric at the end of January – and walks quickly to the café, to sit in the window and read on from where they left off. The fiction soon absorbs her; but looking up now and then, she examines her resolve and finds it firm.

Next morning the bookseller arrives on time. Katrin shows him the two landings, floor to ceiling, her father's books. He nods, looks quickly along a row of titles, opens a volume, nods again at its Gothic script. Then upstairs. The workroom is a terrible shock to her: the humps, ridges, furrows, all sheeted. Yes, she says, I'm going to do some decorating. The other books are in the loft. The sheet in there, over the trunk, looks ghastly, in workroom and loft the whole precaution looks ludicrous and sinister, like the effort of an idiot to conceal something criminal or obscene. Katrin shrugs. And that is what I live with, she thinks. The bookseller is a gentle person. He makes no comment, avoids her eyes, crosses to the books and surveys them briefly. She ushers him out ahead of her, through the low door into her workroom, across the white-shrouded floor and down into the hall, where he says, It's as I expected, Mrs Swinton, I wouldn't be able to sell them. I should have said, says Katrin, I don't want any money. Might you be able to take them away and dispose of them as you think fit? Then, feeling that even this is a great deal to ask, she adds, I'll pay you, of course, for your time and trouble. Now he does look her in the eyes and she sees that he pities her. No, no, he says, I'll take them if that is what you would like, and I shouldn't want any payment. This afternoon, if that would be convenient, I'll come with a van. There's a couple of boys will help me.

They arrive, Katrin leaves them tea, coffee, some cake, and asks will they pull the door to when they go. Then she walks quickly to the café, with her unfinished novel, and reads.

Back home, Katrin climbs the stairs, noting the cavernousness of the landings, the old wallpaper aghast at being seen, and in her workroom at once removes the sepulchral sheets, enters the loft with them in a bundle, adds to them the sheet over the trunk, flings them down against the wall rid of her father, returns to her small table, dons Eric's jacket, and writes:

Eric wrote next day. He wrote (I imagine) that he was full of hope, he would work hard now, and she would, they would have the best of both worlds, in less than a month, his exams out of the way, he would see her again, in Paris, under her skylight, in her big bed, she was the surest thing in his life, ground of everything present and future, he kissed her from head to cold toes, pausing at every beloved place en route.

He applied himself to his studies. He thought he might just scrape through. Better, he began to see how the books he was obliged to read might come to life in him, in how he lived. He talked to Daniel, and understood from him that you might fix on a purpose and make of it (whatever it might mean to anyone else) your own, your saving decision, that by which you fashioned a life you would gladly own up to. In that spirit he lasted a week. But she did not write. Had she written to him as he wrote to her, he would have gone on firmly, seen it through. But he understood after a week, or after a week he acknowledged what he had known in his heart all along, that if she did not write and confirm his faith, nothing in him and no friend or obligation, could help him in the least. He wrote again, trying desperately not to plead, but he was already foundering. A week later came her answer: Je peux pas. Je te demande pardon. Je peux pas. M. He left at once, telling nobody, leaving no message, took out what money he still had, hitched to London and caught the night train, slept not a wink, walked on deck, as though walking would get him there quicker, all in haste, at a run from the Gare du Nord, the métro, the streets, the door. He rang and got no answer and the door was locked. At his back he felt the attentive gaze of Maurice and the two or three others already in place in the Café Amyot. They might know, he went in to ask. Jean-Luc was there. Elle est partie, he said. Where to? Nevers peut-être, peut-être Marrakech. He turned to run to the door, Jean-Luc held him back. Assieds-toi, petit. Maurice pushed a cognac his way across the bar and some bread. He drank quickly, ate. They contemplated him with a sympathy at once tender and remote. He was to them, in that suffering, a fact of life. It was common. They were kind to him in his particular form of a commonplace. Elle avait peur, Maurice said. And muttered something about her freedom. Then shrugged and said again that she was frightened. No they did not know her mother's address in Nevers. Still less where the house with the flat roof was under the stars in Marrakech. He nodded, thanked them, set off fast up the street to Place Monge. There he bought some provisions, caught the 9 out to Ivry and began walking, in a drizzle, towards the N7, towards Nevers, walked, walked, head down, vaguely south. Then at some point, nowhere in particular, he gave up, turned, began walking back again and in the late afternoon, as it was getting dark, found himself on the Pont Neuf, leaning over, staring into the river which, so it seemed, was carting off in one colossal exertion the entire winter's melted snow and ice, so swiftly, such a vast swift body of black water dappled with lights as with some lurid disease. Leaning over, watching the water, he thought seriously of turning again to Nevers and, if he failed there, to Marrakech, and seriously also of climbing on to the parapet and stepping off into the black, thought of both, equally seriously, and not as life or death but as a hopelessness, both. What fetched him back from either, so that he set off dumbly on foot towards the Gare du Nord, was not the will to live but rather a compelling sense that it did not matter either way and that he was tired and might just as well head back to where he could sleep. There, on the bridge, turning away, as it were equally, from chasing after Monique or dropping as a deadweight into the Seine, there in the drizzle that late afternoon, 21 March 1963, Katrin located the beginnings of his resignation into the life he would finish with her.

The spirit has gone out of it. Katrin does not wish to continue with the life of Eric, Monique, Edna and herself. The stuff of it, lying in its heaps, bundles, lines, in order and disorder on the floor and on every other flat surface in her workroom and in the attic room, oppresses her unspeakably. She feels that if she were some remote cousin to whom this house and all its contents had come by mere force of inheritance, no nearer relative living, she would phone a clearance firm and be shut of it all in one day, without compunction, and return with never a backward glance to wherever she lived a life of her own very far from here and with no connection. She contemplates the landings, the bare shelves, the floral wallpaper not seen for many years behind her father's books and now exposed, indecently. The attic likewise: she has made a space, and it oppresses her even worse than the full shelves did. Against it, she has nothing but a bleak satisfaction, a belated vengefulness, that finally she has got her father out of her house. She should have done it sooner, years ago, and might have but for Eric who had never known the man and felt no personal antipathy towards him and who, bibliophile and hoarder, could see no reason why the library should not stay where it was, there were fine old editions in it, he liked to read good things in fine editions and quite often he did, the German at least, taking them into his study for a while. He had even suggested she might teach him Polish so that he would be able to enjoy some of those works too, but there she met him with a flat refusal.

Then one afternoon in early November, coming home reluctantly from the café, she decides that, in the attic at least, Eric should occupy the space left by her father, one dead man hated shall vacate his accommodation to another dead man, beloved, and she begins at once arranging all the letters, those still in the trunk and in the carrier bags, those spilled out on the floor, all not yet carried through into the workroom, she shelves them chronologically, first standing on a chair, reaching up to the top shelf, the most recent up there, working back and down in time through the strata of before she knew him towards the strata of before she was born. The appetite for this removal grows as she performs it. The attic was never a pleasant place, too hot in summer, glacial in winter. Two bare bulbs are its only lighting, and with a sudden savage pleasure she thinks of Monique's slant roof pane that let in the sun, the moon, the stars and skies apparelled in all manner of weather, and she veers in pity, in a bid for friendly kinship, towards Monique in her flight to Nevers or Marrakech or wherever her refuge was against the too-much of love. And having emptied the trunk, put the empty bags inside it, closed the lid, Katrin thinks why not now the shoeboxes? There is shelf-space still. Why not clear the bedroom and the workroom, except for what's needed now and hour by hour, and house it all in an archive, a safe place under the roof, behind a door which she may open, in a darkness she may dispel, if and when she pleases? Why not?

She goes down to make herself a cup of coffee but halts on the first landing and examines the shelving there. Two upright darkly varnished planks set against the recess walls from floor to ceiling, seven planks across on battens. On the second landing she finds the construction to be the same. Eric was no handyman. She remembers they had somebody local in who did a fair job and charged very little. She examines the work more closely. The shelves are glued on the battens, the uprights are screwed into the walls. She passes through the kitchen into the garden and there into the shed, the dank garden, the cluttered shed that smells of damp and of things shoved away out of sight to rot or rust in their own good time, Katrin finds a hammer with a weighty head, and half a dozen screwdrivers, the shafts all rusted but with blades that might fit two or three sizes of screw, slotted or Phillips. She climbs in haste with these tools – left by some previous occupant – to the first landing and taps with the hammer up under the middle shelf close by the left-hand batten: it lifts at once; the right-hand likewise simple. She removes the shelf. In a rush of confidence she feels it is within her power to disassemble and remove the two redundant fixtures. Only now does she go and make her coffee, sits at the kitchen table with her hands around the warming mug. Good. First the shelves, then the shoeboxes. She will have a couple of days of clearance and establishing order. After that, on the landings, she will perhaps undertake the decorating that she invented, implausibly, to explain the dustsheets, in shame and embarrassment, to the bookseller. There at least she will obliterate all trace of her father's legacy, the alcoves, when you climb or descend the stairs, will present a new appearance, they will look ignorant and innocent of him.

By lunchtime Katrin has tapped all fourteen shelves free of their glue and carried them downstairs one by one and stacked them along the dado in the hall. She walks to the café for lunch, a thing she has never done before, pleased with herself, as though an evasion were, against all the odds, proving effective. The café is crowded, she has to share a table, and the young man she eats with, a boy really, at once begins to tell her, helplessly, as it seems, that he has an interview at the theatre at three o' clock, it is his big chance, he is a set-designer, if they take him on he will have some regular income and he and and his girlfriend, she's expecting a baby, will be able to rent a decent flat, she'll have to stop work at Christmas, but if he gets this job, they'll be fine, more than fine, they'll be set up, neither his parents nor hers can help them out much, though they try. He has a large portfolio of his work there with him, leaning against the chair. Would she like to see? Can he show her some? Katrin does her best to attend. But she is in the state she fell into listening to Daniel in the dead of night when he recounted Eric's hitch-hiking to Vizille, it is the tone she hears, all the boy's hope, and his helplessly open face, she can't take her eyes off his face to do any justice to his many sheets of work. But she smiles, nods, praises everything he brings forth for her attention. Then abruptly she comes to the end of her strength, makes her excuses, with all her heart wishes him luck, and leaves.

She forgets him, or tries to, hurries home, resumes her demolition of the shelving, and there, at once, she suffers a setback. She can't turn the screws, her grip, her wrist, is not strong enough. She tries them all, eight on each upright, thirty-two in all, not one can she turn. So four dark upright planks will remain in situ, in the recesses, on both landings. They distress her immeasurably, so fixed, vertical, dark, not to be got rid of after all, faceless, rigid ghosts, sepulchral, pitiless. These planks screwed in tighter than her wrists can loosen seem to her the sign of what she will never escape from, struggle as she may. And for the first time she conceives of selling the house, disposing of everything in it, moving elsewhere, going into hiding somewhere small and very far away.

Later, having wandered around town and along the river, daylight ending damply, the moroseness of winter coming on, she finds herself at the café again, near to closing time. She apologises, not wishing to hold them up, and has reached the door when, to her own surprise, she turns back and asks, That young man I was talking to at lunchtime, he had an interview… Patrick? the waitress says, her face at once all smiles. Yes, he got the job, isn't that wonderful? He came back to tell us, we were so happy for him. That *is* good news, says Katrin, and stands so long in the contemplation of it that the waitress begins to smile at her, as at another thing to be glad about at the end of the working day. He seemed a nice boy, says Katrin. He's *lovely*, says the waitress, her smile becoming complicit laughter.

Next morning she moves the fourteen shelves into the conservatory, Eric's smokehole, among her plants, back copies of the *LRB*, a bicycle, and a couple of chairs in need of mending. Then she walks to the theatre, likes the street, finds a café and watches through the window. She sits there an hour, watching. Then, slowly making for home, she meets Patrick. I hear you got the job, she says. Congratulations. She extends her hand, which he ignores, and hugs her, tight. Sorry, he says. I'm like that. And more than ever now. You wished me luck, he adds, and you meant it. You believe in luck? she asks. Oh yes, I do, he answers. I'm a lucky man, perhaps the luckiest on the planet. I'm glad I met you, Katrin says, to congratulate you. But also I was wondering would you do me a favour. I don't know who else to ask. And in a rush, there on the chilly street, she tells him about her father, the books, that at last she has got rid of them and now she wants to be rid of the fixtures too, those on the landings at least, and she managed the shelves but not the uprights, she can't unscrew the screws, there are thirty-two of them and not one can she move in the slightest, her grip is not strong enough. No problem, he says. I'll bring my cordless. How about this afternoon? Katrin drifts home, musing on the word 'cordless'.

Patrick arrives on a bicycle, the cordless in a pannier. Katrin shows him up. His wrists are as thin as hers. He assesses the screws, fits a bit into the chuck, and beginning very carefully, at the lowest speed, so as not to damage the slots, he loosens and removes all thirty-two in seven minutes. Easy with a cordless, he says. He carries the four planks down for her, into the smokehole. The alcoves are free, out of all proportion is her own sense of liberation. You must let me pay you, she says, standing with him in the sunless conservatory. The very idea makes him laugh. Will you have the wood at least? For your new flat, I mean. Shelving is expensive. It's nice wood really, beech, if I remember rightly, or chestnut, I don't know why we let him varnish it that awful colour, Eric didn't have an opinion and I wasn't definite enough. Patrick would be very glad of the shelves. And he knows someone who will strip the varnish off. Good, says Katrin, they can stay here till you get your flat. I don't use the place, only for my plants, and Eric isn't here now to have a cigarette in it. Patrick looks at her. No, he didn't leave me, she says. We're not divorced, if that's what you're thinking. He's dead, he left me that way, we're divorced that way, but only that way, we're still married really, I'm still his wife, I hate it when anyone calls me his widow. I might see you in the café, I suppose. I go in there quite often nowadays. They are very nice to me. But if I don't see you, do let me know when your baby comes, won't you? Promise me that. He promises.

That evening, 3 November, quite late, Katrin answers the phone and does not catch the caller's name. I'm sorry, she says, who is it? Liz, says the voice, Liz Gracie. And even then in a flurry of mixed feelings Katrin can't take it in. Dr Gracie, she says, in a wonder. How are you? And halts in shame and embarrassment for asking. I'm having a few good days, Dr Gracie answers. I thought we might meet. Would tomorrow suit you? I'd like to know how you are getting on. Is it very late? I'm sorry. My sense of time is a bit awry at present. No, no, says Katrin, how kind of you, it's not at all late, yes I'd love to see you. Do you mean I should come to the surgery? No, I shouldn't like that, Dr Gracie answers. Your café – shall I meet you there? Say eleven. I'm usually all right by then. Yes, says Katrin, still incredulous, tomorrow, in my café, at eleven. How nice. She stands a while by the silent phone, listening again to the sentences still lingering in her head. She can hear an old and local accent in Dr Gracie's voice, West Country. It is the inflexion of her approaching death. And in that voice, Katrin says to herself, she tells me she would like to know how I am getting on.

Next morning Katrin appraises her face as she has not done since Eric's funeral. It alarms her. She puts on the small gold necklace he gave her when they were married. Her neck, her flesh, shows up poorly against it. She takes it off again, ties a blue-green cashmere scarf there instead which he always said he liked on her though she never did herself, it was her mother's. Really nothing in her wardrobe pleases her. No time now. Too late. Make do. Attend to it one day. Perhaps.

Katrin is in the café by 10.30, at her table in the window, watching the street. The waitress smiles at her. You just missed Patrick, she says. He looked in to say hello. But Katrin is watching for Liz Gracie and sick with nervousness. I'm expecting a friend, she says. I'll wait till she comes if you don't mind. She opens her coat, then fastens it again, takes off the scarf and stuffs it in her pocket. What does it matter what she looks like? The morning is bright and cold, the low sun illuminates people's faces, their beauty, their suffering, it shows up how well or ill they can bear to be contemplated. Then a taxi halts outside the café, pauses, Dr Gracie gets out, the taxi pulls away and she stands on the pavement, radically aged, blinking in the sunlight, childishly thrown upon the mercy of the world. Katrin cannot bear to see her even for a moment at a loss. She hurries out, stands before her, embarrassed, bereft of all tact and competence. Briskly Dr Gracie reassures her. This is a good day, she says. Let me take your arm. Katrin sees she must be used to inducing people to credit her still with life. Katrin, the *habituée* of the place and feeling it to be easier and harder because of that, conducts her through the tables to their table in the window. The waitress, become very respectful, takes their order. Now, says Liz Gracie, tell me how you are.

Thank you for your card from Cressbrook Dale, says Katrin. We had a wonderful time, says Liz Gracie. And but for you we shouldn't have gone. Then Katrin tells her that she has no desire to write any more about Eric's life because the rest of it, the final fifty years, seems rather a let-down after the first twenty. Liz Gracie laughs, her eyes are alight with merriment, it shocks Katrin that in amusement she can forget herself, how young she looks, schoolgirlish again, behind her glasses and through the mask of death. Katrin shrugs. I got rid of my father's books, she says. And a nice young man helped me dismantle the shelves. That may be a good thing. And I tidied away most of the letters and papers. I thought I might do some decorating. Perhaps that will help. Katrin, Dr Gracie says, tell me how you and Eric met. She has removed her hat, gloves, scarf, slipped her coat off over the chair back, she shows herself, grey-haired, aged in her hands, neck, face far beyond her years, and alert, leaning forward smiling, a bright silver brooch, an intricate Celtic knot, fastening her soft night-blue dress below her throat. She shows herself truthfully for what she is, so that Katrin thinks, I believe she does want me to tell her how we met, I believe she is interested. We were colleagues for a year, she says, but I suppose you mean how did we fall in love, know it, admit it separately, confess it to one another, act on it? Yes, says Liz Gracie, that is what I mean. Eric had been in post for many years, Katrin says, twenty-five to be exact, he arrived before I was born and there he stayed. Everybody liked him. I came as an assistant, on a one-year contract, saw a good deal of him, he was kind to me, he was helpful, but so he was to everyone, in his fashion. – And what was his fashion? – He came to a sort of frontier with his kindness and his helpfulness and there, so to speak, he bowed, shook your hand, said good-bye, and left you to go across on your own if you wanted to, while he turned away and walked home again without a backward glance. Two or three women told me that – he'll go home again, he won't look back – and offered various explanations. One said, He likes being where he is. Another said, Deep down he's quite a selfish man. A third said, Not selfish – frightened. It was Bettina who told me he was frightened. She left when I arrived. She was ten years older than me, East German with a Russian soldier for a father, so beautiful, Slav eyes and cheek-bones, wide mouth, pale skin, raven-black hair as in the folksongs. She taught him Russian, they spoke Russian together, it was their love-language, they were lovers for three years, then she got sick of the place, said she had to move on, would he come with her, marry her if he liked, or not, just as he liked, but come away with her somewhere with a bit more life in it. But he wouldn't. I can see him backing away, shrugging his shoulders, turning up his hands – a Gitane between two fingers of the left – until she turned away and did not, I suppose, look back. Years later when I asked him about her he shrugged, looked a bit shame-faced and said, Bettina was a gypsy. And that was that. I'm not a gypsy, Katrin says. Whatever else I am, I'm not a gypsy.

I knew all this about how he was with women and very soon I loved him anyway and took care not to show it. And when my time was up, I packed my bags, there was nothing else for me in Britain then, my father wanted me home, he wanted me in a Polish university, things were moving again, he said, there would be a renaissance of Polish scholarship, I would be part of it, I would live at home and he would be so proud of me. Eric came on the bus with me to the railway station and we said good-bye at the barrier. He didn't kiss me and we didn't shake hands. I got on the train, found a seat, and only then did I look out and, contrary to all the stories, he was still there. I waved, opened my book, and when the train pulled away I looked again. He was still there, he didn't wave or smile, only stared. He looked ghastly. My flight wasn't till the afternoon. I met an old school-friend for lunch, she had been an émigrée since the early 1980s and was thinking she might go back. Then I got the tube out to the airport. I hate airports, they make me very nervous, I go over everything fifteen times and even when I'm sure it's right I have my doubts. The check-in for Warsaw was any one of desks 34 to 43, I'll always remember, and when I got there I saw Eric pacing up and down from 34 to 43 and back again, to and fro, to and fro, smoking and staring into the crowds of people like somebody going mad. I stood watching him for a time – ten seconds, ten minutes, I couldn't say – I loved him, how I loved him, and I saw that he was in pain. Then he saw me. No joy came over his face, but a sort of relief. Perhaps a condemned man looks like that when he's waited too long, can't bear it any longer, wants only an end of the torment and the guards to come and take him away to execution. Perhaps. I stood between my two suitcases and he came up to me, trod out his cigarette, stood very close and said, Katrin, don't go, I beg you, please don't go, I love you, I want to marry you. And that was that. I turned away from the check-in with him, back on the tube, across London, out again to where I had left him, all the while he gripped my hand, so hard at times it hurt, scarcely looked at me, only gripped me tight as though if he didn't I might fly away. But I had no desire to fly away. I wanted him gripping me tight like that, so hard it hurt. And like that, gripped tight, him carrying one case, me the other, we went home to his house where I had never been before, and there he stood still and looked at me and waited until I smiled and nodded yes. Then we went to his bed, undressed very quickly, and for me it was as though my life in drought were suddenly given the waters of life to drink and body and soul that had been stifled suddenly breathed the air the angels breathe and I drank deep, breathed deep, and my blood sang through me, rejoicing, oh rejoicing. Contentedly Dr Gracie nods her head and asks, And for him? For him Katrin answers, it was, so it seemed to me, as though his life were saved and not by a god and a religion but by me, a young woman, as though, without my knowing, his life had been in my gift and I gave it him, gave it back to him, so that once more he was in possession of it, to enjoy, and freely now he would share it with me as long as he lived. Dr Gracie smiles. No seeming about it, she says. So it was. I can see it in your face. Katrin wonders at this certainty. Then she continues, I never told anyone before, not the least part of it did I ever speak before now to any living soul but him, and when he began to die and since his death, I let it go out of me, death was stronger than me, death took hold of him, he gave in to death, he turned away from me, he deserted me, he slept with death instead, he went away with death, as though it wasn't true what I felt that first time in his house and in his bed, not strong enough after all, not true enough, and therefore this now, all this now, my account to you, isn't true, isn't true enough, either.

Katrin halts, appalled at her tactlessness. Oh forgive me, she says. You are so ill and I talk like this to you. Forgive me, Liz. Liz Gracie smiles. I shall die without ever having grieved like that, she says. I shall have been spared it. Rob will grieve like that. It has begun in him already and it will be worse, much worse. And the children too, it will be hard for them, but their lives will take them up again, Annie has a child already, Sam has just got married, life will take them up, but Rob will grieve as you are grieving, it can't be otherwise, for so much love, so much grief, it is just, your grief is a measure of your love, be glad if you can, rejoice if you can, grieving you love him, in your heart of hearts you would not want it any different. And now I am tired, Katrin. Could you ask them to get me a taxi, please. She puts on her scarf, her gloves, her chic soft woollen blue-of-the-night beret, fastens her coat over the intricately twining silver brooch. Katrin goes to the counter. She causes a solemnity in the cheerful place. Dr Gracie looked after my little boy, says the manageress. Katrin returns to the table in the window. And the rest, Liz Gracie says. I haven't heard the rest. But I suppose it was only practicalities. Yes, says Katrin. My father was still waiting at Warsaw airport. In the end I phoned my mother at home. Practicalities.

The taxi pulls up in the cold sunlight. One last thing, Dr Gracie says. By February you may feel you are getting over it. But I have seen it sometimes be worse again in the second or the third year. Then cleave to what you told me this afternoon. And think of my husband Rob. Katrin conducts her out through the café in which the voices are subdued. The manageress holds open the door, says, Thank you, Dr Gracie. The taxi pulls away, Katrin watches it out of sight, walks quickly home.

Three weeks later Katrin saw a headline outside a newsagent's: Death of Local GP. She bought the paper. On its front page was a photograph of Dr Gracie, one taken not so long ago, perhaps around the time Katrin first went to see her, when she was in remission, smiling like an earnest schoolgirl. Late afternoon, the streets were cold. Katrin shivered and walked home. She sat in the front room, on the sofa, in a dumb sadness. A day and a half like that, dumb, mechanical, sustaining the life of an automaton. Then a card came from Liz Gracie's husband, Robert. Liz spoke of you, he wrote. Her funeral is on Wednesday. Do come if you would like to. But she would understand you perfectly if you would rather not.

Katrin phoned Daniel. I shall go to her funeral, she said. But please could you be here when I come back from it. I'll make up a bed for you. Please will you come and stay for a couple of days. I'll be in by four. The key will be under the flowerpot on the left. Let yourself in and make yourself at home. Of course, said Daniel. Yes, of course.

# 15

HOME FROM DR Gracie's funeral, Katrin found Daniel sitting in the front room on the sofa, at one end of it, his overcoat folded across his knees and a small travelling-bag at his feet. Perhaps he had been there an hour or more, perhaps only a minute. When he rose and rather formally embraced her it was almost as though he were taking his leave. Sit still, she said. I'll make some tea. Courage, she whispered to herself and in the kitchen summoned up all she had of it. She thought of changing out of her funeral dress but decided not to.

Returning with the tray, she seems, again, to oblige him to bethink himself, make an effort of the will and come in from the sidelines, out of abstraction. This is where the bed was, isn't it? he says. This is where he died. Yes, says Katrin. And where you're sitting now is where I fell asleep listening to you telling me about the fishermen, the larks and the gift of the silver coins. Ah yes, says Daniel. She sets the tray on a low table in front of the sofa and sits down, turning to face him from her corner, across a space. I'm glad you are here, she says. I shouldn't have liked to come back to an empty house. Yes, he says. And I am very glad to be here. And something quickens between them, something other than sorrow; or perhaps it is only one of the shapes of sorrow, a purpose, that they can at least act upon. She pours his tea, and asks, What did she mean when she said 'Je peux pas'? Daniel shrugs. Just that, I think. It frightened her. I felt it that night when they came in out of the snow, into the Wharf. It was the dancing, to that music. And more still in Fred's room, when she couldn't go on with her song and he sang the rest for her. I can't explain it any other way. Katrin nods; but wonders why you would flee from love, however fierce, if it were answered, given and received in equal measure, and you held it there in the flesh enfolded in your arms. She waits, but Daniel only shakes his head, sips his tea, so that not for the first time nor the last, she suspects him of knowing more than he will tell, sparing her perhaps; and hopelessness, always in waiting, stirs in her as though again its time has come.

He hitched back from London, Daniel says. He came straight to my room, said nothing, lay face down on the bed and cried like a motherless child. Then he fell asleep. It was mid-morning, I covered him up with my big coat and went to a lecture. He was still asleep when I came back. I've never seen anyone less willing to wake up. Three weeks later we sat Prelims, which he failed, of course, though he got a distinction in French language. Yes, says Katrin, I found a nice letter to him from his French tutor. The old man liked him, says Daniel. He lectured on the *poètes maudits* and had a soft spot for any of his pupils who 'went off the rails', I suppose because he never had himself.

Katrin stands up abruptly. I'll show you your room, she says. And then I must think about supper. He follows her into the kitchen, past the table where they would eat. She sees him notice Eric's saxophone and Monique's bowl. She sees that he knows she does not want to cook him a meal and eat it at that table. Shall we not go out? he says. Won't you let me take you out? I intended to back in April, you remember, when you came to London instead. Reminded, she says to herself, only just under her breath, the word 'covenant', and turns to him — why should she feel ashamed that he sees her relief? — and kisses him on the cheek. That will be lovely, she says. And now your room.

Climbing the stairs, she points to the empty alcove on the first landing. Gone, she says, and from the second landing too, and from the attic, all my father's books, and good riddance. This is your room. Come and find me when you are ready. I'll be right at the top, under the eaves. There are some things I want to show you and more I want to ask.

Katrin is not ashamed of her workroom now. Still it is the locus of only one idea, Eric; but the materials of that subject, the idea in its abundance and variety, are neatly ordered, nowhere cluttering, and if done with, for the present at least, they are stowed out of sight in the attic on the liberated shelves. She sits at her computer in the window and brings up a photograph she found that morning on the web, of the Cherwell in February 1963. Come and see this, she says to Daniel over her shoulder when she hears that he has climbed the stairs and is pausing at her open door. That's where they walked, I'm sure it is. See the weeping willows, all silver-grey. They walked on the ice, he says, right out of town, to the Ferryman. And now look at this, says Katrin, and crosses quickly to the card-table against the wall where the notebooks are and the last sixteen of Monique's letters and Jean-Luc's photograph of her undressing and the photo of Eric smiling with a glass of champagne to hand after his diagnosis and before the illness took away his appetite. She sees that Daniel notices Eric's jacket on the chair-back. Yes, she says, I wear it when I write about him. But look at this. And she shows him the photo of Edna reclining on cushions in the bows of a punt, smiling, very beautiful, and the long fronds of willow making a cool, airy, sunlit arcade into which she glides, raising a glass. Daniel gives a little cough of laughter, as of wry satisfaction that two things have fallen into connection. Edna in happiness, he says, Edna being steered by an invisible hand towards her heart's desire. Same waterway, might even be the same stretch of it, late May or early June. Yes, says Katrin, he took up with her then, he had his Prelims to re-sit, still he scraped through. You went looking for digs out of college, for October, and you hit on Kingston Road, she had a room at the top, she sub-let the other two, you had the single, Eric and Vince shared the double, but – am I right? – he was already sleeping with her by the end of May. Yes, says Daniel, he stayed out a couple of nights a week and went round to Edna's. Until that started, for the first half of Trinity, I thought he had made up his mind to work, and not just for the re-sits. We had some good conversations, I remember. The books were coming alive. We spoke a lot about comradeship, solidarity, that sort of thing. I was sorry when he said shall we ask Vince to share a house next year. He told me on the hill outside Vizille that of the four of us Vince was the one he'd have found it hardest to be with on his own. And when he took up with Edna, and especially after October when he was sleeping with her every night and hanging out with Vince all day while she was at work, I knew we had parted company. I was surprised when he asked me to be best man at his wedding. Perhaps his brother had refused. I thought of that at his funeral, standing up and saying my few words about him, uneasy on both occasions.

Katrin takes the photo out of Daniel's hand and gives him the last of Monique's letters to Eric that, so far as Katrin knows, he ever opened. See the postmark, she says: Paris, 23 May 1963. Can you tell me was he already sleeping with Edna by then? I found a note from you, 15 May, saying that the 17th suited you to go and have a look at Kingston Road. Daniel smiles. You wouldn't put it past her, would you? A week – time enough. But I don't know. The photo of her on the river might be more than a fortnight after they first met. I agree she looks pleased with herself by then. It's not that, says Katrin rather sharply. I want to know did he go and sleep with Edna after Monique wrote and told him she had made a terrible mistake, she was sorry, could he forgive her, could she come to Oxford at once and make it up with him, she would do whatever he wanted if he would only take her back and they could be for ever as they had been before. Or was he already sleeping with Edna when he read that? I don't know, says Daniel. And I don't think it's critical anyway, for reasons you understand as well as I do, I should say. He loved Monique, he didn't stop loving her for Edna. And I don't think he refused her to be revenged but because she — or it, the love — had frightened him — his spirit, his eagerness to love — almost to death. That's how it seemed to me back then. And perhaps I was included in his fear. I was collateral damage, you might say. I didn't blame him then and I don't blame him now. In a sense he honoured me. He didn't care what Vince thought of him but he didn't like me watching him with Edna. Because I knew Monique and I had seen in him what loving her was like, the joy of it and the desolation.

Katrin is thinking he forgets I am this dead man's widowed wife. He forgets I often wonder do I amount to anything when I am weighed in the balance with Monique. She takes the letter from him and opens a notebook. This is how I proceed, she says. Nobody else has seen it and nobody will. Here is the letter in question. There I have transcribed it in black ink. And there in pencil, you see, is my interlinear translation of it into Eric's — not my — mother tongue. Read all you like, I'm not ashamed of it any more, it's how I am. And I still don't know will it help in the end or not. And while you are reading I'll get ready to go out. Will you mind if I keep this black dress on? I want the occasion of it to continue in me for the rest of the day and to have this outward form. Daniel considers her. Of course, he says. I do understand. And besides, it suits you. Katrin sees that he is unused to complimenting women on their appearance. I don't mean mourning becomes you, he says, embarrassed. I only mean it's a nice dress and you look good in it. Thank you, Katrin says. She leaves him reading in an undertone, Eric, mon amour, c'est atroce ce que je t'ai fait, je ne me comprends pas, j'étais folle, lâche et méchante, chéri, et si tu ne me pardonnes pas…

When we came back in October, says Daniel as they walk to the restaurant, I soon realised that I would be on my own a good deal. I had written three or four times to Eric during the vacation, quite long letters, I remember... Yes, says Katrin, taking his arm, I've read them, I hope you don't mind. I should have loved to have a friend who wrote me letters like those. Did Eric really write you nothing better than the couple of scraps you have given me? No, he didn't, says Daniel, but you mustn't blame him. He was working nights again, in a paint factory, if I remember rightly, in Trafford Park. He owed his mother and father quite a sum of money and he was doing his best to pay it off. It's likely that during those few weeks they began to feel he had pulled himself together and would be a credit to them after all. It pleased his father particularly that he didn't go off to France, nor anywhere else abroad. He hitched to Oxford a couple of times, which they didn't mind, though they would have if they'd known he only went there to be with Edna. He wrote to me, as you know, that he couldn't wait for term to start, but I never assumed that meant he was 'back on the rails', as Dr Maber might have said. He got by for the first three or four weeks but his heart wasn't in it. He spent far less time reading French literature than he did reading the racing papers with Vince. All he really studied was form. They got up late, made coffee, discussed the day's races and went to the betting-shop twenty yards away. He became rather good at it, I must say, far better than Vince, and he was always generous with his winnings. We were in the Wharf most nights – that is, I arrived towards closing time and he, Vince, Edna and the others had been there a couple of hours by then. It was always lively, with the music. Even arriving late, it went to my head. And quite often Eric looked at me as though he wanted me to know that he was thinking, as I was, of the night he and Monique came in like waifs out of the snow and she danced and Pete taught her billiards. I liked living round there. Apart from the betting-shop, which I had no use for, I was glad of the baker's, the post office, three or four nice pubs, and the cinema, of course – I saw all the *nouvelle vague* but Eric would never come with me, not even – or especially not – to see *Hiroshima* when that came round again. I was a good deal on my own, which I can't say I minded very deeply. I sat in St Sepulchre's a fair bit, learned the ways of the owls and foxes in their habitations among the stones. And I loved the canal and the Meadow, that vast opening up, the ways out along the towpath and the riverbank. Most Sundays I had a walk, twenty miles or more. Altogether I liked that *quartier*. I went back there for my final year, found a garret room in the street behind Edna's with a view over the Meadow, I saw it white with snow, silver in the sunny floods, golden with the buttercups in June. After my fashion I was happy enough. Eric and Edna had gone by then, when I wrote to him he didn't write back.

Over their meal Katrin lets Daniel talk. Her affection for him deepens with pity. He is not talking to inform her, to help her in her writing of Eric's life, but because as he talks more and more comes over him of the sadness and struggle of those months that, for now, are her particular concern. He tells her things it would not have occurred to her to ask him, tells them because the force of them inside him, unsaid, is unbearable. Only when, awkwardly, still entangled in the past, he pays the bill and they are ready to leave, does she say, Tomorrow you must come to the café with me, to my café, where they know me, where I feel at home, and I will tell you about Dr Gracie and also about the nice boy Patrick who helped me with the shelves and whose girlfriend is expecting a baby in the New Year.

Back home, Katrin offers Daniel tea, hoping he will say no, her head is full, all she wants is, if not to sleep, at least to lie still in the dark in silence, but he accepts gratefully, she sees the fear of sleeplessness in his eyes and the compulsion to say the rest, the worst. From his corner of the sofa, under the lamp, when she comes in with the tray he apologises, because again what he has to tell her exceeds her requirements and is for his own good, if good it can be called. Towards the end of November, he says, quite late at night, Eric came to my room, which by then he very rarely did, and told me Edna was pregnant. He said she didn't want an abortion but she would have to have one 'for obvious reasons', which strange phrase has lodged in my mind ever since because he looked me in the eyes when he employed it as though he wished me to sanction it, which of course I couldn't. Then he shrugged and said he had found out from somebody who knew from somebody else (called Virginia) in one of the women's colleges, that they could get an abortion done at a place in London for £100. He didn't have that much nor anywhere near that much, he still owed money at home, his grant was used up, but he had a tip on an outsider at Haydock Park next day, Vince would be amazed, he was the one for outsiders, not Eric. So here's hoping, he said and again looked me full in the face. He wasn't asking me for advice, nor for money. And he didn't seem to want my sympathy either. Really, I had nothing to say. I knew nothing whatsoever about such things. I saw that he was frightened and I thought afterwards that perhaps he wanted me to know it. Next day he bet £10 at 20 to 1 and lost. He met me coming out of a lecture – one he should have been at himself – and said, She wants me to marry her but I can't do that, she'll have to go to London, I can't risk another bet, will you lend me fifty, I don't want to ask her, I'll find the rest somehow. I lent him fifty. A week later she took a day off work and they hitched to London and went to the address he'd been given somewhere in the East End. As it happened, I was just leaving the house that evening when they came back. I stood aside, she was pale, she looked mortally sad, she turned her face away from me, Eric, following, raised his eyebrows, said nothing, and they went in and upstairs to her room. That night, three in the morning to be precise, he flung open my door and in a broken voice said, Dan, she can't stop bleeding, get an ambulance. I put my boots on and my big coat and ran out to the phone box by the post office, ran back, left the front door open, I could hear Edna screaming, such a noise of terror and of pain, I ran upstairs, the room was brightly lit, she was lying curled up on the bed in a thin nightdress with a sodden towel between her legs and all around her on the sheet, visibly spreading, was her blood. Eric stood against the wall, shaking, his face a dirty white, staring. I fetched another towel from the bathroom but she wouldn't have me anywhere near her with it. Her head twisted this way and that, the blood seeped steadily through the towel she held, through her fingers, off her legs and over the bedsheet, spreading. Her face and neck and shoulders were so white, truly it was as though all the blood, all the hues, of her body were draining fast and unstoppably out of her. Her screams lessened, it was more a sobbing and moaning, with hiccups and small chokings in her throat and spasms of trembling all through her, helpless, childish, entirely given up to it. Then we heard the siren of the ambulance, and soon the two men came running up the stairs with their gear, glanced at us, and professionally contemplated her, the young woman almost naked on the vast stain of her blood. They shook their heads, said nothing, and began to save her life. By the time they had got her into a fit state to be carried and had managed her very carefully down the steep stairs, half the street was at their windows or on the pavement at their gates, to witness. And only then, ready to close the rear doors, did the older of the ambulance men turn to us and say, Which one of you is it? Eric raised a hand, like a schoolboy. Get in, will you, the man said. Sit by her, she might be glad of it. And the Law will want a word with you, I do not doubt.

Next day, after lunch at Katrin's café, they walk to the railway station and have half an hour before Daniel's train. A dank afternoon, already declining into dusk. The buffet is crowded, he fetches coffee to her in a corner of the waiting room. Will you ever go back to writing your brief lives? he asks. No, she answers. No, I shan't. He says nothing, waits; and into the pause Katrin says, I do think of one of them sometimes, in fact quite often lately, but I shan't write it down. I like it – her – the way she is, floating, unfixed, particularly at nights before I go to sleep if I am very troubled by my thinking and writing about Eric I try to think more about her instead. I know he wouldn't mind that, I'm sure he would encourage me. Again Daniel says nothing, he waits, his face expresses a keen interest but – she feels – he will not ask for what she might not wish to tell him. I've never talked about her before, Katrin says, not even to Eric, I was always afraid she might vanish if I did. But I don't mind telling you, I don't feel she will leave me if I tell her to you.

The waiting room is quiet. People are reading or staring in a mesmerised silence at the monitor. The noises are all outside, announcements, the heavy approaches of trains, the confused heaving of innumerable passengers. Katrin moves closer to Daniel and says, Her name is Marianna Levetzow, she was born on an estate outside Lublin probably in 1795, but when and where she died is not known for certain, accounts vary, most say young – 25 to 30 – in Paris, but at least one has her still alive among other émigrés in London in 1871. She was a poet, but what I like best about her, why my thoughts turn gratefully towards her on the borders of sleep, is that no manuscripts of her poems have ever been found, nor any autobiographical notes, nor any letters by her or to her. She exists solely in the memoirs and correspondence of other people, and the one edition of her work, quite a slim volume published in Paris in 1880, consists entirely of the poems, songs and short lyrical monologues that were written down after her perfomances by listeners whom she touched. She never read from her work, she had it all by heart and spoke it, as though it were coming into being there and then, to small audiences in cafés in Warsaw, Paris, Berlin and London. Sometimes she sang it. And on different occasions she presented herself, or affected people, very differently. She is remembered as forceful, shy, brash, vulgar, virginal, witty, naïve… Most accounts of her performances go back to around 1820, but the publications themselves may be ten, twenty or thirty years later, almost as though their authors as they aged began to realise the significance of what they had been present at when they were young. And of course one publication might inspire another. All the accounts of her childhood and early girlhood, for example, appeared *after* the memoirs and correspondence in which she had, so to speak, already taken shape. So there is – and I have assembled – quite a substantial body of evidence of her life and work, and all in the absence of any writing in her hand, any portrait of her or any relic and memorabilia – a favourite book, a lock of hair, a handkerchief, a pen – such as her famous and mostly male literary contemporaries left behind them, in some cases, by the ton. I am very fond of Marianna L. Every now and then another document turns up, I add it to my stock, and the presence of her in my thinking and dreaming alters a little or a lot. She floats, Daniel. She dims and brightens. One night she is piercingly close and definite, then for many nights following she has become as vague as mist. I like that. I shall never write her down. I know her in the effect she had on people, the evidence for her existence is their saying how she touched upon their lives. Her mother tongue was Polish, as mine is, but she may also have composed and performed in German, French and English since her memorialists who write in those languages sometimes quote her in them. Admittedly, they may be translating her, but if so that is only a further proof of her existence in their lives. I'm glad I have told you about her. I shan't be jealous if now you harbour her in your thoughts as well. Occasionally when Eric was alive I felt a bit guilty that I had never told him about Marianna L., but I don't at all now that he is dead. I feel he knows as much about her as I do and that perhaps he is even involved in the changings of her presence. You should go now, Daniel. It's only ten minutes till your train and you have to cross the bridge to Platform 5.

At the barrier, having embraced her, and standing back, a look of trouble, almost of anticipated shame, comes over Daniel's face. Forgive me, Katrin, he says. I shouldn't ask this: Did you find the pouch of silver coins among Eric's things? No, she says, touching his cheek, no I didn't and I don't at all mind you asking. It has often been on the tip of my tongue to ask do you have them, but I was afraid that, if you did, you would think I wanted them myself, which I don't, if he gave them to you. He didn't, says Daniel. I had assumed he left them to be discovered by you.

This is a bad question to part on, Katrin thinks; but quickly she embraces him again, thanks him for his company and their hours of talk, and hurries away. Glancing back, she sees him still at the barrier like a lost boy, staring after her.

# 16

Katrin writes:

Perhaps he sold them to pay for the abortion?

In the café with Daniel: For some time I have liked the thought of introducing him there. I never thought to be there with Liz but after that one occasion, the few times I went back on my own, I felt changed in the girls' view of me, and between me and the manageress there is now a new connection which we do not need to speak about. And walking in with Daniel, so soon after Liz's funeral, again there is an adjustment in the way I am perceived. Note: the truest life-writing, beyond my ability, would somehow recognise these shifts and make them palpable without ever *fixing* them, because fixing is the way of death and this is so and should be the life-writer's axiom even if the subject in question is dead.

Daniel did not look ill at ease in the café. He looked as he has everywhere I have ever seen him: odd, not belonging, but also – and this is very poignant (and endearing) in him – he looks about him with humility, predisposed to think well of the place and its people, with a lively interest. He resembles Eric in his lack of envy; but in Eric, as I knew him, that came of contentment: truly, as I knew him, he did not want to be anyone else or anywhere else. Daniel is unenvious without being contented by who and where he is.

He asked me about Liz Gracie and listened closely, saying nothing, while I explained what she became to me, how she helped. He listened until he saw that I was talking myself into the fearful contemplation of what I shall do now, without her. Then, in a pause, he nodded and said, Tell me about Patrick, the shelves and the expected baby. So I did.

Now I must write down the rest, till the marriage, in rough outline at least. Also, perhaps even more important, since she risks *fixing* in the view I have of her, I must include whatever else I can glean about Edna from Thomas, from Daniel and Eric, and from her own few letters in the years after the separation. I don't think I need go back to Michael and Sheila. I don't think their views of Edna will change and for my purposes that doesn't matter.

Looking back over the notes I made after my conversations with Michael and Sheila in May I now feel pretty certain that neither they nor Eric's mother and father ever found out about Edna's abortion. In fact, it seems none of them knew anything at all about Edna until Eric wrote in late February 1964 and announced that he was going to marry her at Easter and give up his studies 'for the time being'. Michael remembered that phrase and passed it on to me with a bitterness, as though he were speaking also for the disappointed mother and father, that had endured for fifty years. Both Christmases – 1962 and 1963 – were 'ruined', he said, the first because of Monique, the second because of Edna. Eric came home late and penniless both times, and so preoccupied with his own affairs that the family had no joy in him, only worry and (his father, at least) resentment. He needed money, and since he could earn most working nights that is what he did, coming home to bed just as his family were beginning their day. And early in the new year – both years – he took himself off south again to the place they had grown to hate.

In some ways it distresses me more to write these things than anything else I have had to write. I don't like to watch the man I love behaving badly; and less, if I'm honest, on account of what it did to his family than for what it did to him. By the time he turned twenty-one, in January 1964, he had burdened his life with guilt. And I remember his anxiety when he was dying that there should be nothing left between us for which amends still needed to be made or, if beyond amends, forgiveness asked and granted. I scarcely knew what he meant at the time, or I understood it only as an idea, not applicable to him and me since I had nothing to forgive him nor he, I believed, to forgive me; but in truth, concerning other people, there were things he was to blame for back then, too young, and for which, I suppose he never did make amends and needed instead, and perhaps never received, forgiveness. Edna told Thomas only last week that Eric – 'your father' – had ruined her life, and she never would forgive him. Unfair, unkind; but so it goes on, the bitterness if anything increasing not lessening with the years.

Katrin puts down her pen, takes off Eric's jacket, and presses the place in her left side where the phantom pain lives that will get worse, Dr Gracie said, only if she, Katrin, wishes or allows it to. Death seems to her both final and infinitely continuing. In the living it shuts off everything and nothing. Dwell on a life, a beloved life, and all the longings in it, the regrets, the desire for other outcomes, all stirs, rises, swirls and writhes. Even the done and decided things, proven satisfactions and achievements, dwell on them for a while very closely, even in them, it seems, something may be working for dissolution, there is always a perspective, waiting to be found, which will work on them like a burning glass on ice. When he stopped breathing and lay there getting cold and his limbs and features stiffening and, more so, in the undertaker's parlour when they had made him fit to be looked at before he was lidded over and conveyed into the flames and reduced to ashes – for that interlude he had stillness, a dead stillness, a cold stillness. Since then he has moved continuously like clouds, shaping up and unshaping among all the facts and possibilities of his mortal life. All her writing has done no more than broach his life. Steeping herself in him, now Katrin grieves for him not just in the sense of missing him, wanting him whole and home again, able to be embraced and conversed with; she grieves also for all that, if he had a consciousness, if he lived still as a feeling consciousness, must give him pain.

Katrin goes downstairs, dresses warmly, opens the door – then shakes her head. She has not done enough, she has not yet earned the company of the living. She closes the door, divests herself of her outdoor things, climbs back to the place facing the wall under the roof, puts on his jacket and writes:

A policeman came to speak to Eric in the waiting room while Edna was being seen to by the doctor. Who did it? he asked. Eric told him, and the address. Good, said the policeman. He'll be getting a visit. And you come down to the station when you've had a sleep. You might be lucky or you might not. Depends who's on duty, quite honestly. Eric was lucky. The superintendent reminded him that procurement of an abortion was a serious offence. If the young lady had died, he said, you'd be going to jail. As it is, we'll keep it on the books. So stay out of trouble.

The first thing Edna said to Eric when he was let in to see her – I have this from Daniel who had it from Eric – was, Now you can fucking well marry me. OK, he replied.

Casting out Monique and distancing himself from Daniel was, I should say, part of Eric's decision to buckle down *by his own volition* to the fact of marriage. I have looked again at my notes on Sheila's view of it – when we had our conversation in Cressbrook Dale – and I think, or I am trying to think, that he was a willing partner, with Edna, in his own submission. So it won't do to say that she was the stronger, knowing what she wanted, and that weakly he gave in. Daniel thinks that loving Monique, feeling betrayed by Monique, getting Edna pregnant, procuring the abortion, seeing her nearly killed by it, drove him to an edge over which, like several others of their acquaintance in those years, he might well have jumped. Instead, he backed away, understood, perhaps consciously, perhaps quite unconsciously, what he must do to survive, and did it: married Edna, left Oxford, secured an undemanding job teaching French and German languages at a Surrey polytechnic, took out a mortgage on a Barratt house on a new estate, and 'started a family'. Marriage saved his life.

The first years of it – this marriage – were, for Eric, essentially defensive; he collected himself. 'Reculer pour mieux sauter' comes to mind, but doesn't describe it quite. 'Sauter' is wrong. In my understanding, Eric then and perhaps ever after had no intention of doing any more leaping. Instead, instinctively (becoming the rational hedonist Daniel called him at his funeral), he manoeuvered for a mode of survival which should be as enjoyable as possible.

Sheila was doubtless right to see Edna, at the wedding, not as triumphant but as determined to prove the world (that is, Eric's family) wrong by making a good marriage. True, she had got what she wanted, but so does any woman who marries the man she loves, so did I when I married the same man twenty-five years later. The idea that Edna married Eric for social advancement, to climb into the professional class, is starting to seem to me far-fetched. She was beautiful, intelligent, spirited, and her family was no better or worse than Eric's. Did she really set her sights on an Oxford graduate for a husband? I begin to doubt it. In the event that is not what she got, which at the wedding she already knew; and whether she looked triumphant or determined, certainly at the wedding and in photographs for the next three years, she did not look disappointed. And when she did begin to think him a disappointment, that was not because he had failed to make a banker's or a professor's wife of her. So, yes,

I'm prepared to believe that Edna married Eric for love. And she must have thought that Eric already did, or before long would, love her too. And she had grounds for thinking that, I'm sure.

It was three years before Thomas was born. Edna had trouble conceiving him – for which she blamed the damage done by the abortion to her 'insides' – and the birth itself was difficult. Those first years, themselves without bitterness, did perhaps lay the grounds for the bitterness later. Edna found herself a job as a hotel receptionist in town, worked until she had to leave for the baby, and went back there six months later, arranging the crèche and telling Eric what his duties and his schedule were in that respect. She took her driving test, passed first time, bought a cheap car and used it for her convenience. He had no interest in any of that. He took the bus, drove out in the car with her when she asked him to, and never did learn to drive. At home he did his share of the cleaning, and more than his share of the cooking because he began to enjoy doing that. He mowed the lawn and dug the garden when she asked him to, leaving the cultivation of flowers, fruit and vegetables entirely to her. He was no handyman, Edna did most of the painting, decorating, simple repairs and improvement; he helped as directed and they got workmen in for the rest. They earned enough between them. He was careful with money but raised no serious objection if she was suddenly lavish on herself, the house, the child, a holiday. Visitors – their few friends, family very occasionally – will have thought her the one in charge, the home of her making, and that he did as he was told. His professional work did not much engage or burden him. He got on with it easily, took on more, for more pay; he was co-operative, amiable, a good colleague, his students liked him.

In the course of the first year, forwarded from Heaton Street, Salford 3, Monique's last two letters arrived. She wrote such things as:

Daniel tells me you are married and I suppose for you that means you wouldn't come and see me or let me come and see you even if you did still love me which you don't or you wouldn't make me suffer as I am suffering now. Sometimes when I wake in the night and think about you my main feeling is incomprehension. I do not understand you – it, you, anything really – I don't understand how from one day to the next you could pass from loving me as I know for certain that you did to not loving me or to hating me so much that you could be so unkind. Punishment can't be the reason. I don't believe anyone would punish anyone for so long and so harshly, it is not possible, not for someone who loved me as you did. If Daniel hadn't told me – I wrote and asked him – that you were married and living in a funny English house I would think you must be dead except not even the dead are as lost and silent and unkind as you are to me, I know that much from my mother and my dead father. I made a terrible mistake, I was a coward, I betrayed our love because I was fearful of it, of loving too much, of losing my own life in it, but countless times in these unanswered letters I have said I am sorry and asked you to forgive me and if you would let me I would go on my knees before you and beg and beg you for forgiveness but you won't let me and I do not understand it.

And this:

If you do not write back now quickly I think I shall not write to you any more. Nothing has changed, I have not met anybody else, there is only you, but I have had a new thought about it which I feel to be the truth and it is this: that you are a bigger coward and for longer, perhaps for ever, than I was for a few weeks, and if I did wrong to our love the wrong you did to it is worse, much worse. I made a mistake and you would not forgive me and that is a great cruelty you have done me in return. And this morning when I woke up and you were not there, again and still and always you are never there, I saw very clearly what you were like with me when we made love, how at the mercy of it you were, just as I was, both at the mercy of it, equally, and I saw then and I still see now how good that was, such a good thing, given to very few, and it was ours, in us, and in your heart of hearts, traitor, coward, if you woke this morning and looked in the mirror you would see us standing side by side and naked, wide-eyed, astounded, fearful, at the mercy of it, rejoicing, exultant, wholly given up to it in one another, coward of an English boy, you knew as I did and if you have a scrap of honesty left in you still now you know and will always know that it was glorious, being in it, head over heels in it, laughing and crying and whispering and shouting in it, you knew it was good, you knew your life, like mine, would need it for ever, having loved like that, been *in* love like that, never again could we live without it or only a lesser life, a diminished life, getting by, making do with less when once upon a time not just more but *all* was ours to live and thrive in all the days of our life and have children from who would have been as beautiful as the sons and daughters of the luckiest lovers in any song any poet ever sang. So you have harmed yourself every bit as much as you have me, and why? Because you were too scared to forgive me my terrible terrible terrible mistake. M.

Edna saw both letters, indeed she laid them before Eric on the breakfast table. He shrugged, disregarded her look, took them off with him and added them to the others, unopened.

Occasionally letters came from Daniel. He wrote such things as:

I've been reading Camus again, especially *L'Homme révolté* that the wandering scholar gave you in Vizille. I know I should have passed it on, but I couldn't bear to, I passed on a Brecht instead, to a girl I met on one of my walks. Anyway, Camus. I feel, again, that he is helping me to become the one I am, whatever that is, whatever that will be. I have felt lately, amidst so much that is dull and bad, that my spirit is on the move, I hope towards revolt. For neither the world nor myself in it will do as they are. Neither is anywhere near satisfactory. I love him for making it clear that the one entails the other. 'Je me révolte, donc nous sommes.' Remember that? The better I shape myself, the more I might do for the cause of justice and the dignity of men and women in the world. I accept his atheism, I make it my premise too. And once that is accepted, then, as he says, 'il n'y a plus qu'un enfer et il est de ce monde: c'est contre lui qu'il faut lutter.' But that struggle needs comrades. I wonder do you still think of comradeship, of community? I shan't ever forget our conversations. Another thing in him, of course, another premise or the consequence of the premise of atheism, is love of the earth. I had a walk last weekend, hitched into Wales, walked a good long way and slept out on a hill facing Cader Idris. Cold, of course, but such beauty of moon and stars, the owls calling across me, till the hesitant rosy-fingered dawn. I brewed up a coffee, leaned in my bag against a tree, the rabbits came forth, quite close, the ground was silver-dewy, and I read his epigraph again, from Hölderlin's *Empedokles*, you remember, the dedication of oneself to the earth, to love her faithfully, fearlessly, in her sufferings, in her mysteries, with a love that would last till death. And it's that, the love of the beautiful earth and the making of an answering beauty in art and in deeds, that I'm most touched by at present. Revolt in *jouissance*, in the enjoyment and in the making of beauty, so that men and women will live lives fit to be looked at on the beautiful earth. That seems to be a project worth working for in the time allowed.

At first Eric answered these letters, but briefly, taking up none of the subjects Daniel broached, and leaving such a length of time between his slight replies that the next stage, not replying at all, came easily.

Compliant in all things that did not fundamentally touch him, Eric meanwhile, not in any systematic fashion, not by design and forethought, more like some organism warily but assuredly putting forth, emerging, seeking after what it needs, Eric meanwhile, under the cover of his domestic and professional existence, with a determination at the heart of which was ruthlessness, began to enter into the life he would call his own.

Eric went to fetch Edna and the baby on the bus. He took her suitcase. Now if you could drive…, she said, not unkindly. Back home he had cleaned and made the rooms look welcoming; but she sniffed, she could smell cigarettes. You had company? she asked. No, he answered, it's me. Took a packet of Gitanes out of his pocket and held them up for her inspection. I thought I'd start again. She handed him Thomas – to get used to, she said. They walked out into the garden. He had cut the lawn. She noted what else needed doing. Oh and by the way, he said, holding Thomas on his left arm and in his right hand clutching the Gitanes in his jacket pocket, I've had a vasectomy. Edna turned from the roses to him, to look him full in the face, frowning and appraising. Now why did you go and do that? He shrugged. I thought I would. It's pretty sore still. I thought you might have noticed from how I was sitting on the bus. I'm pretty sore myself, she answered. Giving birth, you know. She looked *put out* – that is, obliged to reconsider him and foreseeing what that might entail. And weakened by the birth, feeling herself to have been in body and soul disintegrated by it, she had no heart at that moment for any such process. Thomas will want changing, she said. Let me show you how it's done.

Eric's other moves, over the next few years, were, each in itself, unexceptionable; only later, looking back on them, you might see what they amounted to. One day, for example,

Edna came in from doing the weekly shop and found that he had hauled his bike out of the very cluttered garden shed, the bike he had ridden home on from Vizille, via Nevers and Paris. He was leaning over it, Thomas sat on a rug close by, placidly watching him. It was Dan's, he said. A woman in Garmisch gave it him. It had been her son's but he got killed. Daniel rode it to Vizille and gave it me. You remember all that? I thought I might get it done up. I see, said Edna. The shopping's in the car, if you wouldn't mind.

Eric reliably did all the things that had become his responsibility; and whatever else Edna wanted doing, he did that too. He arranged his hours at the polytechnic so that he could get home in the early afternoon, collecting Thomas on the way. Then the house was clean and tidy when Edna came in, supper was cooking and Thomas looked content. Edna, glancing round, saw no signs of any dereliction of duty. Not that she was sharply on the look-out for such signs, just that they would have been easy to name and deploy as the grounds for her growing resentment whereas its true grounds were not. She had begun to realise, perhaps only as he realised it himself, that little by little he was establishing a territory in which she would have no say. If she ever did start an argument over his smoking, or the betting slips he left lying on the sideboard, or the jazz LPs he came home with once a week; or if with increasing bitterness she fetched up the outrageous business of his vasectomy, he refused to be engaged, he shrugged, self-deprecatingly he backed away, and all his bearing said: that's what I'm like, we'll have to put up with it.

Edna could never have claimed that Eric annexed for his own sole occupation any zone or activity that was rightly hers, or hers and his in common. He was not encroaching; rather, and in the end hardest to bear, he was opening up places, interests, likings, even passions, that had nothing at all to do with her. His excursions on the revitalised bicycle, always in time that was indisputably his, were an obvious extension of himself beyond her reach. She had her car, she showed no interest in cycling, nor did he ever try to interest her. He cycled to distant markets and came back with jazz records and old books in his panniers. But even within the confines of their small modern house he made domains of his own. Her resentment gathered on this simple fact: he was happy to do all she asked of him in their shared life, and to let her do whatever she pleased in any life she might fashion for herself; quite happy, she began resentfully to realise, because at bottom these areas of life did not matter to him; he had nothing against them, felt not the least disgust or animosity towards them, it was just that he had an elsewhere which engrossed him more. She began to feel that whenever he chose he could always withdraw from her; and that she, for her own recreation, had no such powers of invention and discovery to make for herself a domain of answering life. That, in time, embittered her.

Edna came home one evening – Thomas would be three or four, Eric still only in his late twenties – and found the two of them at either end of the dining room table, quietly occupied, the child drawing with coloured pencils, his father reading and making notes with a grammar and a dictionary to hand. The house was spick and span, the evening meal all but ready to serve, Eric went into the kitchen to see to it. When he came back, to clear and set the table, Edna, still in her outdoor coat, had taken his seat (her usual place for the meal) and was examining the text, the grammar, the dictionary and his notes. I'll move all that, he said. She looked up, hesitant, almost fearful. What's this? she asked. Oh it's the old stuff, he answered. I thought I'd go back to it and start again. No reason why not. It was all in the loft. Lucky I never throw anything away. What language is it? she asked. Middle High German, he answered. It will be hard for a bit, but it will get easier if I persevere. I see, she said. You'll go back and start again where you left off, where I interrupted you. He shook his head. I never really got going. Ask Daniel. It's from the beginning I have to start again. I see, she said. He had seen her resentful and contemptuous, but in her look now there was something plaintive. He shrugged. She rose and went to take off her coat and change out of the smart suit she wore for work.

Thereafter Edna's homecoming was often like that. She found him at the table studying the texts that as a student he had read hastily or not at all but had never sold or given away. And opposite him sat Thomas, intently drawing. She felt that he, and perhaps even also his son, had entered into a life that might continue very well without her.

No literature was taught at Eric's polytechnic, and by now he was scarcely at all in correspondence with Daniel; but he fetched his old set texts down out of the loft, arranged them neatly on the floor along the wall on his side of the bed, and began to work his way through them, making copious notes. Later he got himself a reader's card at the nearest university, cycled there some afternoons and consulted books that helped. And he increased his library second-hand, for very little money. So, catching up, talking and writing to nobody about it, he began to add scholarship in foreign languages to the amenities of the life that was most his own.

Katrin halts in her writing. She has remembered something. But at the thought of it a reluctance, almost a revulsion, starts in her, so that she sits still for a while wondering about herself as the writer of these lives. She has remembered a letter Edna wrote to Eric soon after he and Katrin were married and which, in their agreed openness with one another, he passed to her to read, saying nothing, only shaking his head. Katrin knows roughly where to find it, on which shelf in the attic. But she sits a while longer, rather sickened. Their marriage revived much bitterness in Edna. She wrote at once, telling him he must on no account stop the payments. Old grievances surfaced, and it was as though she wanted paying for each and every one of them.

DAVID CONSTANTINE

Katrin stands on a chair and searches along the shelf of the 80s and 90s. She soon finds half a dozen letters addressed to Eric in Edna's hand. She does not wish to read them all – she has a particular passage in mind – but, standing on the chair, she takes one letter, then another, then a third, out of their envelopes and skims them. Having over the past weeks approached the writer in writing of her own, Katrin pities her. The letter she remembered is the third, posted in Woking, a deep blue second class stamp, 5 May 1990, and the passage, scribbled fast, is this:

You won't remember this, you didn't even notice, I came home and you were sitting at our table face to face with the new French assistant. She was young, of course, and nice-looking but that's not the point, the point is you were talking French and you didn't stop when I came in, you gave me a wave and carried on talking in a language you knew very well I didn't understand, she had her back to me but I could see your face, I should have gone out again and left you to it but instead I stood in the doorway watching you enjoy yourself speaking French and minding me no more than you would somebody on television with the sound turned off. A good five minutes you carried on with never even another glance my way. You won't remember the occasion, it wasn't the worst thing you did to me, not by a long chalk, but it hurt me more than some of those worst things did because it was so like you and so like we were together by that time, you and me.

Katrin folds the letter back into its envelope, back into its bundle which she ties and replaces where it belongs on the black shelf. Enough is enough. She has reached her own stratum with these testimonies, having had no intention of ever doing so. The early deposits, fifty years ago, those few years like a seam of dormant seed now germinating and flowering in the daylight of her own present life, all that is

204

more than enough. She thinks she will go out to the café, or walk past the theatre on the off chance that Patrick might be arriving or leaving there. Instead, giving in to an impulse that feels almost vicious, she reaches for the bundle 1987-89 in which, she knows, are thirteen letters from Bettina Sedakova to Eric, the last written only a week before he intercepted Katrin at the Warsaw check-in.

At her small table facing the wall and wearing Eric's jacket, Katrin unties the letters, removes Bettina's, orders them chronologically and begins to read. A gypsy, Eric called her, she is younger than him, not very much older than Katrin, they overlapped for a year at the polytechnic when Katrin's career in Britain was just beginning. Reading, Katrin remembers her face, her beautiful Slav face, her restlessness, appetite, *hauteur*, ease of movement, insouciance. The letters are in English and German, with some passages, and some quotations from poetry, in Russian, their love-language, which Katrin can manage well enough.

She reads the first half dozen, in gulps, like somebody bingeing. It takes her into the throes of the affair, the romance, the passion, she reads a woman trying to say in her own voice and with the help of the poetry of three languages what it is like when you love heedlessly and the man you love does not, cannot, you outdo him in love, you overbear him. Katrin feels for her, she can see him backing away, a Gitane between two fingers of his left hand and with both hands making the gesture that signifies: What do you expect? You surely see by now what I am like. She reads: At first when we made love, in the lovely hazy dreaminess afterwards, I saw roads climbing with great certainty of purpose to mountain crests that had the dawn behind, I saw an estuary of sunny and breezy water opening out into a whole Atlantic. And even now, despite everything, I have such visions. Some mornings waking on my own I don't care whether you love me or not. Stronger than the coming unhappiness are my pride and gladness that I love you as I do. Is it not my own affair, my glory and my

misery, that I love you like this? And I almost pity you that
you don't love equally and don't know what it's like. I think
perhaps you never have and never will love wholly recklessly
as I love you. But it is bad some days and will be worse. Last
night when you left me as you always leave me, soon, after a
cigarette, after a little conversation and further practising of
your Russian, when you got out of bed and dressed and left
me so that we should not fall asleep together, so that I should
not wake and find you beside me either sleeping or watching
quietly until I should also wake and then –

Katrin folds the letter away, back into its envelope, back
into the bundle which she returns to its right place on the
shelf. She goes downstairs, dresses warmly – it is December,
a cold bright day – and with a feeling of purpose leaves the
house and takes the bus out to the estuary. On the journey,
arriving, walking towards the view she wants of the river
widening to embrace the sea, throughout she is absorbed in
a steady questioning of herself: can she not stop now, read no
more of it, write no more about it, and leave it be? But it
won't be let be, she knows that much. It is all released, and
whatever she does with the letters, cards, telegrams,
photographs and hoarded ephemera, it, the thing itself, will
not go back behind a door in the trunk in the loft nor let
itself be lidded in neat shoeboxes on shelves. It is all released
in her, unstoppably, uncontainably, she must and does see
that. Leave it *being* then, leave it becoming. She did not quit
Bettina in mid-sentence because she, Katrin, lost heart. She
has read three women in love with her dead husband. It
wasn't for self-preservation that she suddenly broke off. The
whole question of whether it helps or harms her to learn
and steep herself in such other lives will be decided, she now
thinks, without her pondering it. The process is under way,
it can't be stopped. In her wish, or decision as it may become,
to cease reading and writing on her subject, there is less a
weighing of the likelihoods of help or harm than the

apprehension of a principle which, though it involves her, quite exceeds her. And this dawning realization thrills and frightens her in equal measure.

For a while, almost unconsciously, Katrin has been watching a small yacht. Now she concentrates. It has a slim white hull and a bright red sail. The tide has turned and is ebbing fast, the river has recovered itself, its own direction, moves with the tide now fast and far into the sea, and the yacht rides with ease and grace upon them both. Katrin's thinking disintegrates, or passes over into the elements of what she is now closely observing, into the steady purposefulness of the outflowing water, the bright catches of sun on it, and the yachtsman's easeful and delighted handling of his small craft as the breeze, the tide, and the river's own gradient hurry him along the way he wants to go. Katrin watches. If asked now, say by Dr Gracie, does she wish to live, does she believe she will? she would answer that on both questions she is edging towards a yes.

Katrin calls in at the bookseller's, just to say hello. He is sitting, as always, reading, with music on quietly. He is glad to see her. He is courteous. In their few minutes of conversation there is a free exchange of kindness and goodwill. Next door, at the cheese shop, it is the same. Katrin buys a local cheese, one Eric used to buy for her among others he preferred himself. The woman asks how she is getting on. Better, says Katrin. Thank you, I'm doing better. I'm glad, says the shopkeeper, handing her the small parcel.

Late that night Katrin phones Daniel. I'm going to stop it, she says. If I can. Ah, he says. Stop it, not bring it to a conclusion? No, just stop and pack everything away, and not because I'm sick of it, not because reading their love letters hurts me too much, not because I've reached any conclusions or think I'll be better if I stop. Why then? he asks. To try and live in truth, she says, and halts there, surprised by the words.

Daniel says nothing, so that after a while of silence Katrin says: I wish you were here. I'm sure I could explain it better if I could see you listening. I *am* listening, he says. Well then, Katrin continues, I feel now that I should break off my writing in mid-sentence because that's the truth of it, truth of the whole project. The process itself – I didn't know this until this afternoon – is what has mattered and will carry on mattering if I let it because in it the truth is by now already proven and more and more proof will only muddle my understanding of it. If I carried on I'd be carrying on in the delusion that there might be an end to it and a final shape. And there really isn't. I haven't finished with any of it and never shall be. I don't even mean that I'd keep on turning up new facts, though doubtless I would if I kept on looking for the rest of my life. The adjustments I'd have to make in the light of new facts would only be the most obvious effects of a process that's working in me anyway and will till the end of my days whether I came across anything new – in that material way – or not. It – my subject – will keep on moving and shifting, and certainly not towards an end if by end is meant any binding final shape. It will move ceaselessly until I cease and even after that versions, strains, fragments of it will continue and continue changing in anyone who knew me and knew anything about my life-writing. There, again, Katrin halts. She is childless, she has lost touch with Poland, she belongs nowhere, she has Eric's few relations, but remotely. And Liz Gracie is dead. Daniel is a year older than Eric was. She feels him thinking her thoughts. Yes, she says. Stay alive, Daniel. I intend to, he says. For as long as possible. Anyway, she says, that's the fact I feel I have understood and among the millions of so-called facts in my archive of the dead husband, that's the one that matters and, by stopping the reading and the writing, henceforth I shall live in accordance with it, if I can. Good night, Daniel. You are my dear friend, I feel that you were listening and that you understand. He mutters something. What did you say? she asks. – Oh just something I remembered. – What, Daniel? – That film, you know: 'la vie qui continue, ta mort qui continue…' Good night, Katrin.

Katrin sleeps at once; but it is a sleep which so torments her she longs in it for release from it, into oblivion. She feels dipped and held under in a mêlée of voices, gestures, faces that come in flurries like snowfall dashed at by winds from every compass point. Is this how she must live: in a hell of hectic simultaneity, the items pell-mell clamouring for her attention, all claiming she has taken too little care of them? Liz Gracie's brooch, the intricate and firmly fastened plait of life, undoes before her eyes into a windy chaos of demands. Thousands of black and white photographs and their ghostly negatives, Michael's catalogued fossils, the ephemera from Eric's shoeboxes, lift and blow about her like aeons of dead leaves. More and more, a blizzard of such stuff, like ghosts, silent, open-mouthed and pestering, like shades who have no vocal cords, they lift their hands in a desperate entreaty: everything matters, every torn-off button counts, every hair-grip, every pressed wild flower, stub of pencil, autograph, bus-ticket, scallop shell, for the hands that held them, owned them, used them, relinquished or deposited them every item counts and begs her: take more care of me, attach me again where I belonged, follow the clues, at every junction go both ways, track every ramification till it is thinner than a hair. All the lives she has touched upon assail her in a deafening interference, the silt and ash of them as they precipitate writhing into shapes undoing even as they form. This is what it is like, your never-endingness. Sleep in its ceaseless petitioning if you can.

Towards dawn Katrin does sleep, and her first sense on waking is of stillness, a profound silence; and only after a while, lying there and wondering at this, does she remember the state that preceded it, and before that her account to Daniel, the estuary, Bettina's letter, the breaking off mid-sentence... And it seems to her all delusion, an ineffectual fiction. She is back in the dark, waking alone, in a grief compounded by the death of the doctor who had begun to help.

# 17

WITH NO APPETITE, in a trance of sadness, Katrin is eating breakfast when the post arrives, one item, a letter from Monique of whom since the funeral she has heard nothing, not even – concerning her present life, at least – from Daniel. It is a thin envelope, postmarked Paris 13 December 2012, the handwriting of fifty years ago, the stamp a slate-blue Marianne among the stars. Katrin fetches a paper-knife, feels for a gap in one corner, very carefully slits along, and takes out the single closely written sheet. Everything she has seen in Monique's hand was addressed to Eric, so it jolts her sideways into a new perspective when she reads: Ma chère Katrin, voilà longtemps que je pense beaucoup à toi... At the funeral it was 'vous' and 'Madame Swinton'. Katrin gets up from the table and stands at the kitchen window, seeing and not seeing the bird-feeder which she has forgotten to replenish. No words going to and fro, no letters, emails, phone calls, solely by force of thinking and unbeknownst to Katrin, Monique has moved into an intimacy with her. At that alone, at the opening half sentence, a great novelty of feeling surges into her, she holds tight to the sill, and the wintry garden swims in a rush of tears. How well she knows this woman in her script, her love and grief! Too well: she has read what she was never meant to read, and things that not even Eric, thinking to save himself, ever read. Worse, she passed her notebook to Daniel, to let him read of Monique whatever he liked. If this is to be a friendship there will be secrets in it that she will never dare, or have the heart, to confess.

Monique writes fast, one closely scribbled side of very light paper; but Katrin knows her writing and the expressive quirks of her French. Though without Eric there would never have been a letter from Monique to Katrin, by name he does not occur, Katrin alone is addressed, in her proper self, Monique speaks only to her and asks, begs her – the long thinking about Katrin has brought Monique to this – that she will come to Paris so they can have some talk together, soon, very soon, will she?

Yes, says Katrin aloud. Yes, I will. Why on earth shouldn't I? I will. She hurries through and phones Daniel. Did you sleep? he asks. No, she answers. Or yes, I did but I'd have done better not to. I woke feeling like death. I'm sorry, he says. Yes, Daniel, but now this: I've had a letter from Monique. Ah, Monique, says Daniel. She phoned me an hour ago, I was still asleep, she wants you to go to Paris, she asked me to beg you to say yes. I do say yes, says Katrin. Then when shall it be? he asks. She understands his tone. You mean you'll come with me? – If you like, yes I will. I won't be in the way. I've things of my own to see to in Paris. Would next Tuesday be any good? Get here by lunchtime, there's a train at 4, takes two and a quarter hours. Leave it with me.

Katrin has a shower; stands naked in the mirror, appraises herself. Nothing in her wardrobe will make a difference. Never mind, she says to her mirrored self. We shall kit ourselves out in Paris.

Daniel phones again. All done, he says. Trains there and back, two rooms for two nights in the once disreputable Malebranche. See you Paddington, Tuesday, 12.23. Daniel, says Katrin, you won't ever tell her Eric never read those letters, will you? And that I let you read them in my transcription. She hears in his silence that there was no need to ask. Forgive me, Daniel, she says. Don't worry, he says.

There are one or two other matters of that kind. We'll talk about them on Eurostar.

The doorbell rings, an uncommon intrusion and one Katrin, when her spirits are low, ignores, keeping still and trying to absent herself until whoever rang goes away; but this morning, without a second thought, on the not yet failing surge of hopefulness, she strides down the hall, and unlocks and opens the door. There stands Partrick. Oh good, he says. You're in and up. She has not seen him for weeks, not in the café nor on the streets around the theatre she sometimes takes a detour through. The sight of him rejoices her; but she also sees in him how far out in her own eccentric course she is, how differently time moves there, how sparse in her haunts are the ordinary human markers. Patrick! she says. What a lovely surprise! Come in. Sorry, he answers, can't hang about. I've come for the shelves, if they're still on offer. We're over there, that white van in Residents Only, Ellie's with me, we've got a new place, lots of room, we're having a house-warming, Christmas Eve, here's your invitation, will you come? Yes, says, Katrin, yes I will. Thank you very much. You know where the shelves are, I'll help you. She carries two out, Patrick following with four. This is Ellie, he says. Katrin leans her shelves against the van and through the open sliding door shakes hands with the young woman whose baby is due towards the end of February, whose face lights with a smile out of a dream, who looks more deeply contented than anyone Katrin can ever remember seeing. Patrick lays the six shelves down on the floor behind the seats, goes back for more. The two women exchange very few words. Each knows a little about the other. How little one needs for sympathy, Katrin thinks. Ellie lets herself be looked at as though she knew impersonally that her pale oval face, its framing black hair, the eyes softly shadowed with fatigue, are a wonder to Katrin, the beholder. Patrick hurries to and fro, glancing for traffic, and in four trips he is done, fourteen shelves and four uprights all laid flat in the back of the van.

What a dismal colour they are, says Katrin. They won't be when you see them next, says Patrick. They're off to Mick the Strip this very minute. Our new place is spacious and sunny and your shelves will be the colour they belong to be. Thanks, Katrin.

Katrin glances again at Ellie, who in that short interval has lapsed into her familiar remoteness, behind the mask of her pregnancy, not discourteously but as of right withdrawing into the centre of her waiting and attending, where she belongs. From across the street Katrin waves good-bye, then closes the door and without thinking goes and sits on the sofa in the front room. She sits there for quite some time.

# 18

AND THE LAST thing, said Daniel – for now, at least – is that her husband, Fortunatus, who is quite a bit older than her – eighty-five or -six, I think – is very jealous of her past and of anyone connected with it, so she certainly won't have told him that she'll be seeing you. She met him – she found him in the gutter, to be exact – it must be forty years ago, and they've been together, on and off, more or less, ever since. They even got married – for the son's sake, she says; but being married only made his jealousy worse. He's very infirm now, not surprisingly, and very dependent on her, and it causes him great suffering, she says, that she still has preoccupations of her own and still flits about. He's Dutch, came to Paris in his teens to be a painter, lived the life of one, drank anything and everything, still paints, no better than he did seventy years ago but no worse either, never learned more than a few words of French, and since she can't speak any Dutch their language has always been a sort of English, pidgin, really, no more than that, but it suffices. I've been with them often enough, but never in my proper person, as you might say. I made up an autobiography in which neither Salford nor Oxford plays any part, and Paris not until my sixtieth birthday. My name, as far as Fortunatus is concerned, is Alfred William Hayfield, I'm a homosexual, some sort of scholar, and I travel a good deal. I see, said Katrin. But the gutter, tell me how she found him. It was 1970, said Daniel. Or thereabouts. Jean-Luc was dead, Eric was married and worse than dead to her, '68 had failed

and nobody felt like trying again. Some of the remnants of it
– myself included occasionally but not on the day in question
– still sat around in the Amyot (not yet gone bust and become
an estate agent's) and one late morning when the mood had
turned especially sad and bad Maurice picked on Monique,
who spent hours and never any money (she had none) in his
place, and said, Why don't you get yourself a man at least? And
everyone looked at her, beautiful, courageous young woman,
too disappointed and beginning to feel old, and there was a
silence, Monique at the centre of it, everybody looking, first
with smiles then sombrely, all eyes on her in silence, until she
said, D'accord. J'y vais. Attendez. And with that, so the story
goes, she left the Amyot, walked up the rue Tournefort, left
along the Pot de Fer and in the Place Monge, just past the
school, under the plane trees, outside the Café des Ortolans,
she found Fortunatus face down in the gutter and fast asleep.
Turning him over, she liked his face – innocent, she told me
– and the smile he gave when he opened his eyes and saw her
studying him. Ten minutes later they stood together on the
pavement outside the Amyot. Maurice and all the regulars
came to the window or the door. Her face entirely
expressionless, like a mime or clown, she pointed to
Fortunatus, he bowed, she took his arm and crossed the street
with him to the door of No. 7. Nobody in the café laughed;
in fact, for some time, so I have been told, nobody said a
word. And thereafter, despite everything, they always spoke of
her, though not always of him, with a wondering and abashed
sort of respect. She did as she said she would do; and what's
more, she lived with the consequences, still does, and never,
to anyone in the café at least, has she ever complained about
Fortunatus, and her flights from him, her escapades, have been
respites and recreations and she has always come back. Then
he must have something in his favour, Katrin said. He can't
be entirely bad. I believe she still likes what she calls his
innocence, said Daniel. Society amazes him, he can't see the
point of it, he can't understand why anyone would want to

live 'like that'. They're two of a kind really, Monique and him, they don't fit any social order and they've never tried to. Unknown to one another, they were both there in the occupation of the Sorbonne, in May, but he was drunk all the time and she was very busy. She did some beautiful posters, red on black mostly. I've got quite a collection at home, should you ever wish to see them. VIVRE SANS TEMPS MORT ET JOUIR SANS ENTRAVE!... L'IMAGINATION AU POUVOIR!... SOYEZ RÉALISTES, DEMANDEZ L'IMPOSSIBLE! Oh dear, how they all come back to me... Monique and Fortunatus have never had any money. She sold a pot now and then or a tapestry or a picture. He never sold anything, not of his own, at least. She did odd jobs, worked on the market for a while. The child was her responsibility, needless to say. Her mother helped, for a few years he and Monique were in Nevers more than in Paris. She gave lessons at the art college there, so I believe. They were doing pretty well then, but Fortunatus somehow found his way to them and begged them to come back. So that's how it was and is – harder now he's decrepit, of course. As a matter of fact, he wasn't always called Fortunatus. He tried several names when he arrived in France. But he settled on Fortunatus after Monique 'rescued him', as he likes to say.

They were slowing through St Denis. Nearly there, said Daniel. I haven't been to Paris for thirty years, said Katrin. Eric never wanted to, so we never did. We went everywhere together, many places, but never to Paris.

It was cold in the Jardin des Plantes, too cold to sit, they walked the length of the long allée, back and forth, three or four times. Monique only had a couple of hours because of Fortunatus who had begun the day cheerfully enough but had turned despondent 'à en mourir' when she told him she would be out for a while. She suggested he went back to bed, and left him. I'm glad Daniel told you about Fortunatus, she says to Katrin. It means I don't have to. But even if he weren't the way he is, I still couldn't have had you to stay, the place is tiny, half the size of rue Tournefort. I hope you like the Malebranche. Daniel found it, you know, on his first trip to Paris, still only a schoolboy, when he and I first met. I'm sorry if I tell you things you already know. – I like to hear them from you, Katrin replies. They are not the same things in a different person's voice. And in French in your voice, Monique, they are quite new. Unimaginably new! It proves the truth she now wishes to live by that the story takes a different shape and tone and works differently on her life as she listens to fragments of it now in French in Monique's voice, in a strange location. And attending to that language, making her side of the conversation in it, becoming more fluent and expressive, she recalls – feels for him – how Eric cycling from Vizille came out of solitude and silence into a rush of speech in the foreign tongue of love. For now at least she feels she is being given new energy as she listens to and replies to Monique. I do like the Malebranche, she says. Daniel hates it, of course – well, sort of hates it – because it is not as it was. But our rooms are on the top floor – he asked for them specially – side by side, with tiny balconies not much bigger than window boxes. Daniel says it reminds him of Eric's room in Oxford, when you climbed through the window and saw the stars and the snowy roof-tops in that terrible cold. But I was thinking it must be even more like your room in the rue Tournefort – Daniel pointed in that direction – so high up, a world of your own. I think I'll walk around there this afternoon. Do you still have your fur coat, by the way? I like you in this – she touches the sleeve of Monique's duffle coat – you came to the funeral in it, but I have been wondering what happened to the famous fur coat that had been your mother's. Fortunatus was jealous of it, says Monique. He kept saying we should sell it, why should I have a fur coat when we had no money? He threatened to take it to the flea market himself so I said I would, but I took it to my son's house, for safekeeping. His wife doesn't approve, of course, but at least she won't sell it. So there it is. Perhaps her little girl will like it one day.

Monique takes Katrin's arm. They are heading towards the river-end. There they will turn and walk back again, into the wind which though not strong, little more than a breath, is glacial. The sun is low, the bare trees glint. There are other pairs, and one or two solitaries, pacing the length of the Jardin des Plantes and back again. The dog-walkers, the joggers, the mothers or nannies with children and babies, the people hurrying towards some business on this or that side of the river, they are human beings too but rather different, today at least, from those who have things to discuss or who need to be alone or who are always alone, pacing up and down on the gravel, thinking, speaking and listening, muttering to nobody, thinking. The lucky can be one sort of human one day, another the next.

See the old places are still shut up, says Monique, and points to the long repositories of geology and palaeontology on their right. I used to go in there often with Olivier when he was little. The attendants were nice to us. He slept and I drew trilobites and ammonites and strange growths of minerals and corals. In winter we spent hours in one place or the other. It was warmer than outside. And when Olivier could take an interest I showed him the creatures and the formations and my drawings of them and he did drawings too. Under the bed there's still a big portfolio of his work and my work together at that time. Did you not want children, Katrin? I did, says Katrin. But Eric had a vasectomy after Thomas was born. Monique halts and stares. Daniel never told me that. Did he not? says Katrin. Perhaps he tells you some things and me others. It doesn't matter. Yes, I did want children when I married Eric, and perhaps what he had done would have been reversible. But he wasn't keen on another operation and I didn't pester him. For a while I thought we might adopt instead and I think he would have agreed to that if I had insisted. But I didn't, so there were no children in the house. But we had one another, as he often said.

They resume their walking. Why did he do it in the first place? Monique asks. I don't really know, says Katrin. I asked him once, he only shrugged. But I've thought about it a good deal for myself and I think it was all part of his self-preservation at that time. In a certain sense he didn't want any more life, or only on his own terms, in ways he could accommodate. That's not a nice thing to say about him, but I can say it to you because you loved him too and you would understand if I explained it properly. Perhaps I will one day. We'll see each sometimes, won't we? It was painful to me at first when I began to realise, in the weeks after his death, what your love was like, yours and his. I felt myself to be nothing in comparison. But lately I have felt less like that. I'm glad he loved you as he did and you him, truly I'm glad. I do want you to know that, Monique.

They turn and face into the wind, bowing their heads slightly, walking slowly. Do you know if Edna had lovers while they were married? Monique asks. I don't think so, Katrin answers. Right at the end, when it was already agreed they should divorce and that Eric would look after Thomas, she took up with a man at work and moved in with him for a while. But it didn't last. I've never felt she was much attracted by that sort of thing. After the settlement she found a place of her own and if she had lovers at all I'm pretty certain she never wanted to marry anybody again. She liked animals. She bought a mare, to ride, and at home she always had a couple of dogs for company. So many years, says Monique. She must have been very lonely. Perhaps, says Katrin. Or perhaps she just preferred being on her own. The worst of it was her bitterness and that only increased with the years. When Thomas grew up he made a point of visiting her and lately she has become rather dependent on him, I think. And Eric, Monique asks, do you know was he unfaithful to her? Katrin considers for a moment how she should reply.

She wishes to be candid; but she shrinks from letting Monique guess how thoroughly she has steeped herself in Eric's past. No, she says at last, I don't think he was unfaithful to her, and not because of his marriage vows but because, as I just suggested, he had become very cautious. When she moved out, he did have two or three affairs but only the last of them, with a woman from East Germany called Bettina, was risky, I should say. And after Bettina – he backed away from her – it was me. So you were the one who brought him back into life, says Monique. That's kind of you, Katrin replies. I wonder if it's true. I should like to believe that what you have said is true. – Why shouldn't you? – Perhaps I will, at least I'll try. But I'm more likely to believe that Bettina showed him the larger life again, and again it frightened him, and he married me because there was no risk in me. That's not what Daniel thinks, Monique replies.

The two women walk in silence for a while. Then, in a rush, Katrin tells Monique about Patrick and about Ellie of the dark eyes whose baby is due towards the end of February, Patrick who got the job he wanted after Katrin with all her heart had wished him luck, and who now earns enough to rent a spacious and sunny new flat for Ellie and the baby to come home to. He helped me get rid of the shelves my father's books were on, she says. They were stained an awful black. But Patrick has taken them away, I gave them to him, and they will look beautiful in the new flat when the black is stripped off and the natural wood, it's either beech or chestnut, is revealed. I'm going to their house-warming next week, she says. And I wanted to ask you, will you come with me tomorrow and help me buy something for the baby, and also something, perhaps several things, for myself, to look better in. I'll never look like you, as you were back then, as you were at the funeral, as you are now, never, I have no flair, no confidence in such matters, but if you will help me tomorrow, I shall at least look better than I do. That is your sadness talking, says Monique. You can't see all the truth of yourself because of the sadness. You can't see the beauty in yourself. But of course I'll come with you tomorrow. We will enjoy ourselves together.

The place – Daniel's suggestion – was a PMU bar in a small street very close to the Gare du Nord. Apart from the *patronne*, they were the only women there. She ushered them into the far corner, under the television which was showing the races with the sound turned off. Là vous serez tranquilles, she said; complained about the bitter cold weather and took their order for two glasses of grog. Daniel likes this place, Monique said. He comes here with a book and sits where we are, under the television, and watches everyone.

The bar was quiet – the men spoke in low voices if at all – but by no means still. A few sat at tables, facing away from the television, studying form and making their bets, and they had the still concentration of scholars in a public library. But they sat no longer than was necessary, stood up, went to the counter, handed over some money, went out for a smoke, came in again, stood watching the silent screen. So the stillness continually disintegrated, into quiet and purposeful comings and goings. And the café extended through its outdoor smokers and their inaudible conversations into the eternal commotion of the street itself. Indoors a subdued decorum prevailed. Nobody shouted, neither good luck not bad was signalled loudly. The men were of all ages, French and immigrant, various in their dress, none well-to-do, some threadbare-poor, and all enthralled in the passion of gambling. Yes, I see why Daniel likes coming here, Katrin said. It is the serious intentness of their studying and watching, the hope in their lifted staring faces, every man unique in his showing what they all have in common. The *patronne* brought the drinks, commented amiably on Katrin's shopping, and left them to their own conversation. Daniel will be here in half an hour, said Monique.

Liz Gracie was beginning to help me, says Katrin. And then she died. But at her funeral, when I saw her family and the room full of people she had helped and who would miss her very badly, I became a bit less selfish, more grateful, less aggrieved, and in that state, which has lasted, I see that she made more than a beginning at helping me, she really did help and still does. So of course I miss her – she was beautiful, she listened, she had patience, she was an extraordinary physician – everyone misses her who knew her at all and for her husband and their children it must be terrible, terrible. But I am better because of her, I feel her help continuing. She told me the truth: that the first Christmas would be appalling, and the first anniversary worse, and that in many cases the third year, when you thought you were coming through, was unimaginably bad all over again. In fact, she did not really allow the idea of getting through it, over it, over him. Why should you? she asked. Why should you even want to? You loved him, you still love him, I don't believe you can want to stop loving him. What you do want is to be able to live, and to do that you have to convert this killing grief into what it came from, into its equal other self, which is to say: into continuing and enlivening love. So that is what I am trying to do. And some days it seems to me a lie. Love in absence can't possibly enliven you. Other days I feel it to be the only truth, and I even feel I am a step nearer to living in it.

Katrin halts, Monique's face, the face of a childish clown unbearably afflicted, has halted her. Oh, Monique, how selfish I am! You see how selfish I still am. And yet these past few weeks I have thought about you so much and so intently often I forgot myself. And now, see, I forget you, as though you were only a sympathising listener. Forgive me.

Monique shakes her head. You are his wife, it is different. Next time we meet I will try to tell you what it is like for me who loved him when he and I were scarcely more than children and slept with him all told, if you count up the hours and the days, for no more than a month. Finish what you were saying.

Katrin shrugs. That's it really. Except perhaps, that knowing it will be very bad again, I suppose what I have been doing lately is making some sort of provision for when that happens, by storing up things inside me that will help. And these two days talking to you will be a wonderful resource, I do know that and I thank you for them. Monique nods. And here's something else, she says. Her voice sounds odd, her look is the oddest mixture of glee, horror, determination and childish helplessness, so that now Katrin attends wholly to her in alarm. Monique has her back to the room full of rapt and studious men. Come closer, she says to Katrin across the small table, lean towards me. Katrin bends so close their heads are almost touching. Now put your hands together and open them. Now close your eyes. Katrin obeys her as a small daughter would, and there under the silent television showing from remote locations the fall of the good luck and the bad, she feels in the cup of her warm hands the rush, the slither and the settling of cool silver. Then she opens her eyes, sees the gift, sees Monique's face, the child, the girl shining gleefully through the old woman at this surprise. The empty crimson pouch lies on the formica table top.

I can't, Monique, Katrin says. He gave them to you. Yes, says Monique, he gave them to me, the day he left, at the end of September, he told me the story and to finish it he tipped them into my hands as I have just done into yours. And he said they were mine. To do what I liked with, he said. And after that he never mentioned them, never asked what I had done with them and in all the bitterness never asked for them back. So they are mine. I hid them from Fortunatus under a floor board. Eric gave them to me. They are mine. I am free to do what I like with them. So I give them to you. Now hide them away quickly before anyone sees our business in this gambling den. Daniel will be here in a minute. He is never late. Tell him on the train if you want to. But most of all, Katrin, write to me, write me letters in French and I will write to you and that will be a help, and whenever we can we will meet.

# Translations

p. 17
*Je suis désolée, oh, excusez-moi, madame, je suis Monique.*
I'm so sorry, oh forgive me, madame, I am Monique.


p. 18
*Je vous ai apporté ça, madame. Un petit souvenir des années soixante.*
I've brought you this, madame. A small souvenir of the 60s.
*Ça vous plaît?*
You like it?
*Tu t'en souviens?*
You remember?
*Merci, Monique, she said. Soyez la bienvenue dans cette maison.*
Thank you, Monique, she said. You are welcome in this house.


p. 37
*'Pour t'encourager.'*
'To encourage you.'


p. 42
*Eric, chéri, j'arrive pas à croire que tu ne sois plus là. Mon corps, le lit, tout l'appartement, nous n'y comprenons rien…*
Eric, my darling, it's not possible that you're not here. My body, the bed, the whole flat, we can't understand it…


p. 56
*'Tu m'aimes?'*
Do you like me like this?

227

p. 64
*Si le fascisme revient, ce n'est pas la peine d'avoir des enfants ou de planter des arbres.*
If fascism comes back there's no point in having children or planting trees.
*Éclosion*
Opening out

p. 73
*'La rue de la vie dessus'*
'The road of the life above'

p. 75
*Qu'est-ce que je vous offre?*
What may I offer you?
*Un petit souvenir*
A little souvenir

p. 79
*'Avant d'être à Paris, j'étais à Nevers'…. 'C'est à Nevers que j'ai été le plus jeune de toute ma vie.'*
Before being in Paris I was in Nevers… In all my life I was never so young as I was in Nevers.

p. 82
*Ça te plaît? C'est beau, hein?*
You like it? Isn't it beautiful!

p. 84
*Bonne nuit*
Good night

p. 84
*Dépaysé*
Disoriented
p. 85
*Viens*
Come

p. 128
*Je suis au lit.*
I am in bed.

p. 129
*C'est bon*
It's OK

p. 131
*T'as bien fait. Je t'aime.*
Well done. I love you.

p. 135
*J'étais le plus jeune de toute ma vie à Nevers.*
In all my life I was never so young as I was in Nevers.

p. 154
*C'est là ton pub?*
Is that your pub?

p. 157
*Farouche*
Shy, like a wild animal

pp. 161–2
*Quand nous en serons au temps des cerises*
*Et gai rossignol et merle moqueur*
*Seront tous en fête*
*Les belles auront la folie en tête*

*Et les amoureux du soleil au cœur*
*Quand nous chanterons le temps des cerises*
*Sifflera bien mieux le merle moqueur...*

When we shall come to the time of the cherries
And glad nightingale and mocking blackbird
Will all celebrate
The girls will have crazy things in their heads
And the boys in love will have sun in their hearts
When we shall sing the time of the cherries
The mocking blackbird will whistle still better...

*Mais il est bien court le temps des cerises*
*Où l'on s'en va deux cueillir en rêvant*
*Des pendants d'oreille...*
*Cerises d'amour aux robes vermeilles*
*Tombant sous la feuille en gouttes de sang...*
*Mais il est bien court le temps des cerises*
*Pendants de corail qu'on cueille en rêvant!*

But it is a brief time, the time of the cherries
When we go in pairs, picking and dreaming
Pendants for the ears...
Cherries of love in vermilion dresses
Falling under the leaves in drops of blood...
But it is a brief time, the time of the cherries
Pendants of coral we pluck as we dream!

*Quand vous en serez au temps des cerises*
*Si vous avez peur des chagrins d'amour*
*Évitez les belles!*
*Moi qui ne crains pas les peines cruelles*
*Je ne vivrai pas sans souffrir un jour...*
*Quand vous en serez au temps des cerises*
*Vous aurez aussi des peines d'amour!*

When you shall come to the time of the cherries
If you are afraid of the sorrows of love
Keep away from the girls!
I, not afraid of cruel afflictions
I shall not live without suffering one day...
When you shall come to the time of the cherries
You also will suffer the torments of love!

*J'aimerai toujours le temps des cerises*
*C'est de ce temps-là que je garde au cœur*
*Une plaie ouverte!*
*Et Dame Fortune, en m'étant offerte*
*Ne pourra jamais fermer ma douleur...*
*J'aimerai toujours le temps des cerises*
*Et le souvenir que je garde au cœur!*

I'll always love the time of the cherries
It is from that time I hold in my heart
A still open wound.
And Dame Fortune being given to me
Will never be able to close my pain...
I'll always love the time of the cherries
Along with the memory I hold in my heart!

p. 165
*Je peux pas. Je te demande pardon. Je peux pas. M.*
I can't do it. Forgive me. I can't. M.

p. 166
*Elle est partie*
She's gone.
*Nevers peut-être, peut-être Marrakech.*
Nevers perhaps, perhaps Marrakech.
*Assieds-toi, petit.*
Sit down, child.
*Elle avait peur*
She was frightened.

231

p. 180
*Poètes maudits*
The poets under a curse (especially Rimbaud and Verlaine)

p. 183
*Eric, mon amour, c'est atroce ce que je t'ai fait, je ne me comprends pas, j'étais folle, lâche et méchante, chéri, et si tu ne me pardonnes pas...*
Eric, my love, it's a horrible thing I did to you, I don't understand myself, I was mad and cowardly and wicked, my darling, and if you won't forgive me...

p. 195
'*Reculer pour mieux sauter*'
Step back, the better to leap forward

p. 199
'*Je me révolte, donc nous sommes.*'
'I revolt, therefore we are.'
'*Il n'y a plus qu'un enfer et il est de ce monde: c'est contre lui qu'il faut lutter.*'
'There's only one hell left and it is of this world: that's the hell we must struggle against.'

p. 209
'*La vie qui continue, ta mort qui continue...*'
'Life continuing, your death continuing...'

p. 211
*Ma chère Katrin, voilà longtemps que je pense beaucoup à toi...*
My dear Katrin, for a long time now you have been very much in my thoughts...

p. 216
*D'accord. J'y vais. Attendez.*
OK. I will. Wait here.

p. 217
*VIVRE SANS TEMPS MORT ET JOUIR SANS
ENTRAVE!... L'IMAGINATION AU POUVOIR!...
SOYEZ RÉALISTES, DEMANDEZ L'IMPOSSIBLE!*
LIFE WITHOUT DEAD TIME! PLEASURE
UNHINDERED!....POWER TO THE IMAGINATION!...
BE REALISTIC, DEMAND THE IMPOSSIBLE!

p. 217
*'À en mourir'*
'Fit to die'

p. 222
*Là vous serez tranquilles*
You'll be nice and quiet there